To: Jenny

THE LEGACY

Best Wishes

Mardi Marsh

MARDI MARSH

authorHOUSE®

AuthorHouse™ UK Ltd.
1663 Liberty Drive
Bloomington, IN 47403 USA
www.authorhouse.co.uk
Phone: 0800.197.4150

Published by AuthorHouse 09/23/2013

ISBN: 978-1-4817-8690-4 (sc)
ISBN: 978-1-4817-8691-1 (e)

Mardi Marsh—was born and grew up in Andover Hampshire. This is her debut novel.

She has three grown up children and four grandchildren. Mardi and her husband Bob live in a village near the beach on the south coast of England where they brought up their children.

Having been diagnosed with breast cancer she knew very well how devastating this could be. When she was given the all clear, she wanted to give something back to help others. Mardi gained counselling qualifications and set up a support group for patients with breast cancer at a local Hospital in 1992, which stills runs today.

She feels that if there are positive's to come from that painful experience it would be to grab life, run with it and make every day count. Have a can do attitude and think positively—and smile.

My first novel I dedicate to—

The memory of my wonderful parents - Eddie and Doris Batchelor.

<u>My Family</u>

Bob my husband, friend and soul mate.
My three Amazing children - Lissa, Emma and Steven.
My gorgeous grandchildren - Jessica, Ewan, Sam and Ellie for the joy
    you bring into my life.
My family are my world - I love you all so much.

ACKNOWLEDGMENTS

I would like to thank my husband Bob for his patience, support and as always his unconditional love.

Thank you to my daughter Lissa for reviewing the finished novel amongst her busy job of being mum.

Thank you to my daughter Emma for keeping me sane and encouraging me when I had bad days.

Thank you to my Son Steven—my guru technical support and for taking my photo for my novel.

To my sister Mary and her husband Barry, thank you for reviewing a section of the final draft.

My sincere thanks to author Catherine King for her advice and help.

I would also like to thank the lovely ladies of the Fareham Writers' group—Catherine King Jean Grantham, Lorna Howarth, Gunvor Johansson, Kaz Clark, Penny Shergold, Linda March, Eileen Robertson and Eileen Stockwell for their critique at our meetings at Portchester library.

Many thanks to artist Eileen Stockwell for her drawing of Cotton Wood Plantation house and for proof reading the second draft of my novel. I enjoyed our many cups of coffee Eileen when discussing my manuscript.

Many thanks to Christine Lissoni for her feedback on my first draft. Christine was the first person to review my novel her feedback was invaluable.

My publishers Author House—Mark Andrews my check-in coordinator was extremely helpful and supportive during the process.

Thank you to author June Hampson my teacher at St Vincent College, Gosport, and the wonderful group of students who attended the course with me.

Let it be said by our children's children that when we were tested we refused to let this journey end, that we did not turn back nor did we falter; and with eyes fixed on the horizon and God's grace upon us, we carried forth that great gift of freedom and delivered it safely to future generations

President Barack Obama
Inaugural Address January 20th 2009 (Daily Mail)

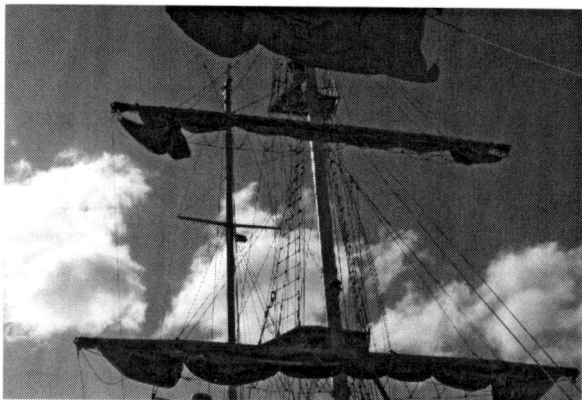

Chapter One

1856

Beth was in a dark and brutal place when she conceived—would she be able to love this baby.

She gasped for air as a wall of intense heat hit her as the slave master threw her down the steps into the lightless hold. This is my worst nightmare, she thought as she froze with fear.

"No! Don't make me," she cried. "Please," she begged.

"Get in there," the slave master, shouted as he kicked her with his boot sending her tumbling into the dark abyss. Beth landed on a pile of hot sweaty bodies. Is this what hell is like? She thought. Terrified she scrambled frantically around in the slimy, putrid mix that covered the floor of the hold. The darkness had engulfed her and her phobia of confined spaces surfaced. She struggled to breathe as the stench overwhelmed her. She was incarcerated, and chained in the hold of the slave ship, 'The Camberley.'

Beth tugged at her chains. I must take control of my emotions; she told herself if I am to survive this terrible place. She felt the pressure either side of her from the slaves wedged around her. She placed her hands on her enlarged tummy to shield it. "It's alright, my little one," she said as she tried to protect it.

Beth watched other mothers with their infants and questioned herself. Would I be a good mother? Will I be able to protect my baby?

The lacerations around Beth's ankles from her shackles had festered from a mix of seawater, excrement and vomit from the slaves, which undulated over her feet with the motion of the ship.

As the weeks passed, it was becoming increasingly difficult as her pregnancy progressed.

Beth knew she must be at least five months pregnant.

She tried to release the seams of her dress to accommodate her expanding waistline. It was difficult in the confined space, if she dare move she would lose the little space she had and end up sitting in the foul water that covered the floor. She knew she had to hold her place at all cost.

Beth began to feel drowsy with the extreme heat and memories flooded her mind.

One particular horrific thought she did not want to relive was pushing hard. She cried "No, No stop! I won't let you in," she said defiantly, as she struggled to push it to the back of her mind.

Then a heart-warming memory took over and she drifted back.

In her mind, she could see Reverend Logan a tall, lean Scotchman in his thirties with a kind, craggy face. He leant forward and patted her on the head as he told her and her mother the wonderful stories about the tribes in Africa they would encounter. His rich Scottish accent mesmerized her as she sat and listened to him in the family church on her father's estate, 'Pendragon Hall' in Somerset.

They left the shores of England looking forward to their adventure and to spreading the word of God.

A movement jolted her back to reality and the sweltering conditions of the hold. It was the first kick of her baby. The young girl chained next to Beth was from the same village, she had been one of her pupils she taught to speak English.

"Afia," she took the girl's hand and placed it where she could feel the movement of her baby.

She smiled showing her bright white teeth. The joy Beth felt knowing that the baby was alive filled her with hope. She was thirsty and craving a drink of water only to find the water butt in the hold had run dry. There was pandemonium all around her women screaming, children crying for water and the plea from the sick and the dying for help. "How can I bear this torment," she thought as she tried to shut out the noise. Then in her mind, she heard her dead mother's voice telling her to be strong.

Beth once more fought hard to stop the flashback of that dreadful day resurfacing in her mind and in flooded visions of her home and she wandered back.

The trees wore their new coat of bright, green leaves and the wind blew through Beth's hair as she galloped through the lush green pastures that surrounded her father's estate. She waited for her father by the grand stone entrance. A pair of carved life sized lions standing on plinths either side guarded this. Her father was returning from London where he had sat in the House of Lords. She always rode her beloved pony Taffy to meet him. He was a gift from her father on her eighth birthday.

"Father, Father," she called excitedly as his carriage came alongside. He gave a broad smile from under his wig and flamboyant hat. He was in his late sixties, a stout man through good living, his face flushed with delight at seeing his daughter. She did not want the vision to end. "Father, father, don't go," she called trying to hold onto his apparition. However, a voice was calling her name bringing her back to reality.

"Missy,—pain," said Afia touching Beth's arm as she held her stomach and vomited again. She had been like this for the last week since she was suffering from dysentery. She was painfully thin but still managed to smile. She was a sweet girl, only sixteen. Beth was very concerned and put her arm around Afia to comfort her.

The flashback came with a ferocity she could not hold back. "Please I don't want to", she murmured but it was unstoppable.

The flashback took her back to that harrowing day in the village in West Africa, which she had called home for the last two years.

The raid had begun at noon on Beth's eighteenth birthday. She had been in the shade of her hut teaching the young women of the village to speak English. Her pupils had given her a necklace of red glass beads, which Beth had placed around her neck to their delight.

Suddenly they heard screaming and shouting that the village was being attacked. The noise and commotion had been overwhelming and terrified villagers were running in all directions.

"Hurry, get inside," screamed Beth. She grabbed a wooden stool and ushered the young women into the hut. She barricaded the doorway with whatever she could find. The women cried and wailed as they clung to one another behind Beth. She summoned up all her courage as she prepared to defend them. Her hands were sweaty. Her body tensed with fear—as she waited. Then a loud noise broke the silence. Beth and the young women jumped at the noise as men with spears broke through the doorway of the hut. A looming and frightening figure stood out from the throng, his muscular black body shimmered with perspiration. He wore an animal skin across his body and waved a spear smeared with blood. His cold eyes stared right through Beth, his smile was menacing. Beth had never felt terror as she did at that moment; her body started to shake involuntarily. She pushed the women further into the corner of the room. All her instincts told her to run—but she was cornered. He pointed at Beth with his spear and spoke in his native tongue to the men that stood behind him.

Moving towards Beth, he ripped the stool from her and flung her to the dry parched floor. Her necklace broke and the red beads scattered through the air as his men dragged the other women screaming from the hut.

All round her, she could hear shouting and screaming; a barrage of noise that helped her to block out the terror—of what was about to happen to her.

With trepidation, Beth scrambled up against the walls of her hut trying to get away from him. His large body overshadowed her. Her body paralysed with fear would not let her scream. He struck her hard across the face; she reeled from the blow knowing the situation was inevitable. I must not resist, for he may kill me, she thought. She felt his weight upon her she could hardly breathe. The smell of his sweaty body filled her nostrils. As he bared his rotten teeth, his stale breath hit her face. She tensed her body as she felt the pain of him invade her. She closed her eyes tightly to shut out the evil grin on his pockmarked face. Gripping hold of the straw mat on the floor of her hut, she prayed for him to be quick. Following his savage attack he dragged her up and shoved her out of the hut where she wandered about, traumatised.

"Beth! Beth!" cried Eliza, putting her arms around her daughter. "I have been searching for you." Eliza knew what must have happened to her from her disconnected behaviour and dishevelled state. Eliza picked up a clump of straw and cleaned away the blood and semen that ran down her daughter's legs.

"Mama, Mama!" She cried inconsolably.

Their captors pushed them roughly and chained them with the other captured villagers.

Eliza grabbed her hand. "My child, push it from your mind. Remember God is with us. You must call on him for all your strength."

"God, you say mother? I should call on God! Where was he when I needed him?" Beth cried.

Eliza tried to calm her and knew that as a mother she must help her daughter to survive by teaching her to be strong and to trust in God.

Reverend Logan watched in horror.

"You'll not be taking these lassies, they are under my protection," shouted Reverend Logan in his broad, Scottish accent. He pulled Eliza and Beth out of the line. A rifle butt struck him several times on the head, and he fell to the ground.

"Leave him alone!" Eliza cried, as she tried to reach him, pulling Beth with her. She felt the sharp pain of a whip hitting her back and pushed back into line.

The last time Eliza and Beth saw Reverend Logan he was lying on the dry, parched, ground, bloodied and motionless as they left the village.

Eliza comforted her daughter. "We must put ourselves into God's hands, my child, and pray for Reverend Logan." Eliza fought back her tears for the man she had become fond of but now had to leave behind.

AFRICA
showing
SOURCES OF SLAVE SUPPLY
and
ROUTES OF DISTRIBUTION

Sources of Slave Supply

Routes of Distribution

It had taken several days to reach the captor's village and on arrival, they herded the slaves into pens and gave them miserly food rations.

Eliza was worried at Beth's silence since they left their village she seemed detached and emotionless.

"Let me wash your feet," said her mother as she took each foot and bathed the cuts around her ankles. Beth stared into space not responding. Eliza feared for the psychological impact the rape had had on her daughter.

There was quite a commotion one morning when slavers arrived. To the delight of the king of the village, they traded all the slaves including Beth and her mother and added them to the already long line of slaves.

Then they started the long journey going from village to village across the African interior, where the slavers traded for more slaves.

Beth asked herself, Why God why me? What did I do to deserve this? She walked side-by-side with her mother mile after mile, day after day, finding the energy to place one foot in front of the other in the cruel heat of the sun. She knew her mother was worried about her, but she was unable to rid herself of the memory of that dreadful day it consumed her, leaving her feeling numb. Then, when she least expected it, she sensed an overwhelming need to cry. The tears flowed and flowed. Her mother was relieved—her daughter was back.

The long column of slaves wound their way along the dusty path through the bush leaving a dust trail in the air.

Weeks passed and Eliza had become ill with dysentery and Beth was very concerned.

She felt that it was her turn to be strong, so she could help her mother. The meagre rations were not enough to sustain them and they were weak and exhausted.

"I cannot continue," said Eliza, as she was violently sick again. She was staggering, so Beth took her arm and supported her. Her mother was defecating, vomiting uncontrollably, and becoming weaker. There was a shout from the slave master to stop and rest. Beth cleaned her mother with a piece of cloth torn from her sleeve and dipped it in the water she had been given.

"Don't waste your water, my child," her mother said anxiously. "You need it to survive."

Beth stroked her forehead. "Mother, please rest."

She fed her the scanty rations, but Eliza could not keep them down.

Beth knew that her mother was too weak to continue the arduous journey to the port and what this would mean. Beth called on God for strength.

She knew her mother's end would be the same as that of the other slaves who were left behind on the side of the road, too weak and ill to continue, shot or abandoned and left to starve to death.

The slave master shouted "Get on your feet." Beth took her mother's arm and struggled to hold her up. Her mother's feet dragged along the ground. Then suddenly Eliza fell. Beth tried to pick her up and keep her walking—as the alternative was unthinkable.

The slave master pushed Beth out of the way, unchained her mother, and threw her to the side of the road.

Beth ran to her mother's side.

"Be strong, my child, God bless you," Eliza said as she held her daughter's gaze—for which she knew would be for the last time.

Beth was dragged away from her screaming, "Mother; Mother!"

"Keep walking!" commanded the slave master as he chained her to another slave.

Beth shouted in despair. "Where are you my, God why have you deserted me?" She screamed hysterically as her mother disappeared into the distance.

A comforting voice broke through her pain and anguish.

"Lean on me," said a voice.

Through her tears, Beth looked up into the face of the man. He seemed to be larger-than-life. His expression conveyed compassion.

Then she heard a distant rifle shot. She knew it had taken her mother's life and had made her an orphan. She felt as if it had entered her body too and she passed out. The slave next to her picked her up and carried her.

Beth came to, lying down. It was a rest period. She could feel him cooling her forehead with water. Beth looked up into his kind eyes.

She touched his hand—"God bless you," she said.

He sat her up and gave her some of their paltry rations.

"Try and eat."

Beth pushed the food away. "I want to die, I want to be with my mother," she sobbed.

"Your mother would want you to survive," he said.

"Start walking!" said the slave master as he poked them with the handle of his whip.

Her companion helped her up and took her arm to support her.

"What is your name?" asked Beth.

"Chief Abel Tukowunu."

"You speak good English."

"I was taught by a priest," he replied.

The slave master struck them with a lash of the whip for talking. They continued in silence feeling the shared companionship. They were grateful for the rest periods at each village while the slavers bartered for new slaves.

It had taken many months to reach their final destination, and many had died of sheer exhaustion. Eventually they had reached the coast; the smell emanating from the slave ships in the port assaulted their nostrils. They descended from the cliff top via a steep path. They could see the throng of activity at the harbour as they saw slaves herded into manageable groups.

They separated the men from the women and children as they queued to board 'The Camberley'

"No No, you cannot take, Abel," Beth cried. She tugged at his arm as they unchained him and dragged him away. Abel gave her a reassuring look and then he was gone. Nervously she scanned the slaves looking for him, feeling vulnerable without him by her side.

As Beth queued to board, the slave ship she heard screams coming from in front of her and then she saw why. They held her and branded her with a red-hot branding iron.

Suddenly Beth awoke in the hold of 'The Camberley.' She had been dreaming, but jerked sharply back to consciousness by a searing pain, which had felt like the branding iron that she had felt all those many months ago.

The intense pain gripped her, spreading throughout her body. "Is this it?" Is my baby coming?' she asked herself. "Dear lord, no!" My contractions must not start! It is too early!" Beth knew from delivering babies in the village that she must be close to seven months and that this only meant one thing in her experience. The chances of her baby being born alive were extremely low. How was she supposed to endure these inhuman conditions and bring her baby into such misery?

Beth's contractions were closer together now and her back was on fire with the intensity of the pain. Her biggest challenge was to deliver her baby, alive or dead.

She was a good Christian and well educated. She knew she could deliver her baby.

Beth had been saving herself for the right one. She had been a virgin and always dreamt that she would have her first-born at her family home, 'Pendragon Hall.'

With the intense heat, Beth began to drift once more into a dream-like state, and in her mind found herself back at her childhood home.

Beth was the off spring of a Duke and his favourite black housemaid Eliza who was thirty. Her father had named her Bethany, which soon became Beth. He recognised her legally and was a loving father to her. Beth and the Duke had matching heart shaped birthmarks on the back of their wrists, which he said showed that she was indeed his daughter.

The Duchess felt humiliated and jealous of the favouritisms he showed Beth over her children. The Duke gave Beth's mother a cottage in the grounds, which he visited regularly. She was educated in the same manner as his other children, her half siblings Charlotte and James.

When the Duke died James as his only son and heir inherited his estate. His mother the Duchess now wanted to get rid of her husband's mistress, Eliza, and his bastard daughter Beth.

"You are not safe here now, Eliza. I would like you and Beth, to come with me to Africa and help me spread the word of God. Please say you will?" said Reverend Logan.

He had been for many years the Minister of the church on the Duke's estate. He knew that the Duchess had plans to sell Eliza and Beth into slavery, so he put his proposal to the Duchess. She had agreed, as she saw this as an opportunity to get rid of this embarrassment.

Reverend Logan was very fond of Eliza and Beth.

"Thank you Reverend, I agree it is not safe here for us, now that we do not have the Duke's protection, so Beth and I will join you," said a grateful Eliza.

They had travelled by cargo ship, which was laden with trading goods.

Beth said as she stood on the deck and looked out to sea, "How I look forward to doing your work, Lord." She could not wait for the adventure that lay ahead of her.

It took several months of journeying over land before arriving in the village of the Setae tribe in West Africa. Reverend Logan had soon built up a rapport with the king and his tribe.

Pain broke through into her dream. Strong waves of contractions brought Beth back to consciousness again. She could not move because of her chains and the overcrowding.

"Please, God, bring my baby safely into the world," she said as she braced herself for the next contraction. The light that filtered through the hatch flickered across Beth's distorted face.

Afia, reached out for Beth's hand, "Hand, Missy?" Beth clasped it as the agonising pain took hold. As each contraction arose, she took deep breaths and as the pains became stronger and closer together, she knew it would not be long. She now just wanted to push. She felt down and could feel her baby's head. Although Afia was very weak, she leant forward and as Beth pushed, letting out an agonising cry, the baby, bloodied and slimy entered the world into Afia's thin, sinuous hands.

It was a perfectly formed baby girl, very tiny, blue and worryingly . . . not crying.

Beth took her baby from Afia fearing it would fall into the excrement. She lay her on her lap and cut the cord with her teeth. Beth hooked the mucus out of its tiny mouth and it coughed, spluttered, and let out a weak cry.

She set about cleaning her daughter as best she could. Beth wrestled with her conscience. Would she feel anything when she held her baby in her arms?

Though her eyes were sunken and her face was skeletal, Afia managed a smile. Beth took her hand—and kissed it, "Thank you Afia."

Beth knew the odds of her baby surviving in this environment were very low. She knew it would only be a matter of time before her newborn succumbed. Her baby might live but she could bleed heavily and leave her baby motherless. All these thoughts flooded her mind.

Her thoughts turned to her mother. This is your granddaughter; I name her after you Eliza. Oh Mother if only you could see her. Beth said emotionally.

Beth licked her finger and did the sign of the cross on her daughter's forehead to christen her.

She held her baby to her breast to suckle. The baby was weak and its tiny mouth struggled to attach itself to feed. She expressed some milk from her breast and directed it into its little mouth. She thought her baby had fallen asleep through the exhaustion of the birth but when she checked her, she found that she had stopped breathing.

"Dear God, help me!" she cried. She felt panic rising in her body and shook involuntary. She laid her daughter on her lap, covered its little mouth with hers, and blew air into her. She kept checking her but there was no sign of life. As she continued, she prayed that the next breath might save her. For if she was trying, then there was still hope.

In panic, Beth shouted. "Mother, help me!" she cried. Afia put her arm around her.

"Missy—no cry baby in heaven." Beth's brain could not comprehend the fact that she could not save her daughter. Now her baby was dead, lying there limp and lifeless.

She picked her up, kissed her and held her close—for she truly knew she did love her, and let out a heart-rending scream as the shock gave way to the reality of her baby's death.

She tormented herself "God, did you take my little daughter because I was raped, or was it because I doubted whether I could love her that you chose to punish me? Why me?" she cried. "I have always tried to be a good Christian. Why have you forsaken me, Lord?" Beth was in a dark and lonely place.

She had to accept that her daughter was now in God's hands as she prayed for her little soul. She had thought that she had shed every tear in her body since she was captured. She felt dead inside, numb, just going through the motions. Losing her baby hit the innermost depths of her soul, she cried until there were no more tears.

During the next few days, her grief turned to anger. My baby stood no chance of survival in these abysmal conditions on board 'The Camberley.' How could one human being do this to another? She must forgive, as Christ had done on the cross. She struggled with her faith and prayed that one day she would be able to forgive, but now she was severely tested and all she felt was revulsion and outrage towards her captors.

"Rest your head on my shoulder," Beth said to Afia. She was emaciated and Beth knew she would not live long. Her heart went out to this sweet girl. Afia managed a smile and promptly fell asleep.

The slave master removed the hatch, flooding the hold with bright light and fresh air. Abel and five other men cleaned the hold of the build up of excrement and clear out the bodies of those slaves that had died overnight.

"Out," the slave master shouted. Beth moved to get up and Afia fell to the floor. She went to help her. "Keep moving," the slave master shouted and shoved the handle of his whip into her side. Beth winced and quietly said, "God bless you, Afia," as she was dragged by her chains. She was unable to cry for her, as she was numb from her daughter's death, the tears would not come.

Beth shielded her daughter's body under her top out of sight. In her shocked state of mind, she talked to her baby as she climbed on deck not accepting she was dead.

With the sheer number of slave climbing out of the hold, they pushed and jostled her. Weak from giving birth and unsteady on her feet from so many hours chained to her bench, her knees and legs almost buckled. Beth held on tightly to her dead daughter, as she knew there would be frenzy as the slaves rushed for the water barrels. The slave master chained the slaves together in pairs to help control them on deck.

Beth chained to a frail old woman found it slow getting to the water butt, by the time they got there the stampede was over. Beth handed a ladle of water to the sick woman and then drank her ration. It was like an elixir to them.

They were grateful to be out of the cramped, hot, smelly hold. They washed themselves with seawater and block of soap left out for the slaves to use, enjoying the fresh feeling of the cooling seawater as it ran down them.

Beth was unaware that the slave master had his eye on her. In her deluded mind she talked to her daughter as she cleaned her, then she felt a hand on her shoulder. Panic stricken she held her dead daughter close to her. The slave master turned her around to face him.

"What are you holding, girl?" he shouted. Realizing her baby was dead he snatched the lifeless baby from Beth's arms and dangled it over the side of the ship.

"It's dead, no good to me," he said through a cruel smile. Beth was distraught, begging him to give her daughter back to her. Although she was weak, she found strength that only a mother finds when her child needs help. Beth tried to get to her baby. She clawed at the slave master but he laughed and dropped the body of her daughter into the sea. Without a word Beth jumped overboard after her and hung over the side of the ship by her chains screaming,

"My baby: My baby!" The old woman caught by the ship's side had stopped her from falling into the sea. The slave master rushed to catch the chains that were keeping them together.

"Quick men, help me drag her back on deck for this is our profit hanging overboard." The deckhands rushed to help him. They hauled Beth up and the slave master unchained her. They found the old woman had gone into convulsions and was frothing at the mouth. She lay dying on the deck. Beth collapsed, motionless and drained of all life. All she wanted was to join her daughter. She begged the slave master, "Please let me die. Let me join my daughter, please!" The slave master examined the old woman and found that she was dead. "Throw her overboard, lads." He was not happy at losing a slave and kicked Beth in temper several times.

Beth dazed and in shock picked herself up and wandered about aimlessly. She tried to pull herself together by plunging her head into the barrel of seawater, hoping it would help her make sense of what had just happened. She did not realise that she had cut her head until the water turned red. She felt no pain. She was in shock. She cried, "Dear Lord, have you forsaken me?"

"Beth, it's Abel," he said in a soft, comforting voice as he sat her against the side of the ship. Abel could not bring her water as a chain to the barrel secured the ladle. Therefore, he tore a piece of cloth from his sleeve and soaked it in the water from the barrel squeezing the water into her mouth. He wiped her face to cool her. Beth looked up at him, traumatised she repeatedly said, my baby I want my baby. "Abel reassured her and said, "You are not alone. I will help you." She sat beside him, lent her head against his shoulder and closed her eyes, exhausted mentally and physically.

She awoke from the shouts of the slave master. He was ordering the slaves back to the hold as a storm was brewing.

Abel helped her up and still traumatized, she entered the hold. The hatch closed and in the darkness, Beth sat questioning her faith. Why do good people like my mother and my innocent baby die at the hands of wicked people?' That cannot be a loving God. To Beth oblivion never seemed more enticing.

With exhaustion, she once again drifted back to her childhood on her father's estate in Somerset, England.

"My sweet Beth, come and read to your father," he said as he patted the seat next to him. Beth was rummaging through the books in the library. "I need to find something challenging father. I will read this one. It is called The Pilgrim's Progress." She settled down next to him and read the book. How the Duke enjoyed his daughter's company. Life was always fun when Beth was about and he sighed with contentment.

When their lessons had finished for the day, they played. Charlotte and James were her half siblings. Beth loved Charlotte and felt very protective towards her, as she had had a weak heart since birth. James considered himself superior to Beth as he had white skin. If he could get her into trouble, he would.

"One, two, three," Charlotte counted with her hands covering her eyes. James, followed by Beth, scurried up several flights of stairs. At the end of a corridor, there were a further few steps, which lead to the attic. James lifted the hatch. "In here, Charlotte will never find us!" He beckoned Beth to follow him. Once in James called to her to get into a cupboard in the far corner. "Quick this is a great hiding place, hurry." Beth reluctantly entered the cupboard. It was dark and cold. Slam went the door behind her. She was alone, her fear of confined spaces surfaced and she could feel the panic rising.

"James, let me out. Do you hear me? Let me out," Beth shouted. Her fingers felt frantically around the dark cupboard searching for the door, only to find it locked. She heard James laugh as he put the key into his jacket pocket and climbed out of the attic.

Beth heard the thud of the hatch closing behind him.

She was now hysterical and let out a heart-rending scream.

Her screaming woke her with a start and for a few seconds her mind did not register the death of her daughter. Then like darkness, the grief entered her consciousness and pushed her into a melancholy state.

A storm was brewing. Flashes of lightning hit the angry grey sea, illuminating the dark sky. The storm buffeted the small wooden British slave ship through the mountainous waves.

The Captain shouted to his crew, "Batten down the hatches, men!" He knew how bad these storms could be crossing the Atlantic. Many Captains had lost their ships and precious cargo, but he would not.

The storm raged for four hours. The Captain and his crew were exhausted and relieved when the storm dissipated and the sun emerged from the clouds lifting the darkness.

He shouted orders to the slave master. "Check the cargo below deck!" He lifted the wooden hatch and reeled backwards as the smell hit his nostrils. Below in the dark was a mass of humanity 280 slaves in total. Crammed into the hold were 190 males, 60 women and 30 children.

As he shone a light down, the crushed bodies of some young children became apparent.

The sound from the tortured souls reverberated around the hold. In strange tongues, mothers were screaming hysterically as they found that their children were dead. All the slaves where brought up on deck and the dead children were thrown overboard to the harrowing cries from their mothers.

Abel caught sight of Beth and was relieved to see she was all right. Beth met his eyes. Abel moved closer to her and smiled, her heart jumped at the sheer joy at seeing again.

"How are you, Beth?" he said his face searching hers. She looked at him and cried for the first time since her daughter's death. Abel held her and the feeling transported her back to her childhood when her Mother would comfort her after her half brother James had cruelly called her a nigger.

Beth was of mixed racial origin, but her features were mainly European. One of her most striking attributes were her large soulful eyes peering from under an unruly head of curly, dark brown hair. Her slight frame made her appear vulnerable, but anyone who knew her would say that she was strong and resilient.

Abel chained in the hold struggled with the memories of his village burning and his parents bodies lying amongst the smouldering ruins on the day his village was destroyed. "Lord, please deliver me from the images in my mind. I ask for forgiveness for letting my people down when they depended on me to protect them." Abel felt remorse. Abel's father had made him both mentally and physically strong. Abel had undergone the tribal initiation ceremony to become a warrior and village chieftain. Father Jose, a Catholic Priest, had taught him to speak English and to read and write. His captor's language would help him to cope with the greatest challenge of all. To survive this ordeal and to help his brothers who had also been prey to the slave traders.

Beth could not bear the wet clothes that clung to her like a second skin, and pushed her wet, sticky hair off her face. I took it all for granted, she thought. To be able to eat and drink whenever I wished, bathe, and wear beautiful gowns. My freedom I swear to you, heavenly father, I will never, never take it for granted again.

To Beth's relief the hatch opened and her thoughts immediately went to Abel, would she see him? She did not always but when she did; they were precious and reassuring moments.

Beth rushed for the water barrel to quench her thirst. The slaves surrounded it. She tried to fight her way through but could not find the strength. Abel appeared and made a pathway through the throng for her.

"Beth," he called as his eyes pierced her very being. Able handed her one of the ladles and she drank her allotted amount. She relished it as it eased her parched throat. She handed it back to him and he drank. Beth looked up at this strong, powerful man who she so adored.

"Come, come," he said when he had finished in his deep, commanding voice, which she just loved.

Able took her hand and guided her to sit down in the shade. Beth felt an overwhelming feeling of oneness with him.

She felt blessed to have such a wonderful man to look out for her.

Beth thought to herself, if only you knew how I feel about you Abel. You make me feel loved and safe as my father did. However, I am tarnished, unclean when you know what happened to me, you would not want me.

The slaver had stopped at many ports to take on more slaves, making life more unbearable in the hold. The slave chained to the left of Abel was from a rival village. His tribe had fought against him on many occasions. However, under these circumstances, Abel now considered him as his brother. Although he helped to feed him he became weaker and eventually died.

The younger boy on the other side of Abel was only 10 years old. He cried for the first two days and kept calling for his mother until he became too weak. Abel did not speak his tongue, so through gesticulation he encouraged the boy to eat and to be brave. The boy looked up at him with his big brown eyes and it made Abel feel very protective towards him.

This had been an arduous journey. Abel heard a deckhand shout. "Land ho, Captain!" The wooden hatch door opened and one by one, the slaves went up onto the deck. Abel heard the slave master order his men, "Get them cleaned up I want the best price for them."

The bright light hurt Abel's eyes as he climbed out of the hold and onto the deck. He had a handsome face with a strong jaw line and was tall and muscular, with a noble bearing. He stood out from the other slaves. The slave master had noted this. They washed him from a bucket of seawater using a block of soap and rags to clean him. They shaved his head and a piece of cloth covered his private parts. Then lined up with the other cleaned slaves was inspected by the slave master, who noted down against his name the comment—Top price ready for sale.

Beth was delighted to see Abel again as she waited for her turn to be cleaned. She prayed that their paths would cross again.

Chapter Two

Charleston—The Quayside

The chained slaves were marched along the dock, their bodies hunched in despair. Abel reflected, Thank you, Lord, for my survival on board 'The Camberley', he looked longingly for Beth. He wanted to see her again, although he knew the odds were against this happening. He felt destined to protect her.

The slaves were marched into a large, dark and damp building. Abel could hear moaning from the sick and dying as they passed a side room. The smell was overwhelming, reminding him of the hold of 'The Camberley'. The slave master undid Beth's chains. "Help in there," he said as he pushed her towards the sick room. He took the rest of the slaves to a large room where they sat in rows on the straw covered floor.

The slaves waited for several days in the warehouse. Abel's stomach had become painful and bloated and he felt nauseous and could not control his bowel movements. They took him to the room he had passed on the way in and laid him down, he could not remember anymore until he opened his eyes. "Beth," he softly murmured. She was cooling his body with water to try to bring down his temperature.

"Yes, Abel, it's me, now shush," as she put her finger to his lips. "Rest now, reserve your strength." Abel thought her eyes were comforting. The roar from the slave master brought him back to reality. He pulled Beth away and checked Abel to see if he would be fit enough for sale.

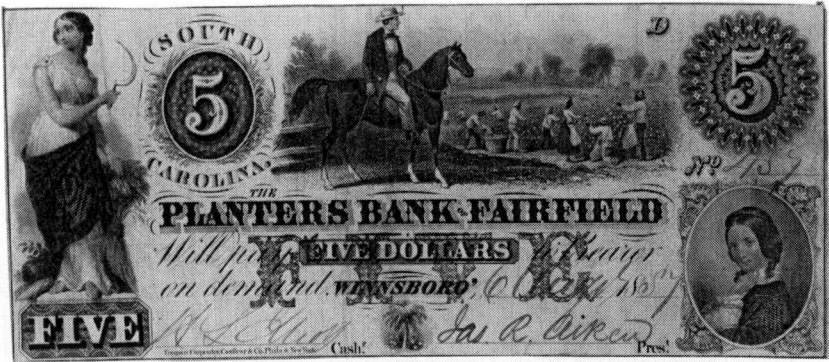

Theodore Jackson - owner of 'Cotton Wood Plantation' Charleston, South Carolina.

Theodore sat at the desk in his study looking at the monthly accounts. Not good, the severe storms last year had yielded a poor cotton harvest, which had badly affected the business. He must have a good return on the cotton harvest this year. He was down on the number of slaves he needed to bring in the cotton next month. He needed to find a quality slave who would replace George, who died last week. George had been a dependable slave running the collection and storage of the cotton. In addition, he required a female to help in his daughter's bedchamber, four young slaves to work in the fields and a young boy to assist in the stables. This was an expensive outlay but he had no choice, so he wrote a list for his visit to Charleston. He lifted his quill, dipped it into the silver inkpot and wrote on the quality paper in front of him.

Slave Market
Four prime slaves for harvesting the fields $ 4,300
One female slave - bed chambers $ 800
One-young lad - stables $ 400
1 quality slave - to replace George $ 1,075

                                        Total $ 6,575

Charleston
Make enquiries for white Arab horse.
Ball gown (for Emma's birthday)

Theodore put his hand into his jacket pocket and produced a bunch of keys. He slid open a draw in his ornate oak desk and lifted out a gold coloured moneybox.

Theodore unlocked it and proceeded to count out the necessary amount of money needed to pay for his goods. He placed the notes and coins in the money belt fastened around his waist. He called to his House Servant Tom.

"Bring my horse and inform Samson, that I wish him to accompany me with the horse and cart."

Theodore heard his daughter Emma's laughter coming from the hallway. She swept into his study in her crimson and black riding outfit. "My Emma, you look so much like your mother." She was his world. She had her mother's blonde hair the colour of golden strands and her iridescent blue eyes. He missed Martha so much, they had been soul mates his first and only love. She had died giving birth to their daughter. He knew he spoilt Emma but she brought sunshine into his life, he smiled at her as Emma kissed his cheek.

"Papa, could you purchase some red ribbons for me in Charleston, please?"

"Of course, my angel now let me call for Sebastian to ride with you. It would make me happy to know that you are safe." Emma put her arms around her father's shoulder; she knew how he worried about her. "Father, I am meeting Georgina at the avenue of trees near the church. We are going to the summer house in the grounds to plan my birthday ball." Georgina was her best friend since childhood and her brother Peter was a Confederate officer. Emma thought he looked so handsome in his uniform; she was a little in love with him. She hoped he felt the same way. Her father was constantly arranging for Sebastian her stepbrother to spend time with her, but there was no way she would ever like him. He was cruel and she was scared of him.

"I will be fine, father," she smiled and kissed him on the cheek.

Theodore was in his early fifties a striking man, tall and handsome with a thick head of dark hair, which was greying at the temples. His eyes were a piercing colour blue, his mouth was full and he had a dimple in his chin. He considered himself to be fair and righteous, a good Christian and neighbour. Theodore rode his horse along the avenue followed by Samson riding the horse and cart. He looked at the sweeping grounds of his plantation. He had inherited the plantation and worked hard to make it the most productive and profitable in South Carolina.

It would be his Legacy to leave for further generations.

He was careful with his money, something his stepson Sebastian was not. He had to monitor Sebastian's spending, for he loved to gamble.

It was a glorious morning and before him laid the cotton fields. The cotton was nearly ready for picking, he prayed for good weather so he could start the work next month.

Day by day, he was feeling better since his second wife Sophia had left him for John Holt, a neighbouring plantation owner. She was a vivacious woman who could turn men's heads. He remembered the first time he saw her at Colonel Hudson's estate; it was at the ball to celebrate his daughter's twenty-first birthday, she had many admirers. Sophia had raven black hair and green eyes that bewitched you, making you powerless. He was standing feeling awkward without a female escort, when he heard laughter and turned to see this stunning beauty. She wore an emerald green dress the colour of her eyes, her dress outlined all her curves. She waved her fan, peeking over the top of it in a flirtatious manner, their eyes met and he was under her spell from that moment.

Her husband had been a Captain who had owned a fleet of cargo ships. He had drowned when his ship had sunk in a storm in the Atlantic.

Theodore married her quickly but soon discovered they had little in common she loved attending social functions whereas he preferred to stay at home. Then they started to sleep in different bedchambers and barely spoke to one another. One day he found a note on his desk in his study telling him that she was leaving. He immediately arranged a meeting with his lawyer to start proceedings for a divorce and to change his will. Her son Sebastian had decided he wanted to remain with his stepfather. Theodore was fond of him and was pleased he wanted to stay with him; he was the son he never had. Sebastian had a quick temper he was also a drunkard and gambler, of which Theodore disapproved. However, he was a great help to him on the plantation, taking responsibility for the slaves.

That suited Theodore, as being a Christian he wrestled with his conscience. The slaves were frightened of Sebastian, but with rebellion threatening on some plantations in the area, he needed a firm control over the slaves. Even if he went too far in his treatment of them, Theodore would turn a blind eye. He had hoped that Emma and he would become close. It would please him greatly to think one day his daughter and heir to Cotton Wood Plantation would marry Sebastian, and run the plantation together after his death.

The Quayside was buzzing it was the day of the slave market which was held on the Wednesday following the arrival of a slave ship. Theodore acknowledged the other plantation owners he knew by a nod of his head.

Theodore was highly respected by the other owners in the area, his family had owned Cotton Wood Plantation for many generations and he had helped many, either with a loan of slaves or financial help.

He had to move fast to get the quality slaves he required for the plantation. The paler coloured slaves were expensive, as they would be required to work in the bedchambers of the large houses. One young woman stood out amongst the rest as she had the palest skin tone with European features. She would be perfect to work in his daughter's bedchamber, and he must have her. There were two men examining her. "$900 for this beauty, a very rare slave, you will be the envy of your neighbours," said the slave master. The men moved away shaking their heads. "Too expensive," they replied. The slave master pushed Beth's chin up with his whip, holding it there while Theodore looked over her body. He decided he would buy her for his Emma.

"$850 and I will buy her." He said in his southern drawl. "You drive a hard bargain, Sir." The slave master paused thoughtfully. "She is yours, Sir. You have made a wise decision." Theodore was pleased with his purchase although this had exceeded his budget. He comforted himself with the fact that he had purchased a quality slave that would fit in well in his household. Samson took charge of her while Theodore set about the business of examining some young males when Oliver Stanton, a regular slave master at the market approached him.

"Good morning, Sir. I have a fine specimen from good stock who was the chief of his village, he also speaks some English let me show you, please follow me." Theodore followed him eagerly to where a crowd was forming. Matthew had been shrewd in getting so many buyers interested, as it would drive the price up.

Theodore pushed his way forward through the throng. He placed some dollars discreetly into Matthew's hand asking for some time to look at this slave on his own.

Matthew obliged and the shouts of outrage resounded around him. Theodore examined Abel checking his teeth, tongue, limbs and penis. Abel gritted his teeth at this demeaning inspection.

He considered him a fine slave, a slave that would no doubt eventually produce offspring that would improve the general stock of slaves held on the plantation.

Theodore spoke to the slave, "What is your name boy?"

"'Abel," he replied.

"How old are you?"

"30 years."

Theodore took the slave master to one side and offered him a higher price than he had intended.

Samson tied Beth's hands behind her back and placed her on the cart. There were four male slaves and a young boy sat opposite her. She smiled at the young lad who appeared to be very nervous. Her heart soared when she saw Abel. Beth tried to disguise her obvious delight at seeing him. Samson secured him to the cart next to Beth. Their eyes met and they held each other's gaze. They had a real connection because of the ordeals they had suffered together. Thank you god for bringing Abel back to me, she said to herself feeling more positive about the future.

Beth had only witnessed her new master bartering for slaves, but could not yet judge whether this was a cruel or compassionate owner. Was this to be a further trial or a period of stability in her life, only time would tell?

Abel could not believe how fortunate he had been that the same master should buy Beth. For he could not imagine his world without her, he had become very fond of her. Now he could look after and protect her. The young lad who had travelled with Abel on The Camberley smiled back at him when he climbed onto the cart. Abel was relieved that the boy was still alive, as he had feared what would become of him.

As Beth first caught sight of Cotton Wood Plantation from the cart as it trundled down the avenue of trees. She thought what new trials and tribulations await me here.

Theodore ordered Samson to take the new slaves to the stable to have their chains removed and tags placed on them. Then he was to inform Sebastian that the new slaves were ready for his inspection. He finished placing the metal tag around their necks and told them to stand in a line ready for the Master.

Sebastian Theodore's stepson put on his monogrammed white cotton shirt and his black riding britches, which emphasised his toned thigh muscles. He had turned thirty he was tanned and rugged in looks and wore his thick black hair tied back.

"Hand me my riding crop," he ordered his servant a young boy called Lawrence.

Lawrence rushed to retrieve it from the table on the far side of the bedroom and handed it to his Master. Sebastian struck him across the face with it. "Be quicker next time, boy." Tears fell from his eyes. He could hear his master laughing as he descended the sweeping staircase

All the slaves feared Sebastian who employed two slaves called Rufus and Gideon. They were the master's eyes and ears amongst the other slaves. Their skin colour was paler than that of the rest. They were also better dressed than the others and administered the punishments. Rufus was head field slave and Gideon was head slave married to Lottie, the head cook in the big house.

Abel noticed that Samson was very nervous. He was in his late sixties with greying hair and a deep scar across his face and seemed to have difficulty walking. He poked and prodded Beth to stand up straight. He said, "If de mas' speaks yar all say ye mas'." (Usually with the passage of time, those that still spoke in their native tongue learnt to respond in the same manner as the others.) Sebastian walked along the line of slaves stopping at Abel. To him, it felt that he had stood there for an eternity there was an air of intimidation about him as he looked into Abel's eyes. Then he moved on to the female and with his riding crop, he lifted Beth's chin, so he could see her face more clearly. He moved the crop slowly over her body, stopping at her lower legs and lifted her skirt. Beth winced. Sebastian laughed. "Remember you are here to work and do my bidding, those who do not will be punished severely as Samson found out." He mounted his horse and galloped away down the avenue of trees followed by Rufus and Gideon.

Samson touched his scar. "Do as mas' say." He took them to the wooden cabins near the cotton fields. He told the slaves that they would have to become Christian. Abel and Beth replied that they already were. A service to christen the slaves took place on Sunday much to their bewilderment.

Theodore believed his duty was as a forward thinking owner to bring the word of God to his slaves. He had already erected a wooden Church for them on the outskirts of his plantation and allowed them to worship there on the Sabbath. Theodore felt that if he allowed them to marry this would encourage family bonds. Adding stability and would make it easier to control and run the plantation. Only whites and the free slaves could worship at the large white timber clad church near the house.

How can I continue day after day seeing the slaves that are God's children endure such treatment? Theodore reflected. It torments me even in my sleep, I ask god's forgiveness every day but I continue to enslave them. This plagued Theodore, as he was deeply religious.

During his childhood, his father would chastise him for being friendly with the slaves, particularly Jacob and his sister Clara. Theodore was the same age as them and they would meet secretly. As they grew up, he found himself falling in love with Clara. One day his father called him to his study. "Son, I have sold Jacob and Clara," he said. It was not fitting for the heir to Cotton Wood Plantation to be so familiar with the slaves, they are your property and you are their

Master, remember that." Theodore had run to his bedchamber put his face into his pillow and sobbed.

He was the only child and his mother had died when he was fourteen years old, he loved her so much. She was a gentle soul and very Religious. When he sat next to her in the church, she would always hold his hand and smile warmly at him. He always remembered the affection she had shown him. He thought his father was sometimes jealous of their close bond. A portrait of her hung in the study and he would go there to confide his thoughts to the only reminder he now had of his mother. In the hut, Abel sat down on the edge of a wooden bed next to Beth. He turned and looked at her. He really wanted to get to know her more. "Thank you for the kindness you showed me when I was ill in the warehouse." Abel said.

Beth felt his penetrating look she felt self-conscious and looked away. "You saved my life Abel," she knew she would be forever in his debt. She tried not to show her delight at him noticing her, for she would be encouraging him. She could not bear him finding out what had happened to her for he would reject her as she considered herself impure. She decided she would remain cold to his advances.

"Where do you come from?" Abel asked.

"I came from England, which is far across the sea." Trying to explain simply to Abel, as she knew he would not really understand. My mother was a servant working for a Duke in his country estate. When I was born the Duke, gave me his name." Beth showed Abel the heart shaped birthmark on her wrist. "My father had one in the same place and would always say no-one could deny I was his daughter, and that I was marked forever with his love."

Beth could not believe she was telling him so much about herself, but somehow she felt completely at ease with him.

Samson interrupted them. "Yar go see the head cook for yar food."

"Give dem food quick about it girl!" Shouted Lottie the head cook. Kate was obviously fearful she had bruises on her arms that she had received from a stressed, intolerant and impatient woman. Kate was reluctant to make eye contact with her, for fear of another beating. She produced a large bucket of cascara and a bowl of biscuits. Abel and Beth held out their food bowls and Kate proceeded to put some food into them. She added a piece of salted beef to both bowls. "No." shouted the cook. "Dem no work." Kate jumped at Lottie's raised voice and looked at them, apologising with her eyes as she removed the meat from their bowls and poured limejuice into their beakers.

"Me Lottie, de head cook in this house," said Lottie in a superior tone. "Yar all line up in de morning and de evening," she shouted.

She was rotund in shape and always looked unkempt. Her hair tumbled out from under her hat and perspiration ran down her face. She was constantly in a bad mood. She shouted at her four children to get out of her way, as they constantly ran backwards and forwards through the kitchen getting under her feet. The baby tied to her back by a large shawl was crying, adding to her anxiety.

Gideon her husband was a demanding and difficult man to live with. He had a roving eye and Lottie found it difficult to keep up with his sexual demands. She needed to keep on the right side of him or he would beat her.

Sunday morning all the slaves attended Church. The Minister took the Christening service and they were all given names. Later they settled in their cabins.

John, Mark, Soul and Peter had bunk beds on one side of the room whilst Abel and Louis took the remaining two single beds.

Chapter Three

⌒⌒

Tom, the House Servant took Beth to meet her mistress, Beth thought he had a kind face. He was smartly dressed and advised her that he would be overseeing her duties within the household.

Mistress Emma asked Tom to send in the new chambermaid. She looked Beth up and down and said "Beth, you will be trained by my other servant Jenny. You will share a room with her and there will be new clothes laid out for you there. I will expect you to come to me when I call, you must always be clean, neat and tidy in your appearance."

"Yes Mistress," Beth replied and curtsied. Jenny took her to their room where Beth washed herself and put on her new clothes. How wonderful to feel clean and have fresh clothes thought Beth, as she admired herself in the mirror on the wall in the room.

She found Jenny both cold and unfriendly she had made it quite clear to Beth who was in charge. Beth soon picked up her duties. On one particular occasion, Beth started work as usual changing her Mistresses' bedding. She had gone to the cupboard to collect fresh linen, on opening the door she found Sebastian astride Jenny on the floor. She turned quickly and closed it feeling very uncomfortable with what she had seen. She knew as a female slave you could not say no to your master. Later in their bedroom, Jenny approached Beth. "I hate the Mas' he hurt me."

The slaves in the fields had to pick the cotton from Sunrise to Sundown. This was back-breaking work. The bell rang at four in the morning for breakfast, and half an hour later, they started work. If they were late, they would receive five lashes. Rufus, the driver, loved the power he wielded over the field slaves and he would whip them over any slight infringement.

The sun was fierce, a new slave called Soul was not picking fast enough for Rufus. He told him to stand against the cart with his arms and legs spread and proceeded to whip him until the blood poured from his back. Soul then had to continue to work.

"Beth, go and tell Samson that I will need a horse ready to ride this morning?" said her Mistress.

"Yes, Mistress Emma," replied Beth. She looked in Samson's hut and tack room, but there was no sign of him. She went to the stables unbeknown to her Sebastian had seen her enter.

"Samson." Beth called looking in all the stalls. She heard the stable door close behind her and she turned and came face to face with Sebastian.

Please lord, not again she thought, her heart pounded in her chest.

"Well girl I have you alone," he said menacingly to Beth as he circled around her. She backed away from him only to find the wall of the stall behind her. Sebastian placed his large powerful hands either side of Beth's shoulders. There was no escape for her. She started to shake with fear. All her emotions from that dreadful day she was raped, returned

Sebastian put his face close to hers; she could feel his breath on her cheek.

"You know you cannot say no to the Master." Beth found him repulsive as he pushed his body into hers. She could feel his excitement throbbing against her as she tried to push him away. He knocked her off her feet onto the straw covered floor of the stall. Beth let out a scream as Sebastian pushed his hand up her skirt. She fought him managing to get one hand free she clawed at his face. He winced from the pain her nails had inflicted she had drawn blood. Sebastian grabbed her hair and banged her head several times on the stable floor.

As Abel was filling in the ledger in the collection shed next door, he heard the screaming. He rushed into the stable. He found Sebastian straddled across Beth. Abel grabbed him, pulled him away, and pinned him against the wall. "Run back to your Mistress, Beth—run!" He shouted.

"You will pay for that," said Sebastian breathlessly. He staggered to the stable door. "Rufus Gideon! Here now!" he shouted.

They both appeared at the same time.

"Hold him," Sebastian ordered. He vented his anger and lay into Abel leaving him bloodied on the stable floor.

"I am sorry Mistress . . . ," Beth said in a distressed state.

"What has happened?" asked a concerned Emma. Beth explained what had taken place in the stable.

"I am not having this, go and tidy yourself up Beth." Emma went down to see her father in his study.

"My angel, how lovely to see you," her father said, looking up from the paperwork on his desk.

"Papa, I must insist that you reprimand Sebastian for mistreating my servant Beth, she is under my protection. Please say you will have a word with him about it, please, as she put an arm around his shoulder.

"Don't upset yourself, my angel, I will speak to him."

Theodore shouted for Tom.

"Tom, tell Sebastian to come to my study immediately."

"Yar, Mas'," said Tom.

Sebastian entered Theodore's study. "You wanted me?"

"You are to leave Beth alone find your fun somewhere else. Is that clear?"

"Yes, Sir," replied an annoyed Sebastian, he knew Emma could always wrap her father around her little finger.

The collection shed was large and as part of Abel's duties, he had to note down in a heavily bound ledger the weight of cotton collected each day by the slaves. They had an established quota they had to achieve or the master punished them.

Abel could not work out why his relationship was not moving along with Beth. It had been six months since they arrived and she was only just acknowledging him. Why was she so cold towards him? It did not make any difference how many times he tried to talk to her at Church on Sunday. He had definitely felt a rapport with her during their previous trials and tribulations. This had been particularly evident when she had looked after him in the warehouse. What had he done?

Theodore looked at the white Arab stallion he was pleased with this fine specimen. He was expensive but worth it, just to see the pleasure it would bring to his daughter on her birthday.

"Samson, I want him broken and ready for riding by next Saturday. The stallion must be safe for Mistress Emma, to ride, do a good job and I will reward you."

"Yar mas'," replied Samson.

Gideon overheard the conversation and was determined that Samson would not benefit from the task set by his master.

Every day Samson set about breaking the stallion, he was progressing well. Gideon knew his master was away on business. While Samson was busy unloading stores he had collected from town for Lottie, Gideon went into the stall where the white Arab was tethered, and started to whip the stallion. It reared and foamed at the mouth trying to get out of the stable.

Louis was in the tack room cleaning the saddles when he heard the commotion, and went to investigate. Louis charged at Gideon with no fear to stop him mistreating the stallion.

Gideon knew that he had to deal with Louis, for if his master found out that he had harmed this special gift for Emma—his punishment would be severe. He grabbed Louis and pushed him towards the frenzied horse. Louis screamed as the stallion repeatedly kicked him. Samson and Abel heard the screaming and rushed to the stables to find Gideon holding the door with Louis inside. Abel struck him and pushed him to the stable floor while Samson calmed the Arab horse and dragged Louis' lifeless body out. Abel carried Louis to his wooden hut. He tried to revive him but Louis had stopped breathing. Abel cradled him and wept. Meanwhile Gideon had recovered and had informed Sebastian that he had found Abel and Louis ill-treating the stallion. On the orders of Sebastian, Gideon and Rufus marched into the hut, dragged Abel out and tied him to the whipping post, where they both laid into him with their whips until Abel became unconscious. His back had deep wounds that were open and bleeding. As an example to the other slaves, Abel languished for two days without water. The temperature during the day was stifling. At night, Peter and Samson crept out and poured some water into Abel's mouth. The other slaves revered Abel as he always came to their aid if they ever needed help this was their opportunity to help him in his hour of need.

The next morning Gideon untied Abel and threw him into his hut.

"Help me please?" Beth shouted to Samson. They placed Abel on his bed face down so Beth could bathe his wounds.

Abel murmured.

"Abel, it is Beth and Samson," she told him. It hurt her to see him in such pain. She had strong feelings for this wonderful man, but she needed to guard her emotions. She was on her own now, she must be strong and never let anything or anybody hurt her again.

At Louis' funeral, Abel read a passage from the bible at the service. Beth laid flowers at his grave.

Abel erected a wooden cross at the head of his grave, engraved with Louis' name. Lord, I let the boy down, I did not protect him, he said to himself. Please forgive me.

Beth could not bear to see Abel so inconsolable her instincts were to comfort him. "You did your best to protect Louis Abel, God knows that and so do we. Please don't be so hard on yourself."

"You are kind," replied Abel.

"You are a fine man Abel."

They walked back from the graveyard together through the plantation.

A week later, it was Harvest Festival and Theodore gave the slaves a day off. Everyone decorated the area outside the wooden Church, ready for the barn dance that evening.

"Let me plait your hair Kate," said Beth as she waited for her to change in her hut. Beth had brought some old ribbons from her drawer that Mistress Emma had given her. "Which colour would you like Kate?" Beth asked. Kate pointed to the red one and beamed as Beth wove it into her hair. They wore their best clothes and arm in arm set off for the Church. They could hear the music floating through the night air, and the laughter and chatter from everyone enjoying themselves. There were candles glowing in the trees surrounding the church, and paper decorations strewn across the branches.

Samson was playing his penny whistle, Peter the drums and Soul was on the washboard. Lottie was in full swing, dancing, her larger-than-life body swaying to the music. On a long table was an array of food and drink given by the Master for the festivities, to show his appreciation for such a good yield this year from the plantation.

Kate and Beth were dancing when Abel tapped Beth on the shoulder.

"Would you dance with me, Beth, please?"

Beth tried not to show her delight at him asking her. She so wanted to be close to him but scared she might weaken; her fear of intimacy was a real problem.

"No I must go back to the house," she said looking up at his disappointed expression.

"Please let me get you a drink and I will walk you back?" Abel said. He just had to get her on her own.

Beth nodded and walked over to the table with him, admiring his fine toned body as he poured her a drink. They strolled along with their drinks in their hands listening to the music and the laughter as it filled the warm night air.

"Tell me, Beth, have I upset you or offended you in anyway?"

"Why no Abel, why do you say that?" she looked at his face searchingly.

He was silent for a while, and then said, "I feel a strong connection to you and hoped you felt the same way?"

Beth leant against a tree looking up at him, the moonlight caught the outline of his face and she thought how handsome he was.

"I have learnt to keep an invisible barrier around me to shut out my emotions and feelings. It is the only way I know how to survive," Beth said.

He touched her arm—she pulled away.

What have I done? Abel thought.

"Beth, I will always look after you and protect you, please let me, we are destined to be together."

Beth had conflicting emotions. Yes, she loved him and felt safe, but what if she lost him as she had her daughter, her mother and Reverend Logan. It would destroy her if she allowed her feelings to surface.

Abel sensed her hesitancy and kissed her gently on the cheek not wanting to frighten her away.

"I must go now, good night Abel," she said as she wrapped her shawl tightly around her shoulders and left.

Abel had seen how the other men looked at Beth they desired her. He had wanted her from the moment that he first set eyes on her, he would not give up—she was his.

It was Sunday and Beth sat in the Church.

"May I sit next to you Beth," asked Abel. Beth nodded her head, she so adored this man. After the service, Abel asked her if he could walk her back to the house.

"Yes." she replied.

It was a glorious day they walked side by side through the cotton fields, laughing and talking.

"Please sit awhile," Abel beckoned to the wooden chairs out-side his cabin. He poured her some water in a wooden beaker and handed it to her. They sat in silence and when Beth had finished her drink, she stood up and handed the empty beaker to him.

"I must go," Abel took hold of her hand. "Wait! Please marry me Beth, I cannot bear to wait any longer, we are meant to be together?" he blurted out.

She went quiet. Oh Abel I so want to say yes, she thought. Why should I not take the happiness he offers me, she struggled with the decision—would he reject her when he knew she had been raped.

Abel tried to judge what her answer would be. Beth bent down, cupped his face in her hands, and said, "Yes Abel, I will marry you." Abel picked her up and twirled her around his face an explosion of joy at her answer.

Beth prayed their love would overcome her impurity and that he would understand her fear of intimacy for she loved him so much. Her guard was down, and her tears flowed she was so happy. Her heart flooded with love for the man who had saved her and excitement filled every part of her body. She said to herself. "Please,

God, do not take Abel from me I could not bear to lose someone else I love.

"Mistress, I would like your permission to marry Abel?" Beth's hands shook as she brushed her long hair.

"Why, I have no problem with it but I must ask my father," Beth thanked her Mistress.

The sun flickered through Emma's bedroom window, dancing on the mirror opposite her bed. She stretched out in her large soft bed. It was her twenty-first birthday and with excitement she jumped up and called to Beth to get her dressed, and then she rushed down the staircase into her father's study.

"Father, I am so excited, what have you bought me for my birthday?" Theodore hugged his daughter.

"Happy birthday, my angel, you will have your surprise before your birthday ball this evening."

"Oh, father, I cannot contain my excitement, what is it?'

He laughed. "You must be patient, my angel," he said as he hugged her. How he wished her mother could be here to enjoy this special moment.

She sighed, and giggling ran down the hallway and into the kitchen. "Have you started preparing the food for this evening?" she shouted to Lottie. "Tom, have you prepared the floral decoration yet?"

Beth laid out the Mistress's new dress her father had brought back from Charleston. Beth could not resist sliding her hand gently against its soft silk fabric. It was scarlet with white lace around the neck, puffed sleeves with pearl buttons down the back and on the bodice. She held it against herself and imagined what it would be like to wear it on her wedding day. She quickly came to her senses and laid it down on the bed.

That evening Emma stood in front of her full-length mirror, her golden blonde hair was pinned back at each side of her face with a diamond clip in the shape of a flower. The rest of her hair tumbled over her bare shoulders. The dress outlined her shapely figure; the top of her breasts overflowed out of her bodice. Beth placed the mistress's diamond and ruby necklace around her slender neck.

Emma turned towards Beth. "Beth my father has given his permission for you to marry Abel."

"Thank you, Mistress," said a very happy and relieved Beth. Her heart started to race she could not be happier and could not wait to tell Abel.

"Now pull me in as tight as you can, Beth, I want my waist to look as tiny as possible." She wanted to look her best so Peter would not be able to take his eyes off her. He would surely want to dance with her all night. She had a crush on him since he came back from his duties as a Captain in the Confederate army.

Last summer he had looked so handsome in his uniform. It would make her birthday if only Peter would ask her to dance. Her father was so protective and would discourage any attention from men, but kept encouraging Sebastian to spend time with her. She despised him, as he was hateful and always jealous of the attention her father gave her. He may have been able to deceive her father but not her.

Theodore called upstairs to his daughter "Emma, my angel, your surprise is waiting for you outside." Her beauty astounded everyone, her striking gown glided over each step down the sweeping staircase. Her father looked at her and for one brief moment saw his beloved Martha.

"Father, he is beautiful I will call him Star," Emma said as she hugged her horse. Then she ran and embraced her father, her eyes shining with delight.

Theodore smiled with contentment.

The house was alive with music and laughter. At every window, there were candles and flowers placed around the large impressive front door, which gave a warm welcome to the guests.

The carriages arrived one by one and passengers alighted in their finery.

That night Emma's wish came true. Peter asked her to dance and she thought she was in heaven. The dance floor was an array of coloured dresses swirling to the music. Sebastian was drunk and behaving badly, he kept trying to dance with Emma.

Theodore went over to him and grabbed his arm to keep him upright. He took him into his study and warned him to behave and not to spoil Emma's party or he would reduce his allowance.

Intoxicated Sebastian asked his stepfather for a loan to repay his gambling debt.

"What again, no more Sebastian, I will not give you another penny. Now get out of my sight and sober up!"

Sebastian returned to his room and tore it apart in temper. Who does he think he is to deny me the money I so badly need? He felt he deserved a higher allowance for the hours he had put into the plantation. It would have been different if he were the heir. He must pursue Emma to become his wife and then the plantation would be his, but this was proving to be difficult.

He had a deadline to repay the money he owed, these were business people you did not cross. They had murdered his friend Thomas he must get the money at all costs.

It was Beth's wedding day and the weather was fine. Grace, Samson's wife set about decorating the wooden Church with flowers.

"Beth" said her Mistress. "I have no further use for this gown, perhaps this could be your wedding dress?" Emma had become very fond of Beth.

"Thank you Mistress." Excitedly Beth took the dress to her room. Dressed in this gown I will feel as I did back home, she thought, at least on my wedding day. She thought how different her wedding day would have been had she been living at home on her Father's estate. Her Mother would be smiling with pride as she fussed around her helping her get dressed. Her Father would have given her away and her sister Charlotte would have been her bridesmaid. The saddest thing of all is that they would never meet her beloved Abel. She buried her head in her hands and wept at what might have been.

Beth looked at her reflection in the mirror and transported back to Pendragon hall and her youth.

"Missy," Kate started to cry at the sight of Beth in her wedding dress and hugged her, and set about plaiting her hair for her.

Lottie prepared some food for the wedding feast. The Minister arrived to take the service. Tom the House Servant gave Beth away, how he wished it were he who was marrying her.

Abel turned and watched Beth walk down the aisle towards him, thanking God for giving him this wonderful woman to share his life.

"You may kiss the bride," said the Minister to Abel.

He looked into her beautiful, dark eyes that shone with happiness and kissed her gently on her lips. He knew he would love this woman forever.

They signed the register and walked hand in hand to the festivities that had been organised by Kate and Lottie. They all danced and laughed until late.

Beth and Abel walked in the warmth of the evening to Abel's large wooden hut that had come with his position in charge of the storage shed. Theodore was very pleased with him and rewarded him with a larger cabin. Beth would live with him there.

Abel touched her face—she backed away. Abel felt her nervousness.

"I can't," Beth cried.

"I'm sorry. I did not mean to rush you. We can just hold each other," he said as he tried to reassure her.

Beth wished she had told him before their marriage.

"Sit down Abel I need to tell you something." She summoned up the courage and told him everything that had happened to her.

There was an uncomfortable silence. Beth panicked would he reject her. Abel reached out to her.

"Do you think so little of me to think I would not want you because of what happened to you? I so wish I could have been there to protect you. I do understand it will happen when you are ready. I love you with all of my heart and body and just having you by my side is enough for me." Abel took Beth's hands and held her. Beth felt that at last she was loved and not alone anymore.

Life at Cotton Wood Plantation went on.

Beth snuggled up to Abel as usual, but this time she was ready for more. She took his hand and placed it on her breast.

Abel looked at her. "Are you sure Beth?" he said.

"Yes very sure."

"I will be gentle, just tell me if you need me to stop."

"Close your eyes my love."

She did as he asked feeling apprehensive. He kissed her forehead tenderly and with his lips slightly parted, he slowly glided them towards her generous mouth and kissed her. Then his moist tongue moved down her neck teased her as he moved to her breasts and played with her erect nipples. "Oh Abel," she moaned with pleasure her body relaxing and succumbing to his soft touch. He then traced the curve of her waist. She arched her back and whimpered with pleasure. Abel caressed her thighs and finding her pleasure spot caressed it rhythmically until she climaxed, she cried with delight. Abel repeated it and her groans grew louder and louder, and then he entered her. Her body glowed in the candle light. To him she was such a thing of beauty. They kissed passionately and fell asleep in each other's arms.

The months passed, this was the happiest Beth had been since she was taken into captivity. Abel was elated when Beth told him she was with child.

In the New Year, she gave birth to a son. Thank you for the safe delivery of my son Lord and bless my daughter Eliza. Her thoughts returned to the 'The Camberley' and the child that had died at birth.

Beth held Will tightly kissed him and handed him to his father. Abel raised him up thanking God for a son. "This is my son, William Tukowunu, son of Chief Abel Tukowunu of the Manitou Tribe. May God and his ancestors look on him kindly and protect him."

Captain George Johnson, Theodore's neighbour had requested the loan of a slave for a month to help with the cotton picking on his plantation. He was prepared to pay well. Theodore agreed to loan him Peter one of his new men, he had often found this business to be profitable. Abel had become close to Peter and was concerned how he would cope, since he had heard reports of the cruel treatment of the field slaves by the white overseer. He watched as Peter climbed onto the cart to take him to his new master.

Peter went straight to work in the fields. The White overseer constantly whipped him, shouting "Faster nigger." At the end of the day, he had fallen short of his quota and the overseer had punished him. This treatment went on day after day until he could not take any more.

He must escape while he still had the strength. He took his chance at night and made for the swamps, he knew of other slaves that had escaped and hoped to join them. He kept going all day under the blistering sun, his mouth was dry and he craved water. He fell asleep exhausted on a sturdy branch over-hanging the water. He awoke to the sound of barking dogs. He fell from his sleeping position into the water and scrambled through the mangroves. The dogs caught up with him, tearing at his legs and arms. He tried to fight them off but they dragged him into the swamp. Peter returned to Cotton Wood Plantation. Theodore was furious, as he had to repay the Captain's money.

Theodore left Sebastian to deal with the situation as his conscience troubled him. That way it was easier to pretend that inhuman treatment did not happen on his plantation. There was talk that slaves would receive their freedom soon, how safe would he and his family be? He thought.

Abel saw Peter's return from the window of the sorting and storage warehouse. He watched Gideon and Rufus lift him out and carry him to the punishment hut. The days passed and Peter had no food or water. Abel prayed Peter would make it. After three days, they removed him unconscious from the punishment hut. When the coast was clear, Abel slipped into Peter's hut. He was delirious and weak, and suffering from dehydration. He lifted Peter onto his bed and cleaned his wounds that had festered. He placed wet cool cloths on his forehead, "Rest I will be back later." Beth put a healing mixture on Peter's wounds, something her mother had taught her. She raised his head up and gave him sips of water.

"I must return to the house before I am missed," Beth said.

Abel and Beth between them helped Peter regain his strength and then sent to work in the stables. Sebastian had a weighted bell collar fitted around Peter's neck to stop him from escape.

Jenny had missed her periods.

"Me t'ink me wid child," she said to Beth as she held her stomach." She started to cry. Beth put her arms around her and comforted her.

"Don't worry, Jenny, I will help you. Now dry your eyes."

It had always been just Jenny and her parents. They had died when she was twelve, she continued working in the kitchen needing no one. She was so grateful for Beth's kindness.

During the day, while Beth worked she used a shawl to secure Will to her back. The evenings were a very special time when she breast-fed him, she was able to cuddle him and interact with him, which was wonderful. He was a gift from God and she dreamed that someday soon, they would be set free, and they would be able to bring him up on their own farm somewhere in the country and be a family free of persecution.

It was spring and Jenny was six months and looking forward to having her baby, someone for her to love and to love her—her family.

"Me unwell." Jenny told Beth.

"Look it's late I will see to the mistress you get to your bed. I will check on you later."

Beth knocked on Jenny's door there was no reply. Beth let herself in quietly in case she was asleep. It was dark so she pushed the lantern she was holding forward so she could see if Jenny was all right. Her face was partially covered and she appeared to be asleep so Beth turned for the door. She slipped and fell to the floor. She was annoyed with herself at being so clumsy and that she would wake Jenny up. Her hand and legs felt wet. Beth fumbled to find the lantern that had fallen from her hand. To her horror, the light shone on a pool of blood that had seeped from the bed covers. Beth checked Jenny, she was not breathing.

"Tom, Tom," Beth shouted as she banged on his bedroom door. "Come quickly its Jenny, she is not breathing, I fear she is dead?" Tom followed Beth along the corridors. He lent foreword and checked her breathing. "Yar right Beth," he said as he covered her face. Beth was exhausted she cried as soon as she saw Abel. "I could do nothing to help her." Abel held Beth in his arms. They both looked at their son knowing how lucky they were to have a healthy infant.

There was a Church service on the Sunday at the slaves' church for Jenny. Beth lent into the open coffin and kissed her, and laid some flowers around her head.

Beth was now in charge of her Mistress's bedchamber.

Chapter Four

Sebastian rode into Charleston to Madam Collette's house of ill repute, which he frequently visited. "Well good evening, Sebastian," said the Madam. "Would you like Bella your usual or another?"

"You know I only have Bella," Sebastian replied impatiently.

Captain Gray had hired some thugs led by a brute called Striker to menace Sebastian as he had reneged on his gambling debt. Striker had been observing his movements around the town, particularly his frequent visits to the whorehouse. He had paid Madam Collette to let his men hide in Bella's bedchamber so that they could surprise him. Sebastian opened the door it was dark, and then they pounced on him. Shutting the door Striker said, "Hold him firm men. Do you have the money?"

A frightened Sebastian replied, "No, I beg you give me more time?"

"This is a message from Captain Gray." Striker and his men laid into him knocking him to the ground and continued to kick him. Striker shouted, "Hold him still." He took his knife out and slashed

Sebastian's face. "This is a warning, next time it will be your throat." They pushed past Bella as she came through the door, she screamed when she saw his bloodied face. She tried to clean it for him but he threw her aside. "Get out of my way you, whore. "He struggled down the stairs and onto his horse.

Sebastian returned to the plantation house holding his cravat against his bloodied face. He read the note left for him on his desk telling him that Theodore would be away for two days. I leave you in charge be sure to look after Emma. This gave him the opportunity to get closer to Emma. He cleaned himself up and examined the wound. He went to Theodore's study to look for the moneybox but it was gone. Theodore knew Sebastian would be looking for it while he was away so he had placed it in his strongbox. Sebastian searched for it, pulling everything out in frustration. He drank more Whisky and continued until he was drunk. He shouted through the kitchen door "Gideon, come here—now!" Lottie was very nervous when the Master was drunk. She went outside to find him chopping wood.

"Gideon, de Mas' wants you, he drunk." He went to the study to find his Master swigging a bottle of Whisky and the study wrecked.

"Stand by the Mistress's door and let no one in, if you value your life you will do as I order."

"Yar Mas'," replied Gideon. He followed him up the stairs. Sebastian barged into Emma's bedchamber as Beth was getting her mistress ready for bed.

"What do you think you are doing entering my bedchamber? Get out! Or I will inform my father how you've behaved in his absence," said Emma.

"Girl get out—Now!" Sebastian commanded Beth.

"No do not leave," ordered Emma.

Sebastian grabbed Beth and threw her out of the bedchamber onto the landing. She fell hitting her leg hard on a chest. She tried to stand up to help her Mistress but the pain was excruciating. "Mistress, Mistress," cried Beth. She crawled to the bedchamber door and Gideon threw her back against the banisters. Emma tried to pass Sebastian but he would not let her. He grabbed her ripping her gown and forcibly kissed her, she struggled but Sebastian was too strong. He pinned her against the wall with his body and pushed his hand up her dress, she struggled to fight him off. Beth dragged herself up again and cried,

"Mistress, I am coming."

Sebastian turned to Gideon, "Keep her out."

Gideon did his Masters bidding and stood guard at the bedchamber door. He pushed Beth against the landing wall and she fell to the floor dazed. Emma picked up a hatpin from her dressing table while Sebastian had turned away and hid it behind her back. He turned towards her and said, "There is no point in fighting me—no one can help you. Where is your father's money box?"

"I do not know," she cried. He walked towards her; Emma tried to keep her nerve holding on tightly to her hatpin. He grabbed her and pulled her towards him. In a menacing tone, Sebastian said, "You know you want me Emma, your father wants us to be together, so do not fight me." He threw her onto the bed and brutally kissed her bruising her mouth and ripping at her clothes. He wanted her there and then. He held her with one hand, undid his belt with the other, and lent into her. With one quick movement of her arm, she stabbed him lodging the hatpin in his neck. You slut he cried grabbing her from the bed and with the back of his hand slapped her, she fell striking her head against the marble fire surround. Sebastian tugged the hatpin from his neck and seeing Emma's lifeless body on the floor suddenly brought him to his senses. He lifted her onto the bed feeling the warm blood from the gash to her head. He noticed that her lips had turned blue. What had he done? Panic set in. He checked her breathing—there was none.

He shouted for Gideon. "Ride fast to Doctor Lloyd's house and bring him back." Beth recovered and could see her Mistress on her bed, her white bed gown covered in blood and she was not moving. With Gideon gone, Beth hobbled over to see to her shouting "Mistress!" Sebastian grabbed Beth and putting his hands around her neck said threateningly.

"Girl, if you tell anyone what you have seen, I will kill you and your child, do you understand."

Beth struggled to breathe, she managed to squeal, "Yes, master," he then released his grip.

Sebastian was certain of one thing he had had enough of his stepfather. His own father had treated him brutally throughout his childhood. He needed to be independent. If only he could get his hands on Cotton Wood Plantation. He had messed up. Now he must use his wits.

Sebastian felt that his father's death was the best thing that had happened to him. He remembered well, the fear he felt every time he returned home after each sea voyage.

Captain Augustus Pike was a very religious and an authoritarian figure, he ran—as he put it a very tight ship at Harbour Ridge Plantation. The life for a slave was very short he was inhuman and cruel. His son's life at home was not much better. His mother was indifferent to him and his father would punish him for any minor infringement of his rules.

On many occasions in fear and trepidation, Sebastian stood outside his father's study sometimes for many hours in his under garments. "Get in here," his father would shout. "Bend over that chair," he would order. "Read," he commanded as his father placed a bible opened on the seat of the chair for him to read during his punished. Often his wounds had not healed from the previous caning. He was a result of his upbringing, becoming devoid of feeling.

Beth limped along the landing to get Will from his Moses basket in her bedroom she could hear him crying. She overheard Sebastian giving orders to Rufus.

"Rufus, I want you to collect together six slaves and Abel and chain them and watch over them in the stable?"

"Yar, Mas'."

The doctor examined Emma. "I am afraid she is dead, what happened here?" he had noticed that there was a ripped to Emma's gown.

"Well doctor, I returned from a visit to Charleston to find slaves in my step fathers study. They fled at my arrival pulling everything off the desk looking for money I searched around the house and went upstairs and found Emma on the floor of her bedchamber."

Sebastian broke down in tears "My poor Emma." The doctor consoled him.

"I have everything under control now, we have captured the slaves responsible and they will be dealt with on my Stepfather's return," said Sebastian. The doctor advised him that he would be reporting the circumstances surrounding Emma's death. Beth rushed across the yard to Samson's hut, catching sight of Abel, the other slaves chained, and thrown into the stable by Gideon.

"Help me please, Samson, they have Abel and six others, they have been chained and are being held in the stables," she told him what had happened.

"You no worry, Missy, me find keys." Samson reassured Beth. "We run Missy wait by de chu'ch." Samson knew that the mas' would not believe it was Sebastian, who killed his daughter. Moreover, he would want Abel and the others to pay with their lives. Samson kissed his wife Grace. "God go with you my love," she said knowing that asking him not to go would be pointless. Samson knew he was taking a great risk. He hurriedly crossed the yard with the keys. "Mas' Sebastian he wan' Rufus, Samson stay here." Rufus did not query it and left. Samson quickly unlocked Abel and the other Slaves.

He told them to head for the forest while he and Abel took horses and some water and headed for the wooden Church.

"I will not leave my wife and son," Abel said to Samson.

"No worry Abel, Beth meet us by de chu'ch," replied Samson.

Beth was nervously waiting, it was cold and she could not stop shaking. Will started to cry, she rocked him to quiet him and was relieved when Abel arrived. He pulled her up behind him on his horse. They galloped at speed away from the plantation towards the forest. Sebastian watched them ride away through the window of Emma's bedroom.

"You fool, Rufus," he said angrily as he hit him in the stomach. "Find them or you will forfeit your life," he said. Rufus was winded and had difficulty replying, "Yar, mas'."

Rufus and Gideon made chase at first light with the hounds trained to seek out and corner escaped slaves.

Theodore returned home, to find his beloved daughter was dead. He was devastated. "Emma, my angel," he clung to her and wept uncontrollably. How does a parent react when their child dies before them! He had not been there to protect her, why had he gone away leaving her defenceless. He called her name repeatedly, his face awash with tears. Theodore confronted Sebastian who flinched nervously he knew he had to stick to his story. Theodore raised his hand, struck him hard across the face, and then pinned him against the wall of the study. He shouted angrily looking him in the eyes and said, "I left you in charge Sebastian, and you let me down. I left my precious daughter in your care and you leave her to visit Charleston. Why, why did you go and leave Emma?" he said heartbroken.

Sebastian played the role of the grieving stepbrother convincingly "Sir, I went to Charleston to look at an engagement ring for Emma, I was going to propose to her. If only I could turn back the clock, I would."

"Well you can't and every time I look at your face, I will know it was because of you my daughter was left defenceless. I despise you, get out of my sight."

The funeral service took place in the white wooden Church next to the house many had come from the surrounding area to pay their respects.

Theodore had Emma buried next to her mother in the family churchyard. Her grave covered in red flowers, her favourite colour. An angel carved in marble towered over the family plot. Theodore said "Rest in peace, my angel, your mother will watch over you now."

Theodore felt empty inside his whole world had collapsed. When Martha died, he had to go on for the sake of their daughter but now he just wanted to join them. Melancholia engulfed him.

Abel and Samson rode hard for many hours, stopping for nothing. Beth had explained all to Abel, this was not what he wanted it was so dangerous for Beth and their son. He made Beth promise not to risk her or her son's life to save him.

He came into his own using his bush skills they found water and rested. He did not want to endanger his wife and son. They had to find safety and put distance between themselves and the trackers. They removed Wills tag from his neck and then theirs, as they must pass as free slaves.

"Samson, how did you get your limp?" said Beth.

"Me punished," Beth held Will close to her.

Abel said "Sleep!" we have a long day ahead of us." The men took it in turn to keep guard.

"I can see lights in the distance." Abel told Samson.

"Get on your horses," he said, "Time to move on."

They were weary and desperately wanted to sleep now but Abel knew they had little time before the trackers caught up with them. While Beth suckled Will, Abel approached Samson.

"I need to speak to you," he said quietly, so that Beth would not overhear him. "I need to lead the trackers away from us. I want you to take Beth and my son in the direction of the mountains to the North. You have a good chance if I lead them in another direction. I cannot tell Beth because she will not leave me. I will just take off and you must make speed and hide in the mountains, I will find you."

Samson said, "Me go?"

"This is second nature to me, I am the best person to do this, just please protect my family," said Abel.

"Gawd be with you," said Samson.

Abel took Will in his arms, kissed him, and held Beth tightly.

"I love you and our son so much," Beth stroked his face.

"You must ride behind Samson, for a while as I need to ride ahead to check our way through the forest." She did as he asked, an hour past and Beth was getting worried."

"Abel should have returned by now, Samson," she said

Samson did not answer.

"He has gone hasn't he?"

There was quiet and then Samson replied. "Missy, Able give us a chance, we go to de mountains."

Beth cried as she clung onto Samson's back thinking how typical it was of Abel to want to protect his family. She was so proud of him and prayed for his safe return.

Abel had left a series of false trails near the river to confuse the trackers and their hounds.

He watched from the hilltop as the trackers followed each trail, their lights shining in the distance. They turned repeatedly to follow his tracks. This will now give Samson more time to get his wife and son to safety he thought.

This was second nature to Abel. He remembered well his initiation ceremony from a boy into a man. He had to survive in the bush for thirty days, but this time it was different he could not afford to fall asleep. Abel stopped to rest his horse, finding it increasingly difficult to keep his eyes from closing. The next thing he knew he felt a knife against his throat.

"Wuh yar name?" Abel looked up into the face of a male negro wearing a bandana. He had at least twenty men surrounding him.

"My name is Abel I have escaped from my Master with my family. I am not guilty of a murder."

"Were de others? Asked the leader

"We decided to split up, and go in different directions," said Abel. The leader accepted Abel's explanation and removed the knife. Two of his men held him; he explained that they were also escaped slaves on the run and that his family were welcome to join them.

"I cannot join you I must keep going and catch up with my family," said Abel.

The leader of the group was convinced that Abel was telling the truth and therefore would be unlikely to reveal the slaves whereabouts.

The leader raised his hand for Abel to follow him." They rode at speed until they came to a track. They stopped and the leader nodded his head at Abel and the gang then disappeared into the forest.

Rufus and Gideon were worried it was no ordinary slave they were following. This was the third day and they were no closer to catching him, their lives were on the line.

The trail had turned cold so they decided to return to the area that the hounds had found the strongest scent. The dogs soon picked it up and charged ahead with Rufus and Gideon following.

Theodore had posters placed in and around Charleston, offering a reward for the capture of his slaves. He had contacts in many States and notified them of their descriptions.

Abel came to the outskirts of a town, he needed money for supplies if they where to survive in the mountains. He rode into town nervously. He stopped at the stables where a man was shoeing a horse. "Mister, do you know of any work going in these parts?"

"I believe Mistress Baker is looking for a hired hand, just for a few days to clear her back yard." he pointed down the road in the direction of the house."

Abel knocked on the door, a young black girl answered. "I am looking for work for a few days. I was told your Mistress, might be in need of help?" The girl went away and returned.

"Mistress, say you to go to de back yard and see Jacob, he will show you wuh needs doing." Jacob was black and in his seventies, hunched over, with a wary look in his eyes. "Yar pay be five dollar if yar do a good job, there is wood to chop and de yard to be cleared, about two days work I reckon. You can sleep in de shed for the nights you working." Abel kept his head down and worked hard. Jacob came over to him the next day with some bread and cow's milk. "Weh are yar from?" asked Jacob. "Down South, I like travelling when I find the right place I will settle down and take me a wife." When Abel had finished the work in the yard, he collected his money from Jacob. He went to the general store for supplies and then headed north.

Linchman walked into the saloon, he was a tall man, his face tanned and his skin looked liked leather. His hair was long, and greasy under a crumpled Stetson. It was dirty with sweat marks around the rim from months of wearing in the heat. He had two guns one in his holster and one tucked into his black leather belt. His metal spurs made a clinking sound every time he took a step. Everyone turned and stopped speaking. There was no mistaking—a bounty hunter.

The man behind the bar nervously asked him what he wanted to drink. "Whisky," he said in a gruff voice. He drank it down in one go and pushed his glass towards the barman for another.

"Have any nigger's passed through lately?"

"None that I know of," he replied. He went to the boarding house next door, asking the owner the same question, and got the same answer. He then went to the stables at the top of town, "I need my horse shoeing as soon as possible?"

"I can have him ready in an hour." Linchman left his horse and walked down to the stores to get supplies, where he asked the same question. "Well we had one come in for supplies two days ago, he worked for Mistress Baker," and he pointed the house out to him.

Linchman found Jacob working on the veranda. "Boy, where's the nigger who was working for your Mistress?"

"He left two days ago." Jacob knew that this man meant trouble for Abel, he had cold eyes, and he knew meanness from experience. Linchman showed him a drawing of Abel. "Is this him?"

"Yar that's him," Jacob replied.

"Did he say where he was travelling to next?"

"No"

Linchman put his gun to Jacobs head. "Are you telling me the truth nigger?"

"Yar," replied a frightened Jacob. Linchman put his gun away and walked back to the stables to fetch his horse, he smiled he could feel the reward money in his hand.

Chapter Five

◌

"**D**e horse is lame," said Samson to Beth. "It slows us down."
They were feeling exhausted and hungry. They found a wooden cabin that was empty near the river crossing, they would be glad for some shelter.

"Stay in de cabin I catch a fish to eat." Beth squatted on the floor and suckled Will. Her thoughts were for her husband and she prayed he would return to them.

Samson returned with some fish he had caught, and decided to take the risk of lighting a fire. They had not eaten for several days and they needed the warmth, as the nights were getting cold. Beth cooked the fish, at last, their stomachs were full and they fell asleep feeling warm for the first time in days.

Samson awoke he thought he heard a noise perhaps it was his imagination. Trying not to disturb Beth and the baby, he crept outside. He knew the distinctive sound of hounds that meant one thing the trackers are closing in. It was first light they must move quickly. Samson let the horse go; they went upstream and turned into the dense forest. The barking became louder and louder. Beth held

Will tight and tried to keep up with Samson. Her heart was pounding and sweat poured from her.

"Missy, keep up." Samson said breathlessly as he hacked a path through the undergrowth. With panting breath she replied, "I'm trying." She suddenly lost her footing and put her hands out to protect Will. Samson rushed back to help her.

"Climb de tree quickly." He shoved her up into the branches of the tree as far as he could and took out his knife. The hounds caught up with them and Samson fought them as they tried to get to Beth. The hounds ripped at his arms and legs.

Rufus and Gideon confronted him they both had knives. "De Mas' be pleased to see yar," said Rufus.

Gideon stabbed Samson in the arm making him drop his knife. Rufus grabbed his bloodied arm and twisted it making him cry out in pain.

The noise of the hounds filled the air. "Quiet!" shouted Gideon who hit them to make them obey. They dragged Beth down from the tree with Will. They secured Samson to the back of one of the horses whilst Beth walked along side carrying Will. That night when they had set up camp Rufus and Gideon drank from a bottle of Whisky celebrating the successful capture of Samson and Beth.

Linchman was finding it difficult to follow the slave's tracks he had never come across this before, and had to admit this slave was good. Abel kept going, not stopping to rest, he was pushing his horse hard, and the ground was rough and rocky. It reared up and threw him off.

He did not know how long he had been unconscious but pain filled every part of his body. Abel tried to get up but his legs would not hold him, he looked down to find his left leg had the bone protruding from it. He must strap it up; dragging himself along the ground, he found some broken branches. He tore strips from his shirt and strapped his leg as best he could. As a warrior he was use to pain it was something he had learnt to cope with. Pulling himself up onto his horse, he rode for several hours, and then exhausted Abel stopped to rest up for the night.

Linchman was getting frustrated with how long it was taking to find this slave. He suddenly spotted marks on the ground, getting down from his horse, he saw what appeared to be blood—I have him he said to himself, not long now.

Abel heard the sound of twigs breaking, he knew someone was out there; he placed a blanket over his saddle on the ground to look like he was sleeping and with his knife drawn hobbled behind some rocks out of sight and waited.

Linchman crept slowly towards what he thought was a sleeping body, and jabbed his gun into it. Although Abel was in great pain, he managed to creep behind him and put his arm tightly around Linchman's throat. Linchman threw him over onto the ground and pointed his gun against his head.

"I am not going to kill you, boy; I need you alive to get the reward. I will leave the killing to your Master." With the butt end of his gun, he hit Abel on the head knocking him out. He tied his hands behind his back and lifted him onto his horse for the journey back to Cotton Wood Plantation.

"Mas', Rufus has returned with escaped slaves," said Tom. Theodore thought he would feel better for the capture of those responsible for the death of his beloved daughter. He looked at the pitiful sight in front of him. An old man, exhausted and bleeding from his arms and legs and his fearful daughter's slave with her crying baby strapped to her chest. He knew that Emma had become fond of her and had been able to confide in her. How could these trusted slaves have any part in what had happened? Would revenge on them bring his beautiful daughter back?

Sebastian joined him. "Sir, I will make arrangements to hang these slaves who assisted in the murder of my dear sister." Theodore hesitated and said.

"No lock them up for now," said Theodore.

"But, Sir . . . "Theodore left Sebastian standing there. He was a troubled soul forgiveness was the main stay of his religion. He had been leaving more and more of the day-to-day dealings of the plantation to Sebastian he was overwhelmed with grief. He kept asking himself why my only daughter? He went deeper and deeper into despair, isolating himself in his bedchamber.

Sebastian decided to take matters into his own hands he was no longer scared of his stepfather. Since the death of Emma, he was now a weak and pathetic old man, and besides, he practically ran Cotton Wood now.

"Throw Samson into the punishment hut and take her to the whipping post," he said pointing at Beth. This was a chance for him to silence Beth for good, she knew too much.

Sebastian ordered Rufus to summon all the slaves to witness the punishment.

Gideon pulled Will from her arms and gave him to Lottie, he started to cry, and she held him close to her ample bosom to comfort him. Gideon seemed to get pleasure from the situation, how Lottie hated him.

He ripped the back of Beth's dress, and tied her to the whipping post. Beth prayed for strength to endure this. She could not control her body shaking through fear at what was about to happen to her. Beth closed her eyes and braced herself for the first strike. Gideon raised his hand and struck her. Beth let out a piercing scream as the whip cut her skin. Tom felt helpless, how could a man watch unable to help a woman he cared about, he felt emasculated. He had feelings of guilt, how would he be able to look her in the face again. At the sixth stroke of the whip Beth had passed out with the intolerable pain, her back was a mass of red cuts running with blood that had formed a pool by her feet.

Sebastian threw a bucket of water over her to bring her round. He wanted her to suffer so that she would not open her mouth and tell Theodore his secret.

"Stop! Immediately," commanded Theodore, his face like thunder as he pulled the whip from Sebastian's hand. "Disband this gathering Rufus, return these slaves to their duties."

"Yes Mas'."

"Kate, see to Beth." Looking into Sebastian's eyes Theodore said in a threatening tone "Sir, I wish to see you in my study immediately," and strode off towards the house in an agitated state.

"How dare you, disobey an order I gave you concerning the escaped slaves?" said Theodore to Sebastian.

"Sir, I thought I would help you by taking the burden off you by dealing with this situation myself. You are still distressed from the death of Emma as I am Sir, and I was only trying to help you."

"I understand you feel the loss of Emma but do not forget Sebastian, I am the owner of Cotton Wood Plantation—not you! You will do my bidding or go to live with your mother, now I am busy leave my study." Theodore just wanted to grieve for his daughter and not have to deal with a disobedient stepson.

Sebastian was furious his head was pulsating with anger. He went to the stables, saddled his horse and raced down the avenue into Charleston.

Theodore went to see Beth in her cabin.

"Beth, I know you are now in great pain but when you have recovered I would wish you to return as a chambermaid. My daughter had put great faith in you and she was never wrong. She was a good judge of character I do not think you or Samson was involved in the murder of my daughter.'

Your first duty will be to sort out Mistress Emma's gowns and other items and box them up. You will live in the house in your old room. "Thank you, Sir." Beth desperately wanted to tell Theodore what had happened, but she could not risk it. She would never forget Sebastian threatening to kill her and her son. She prayed Abel had made it to safety, how she missed him.

It was a week since her beating and she was recovering with the help of Kate. Beth loved Kate as a sister. The Master had allowed her to leave her duties for a couple of hours a day to look after Beth. Lottie sent food for her and the baby it was her way of saying that she respected her courage.

Theodore's ordered Samson be released from the punishment hut, he was in a bad way. Grace his wife bathed his head and body trying to bring down his temperature, her tear's dropping onto his face, he awoke and focused on her eyes.

"I'll be alright," he smiled thanking god for the gift of a loving wife. He lay in his hut with everyone doing all they could to care for him between their duties. All the slaves treated Samson with respected a man of God.

He had gone to the aid of an escaped slave four years ago who was injured, his mother had gone to Samson in distress. "Samson, my son needs help. He on the outskirts of the de plantation near de river, his friend is hiding in my cabin he will take you to him." Samson grabbed his herbal bag and followed his friend back to the injured slave. The boy lay there with an animal trap clamped around his leg, the boy's friend and Samson prised it open. "Son, I will do my best to help you." Samson could see the terrible injury it was a deep gash exposing the bone. Samson did his best to staunch the flow of blood from the wound.

"I will pray for yar both, Gawd go with yar." The young lad touched his arm.

"Please look after my maamy for me, she is all alone now?"

"I will," replied Samson. His friend was getting nervous.

"We need to go quickly." They lifted him onto the horse, which they had stolen and disappeared into the woods.

Rufus had observed everything, reporting it back to Sebastian, who sent him and Gideon out to apprehend them. When they had found Samson, they threw him to the ground, Rufus and Gideon repeatedly struck him. They dragged him up and tied him to a tree.

"Well, where are they?"

Samson did not reply. Rufus drew his knife and slashed Samson's cheek.

"I will ask you again, where are they?" Samson did not utter a word.

"Hold out his leg, Gideon," Rufus found a log lying on the forest floor and hit Samson's knee repeatedly. His screams resounded around the forest but Samson was not going to tell.

"Stop! This is getting us nowhere, he is not going to speak," said Gideon. They laid him over their horse and took him back to Cotton Wood Plantation.

Theodore was furious.

"These slaves cost me money and you injure them so they cannot work. I want you to inform me from now on when you catch any escaped slave, do you hear me?"

"Yes, Sir," replied Sebastian,

"Now get out of here and find the two missing slaves they can't have got far and remember what I've said."

Rufus and Gideon found the young lad dead from his injuries his companion had left him. Samson had kept his promise to the young lad and looked after his mother Grace. They had eventually fallen in love and married. Grace returned to their cabin from working in the big house. She walked over to him lying in his bed.

"Samson . . ." then she noticed he was blue around the mouth and shook him. "Samson, don't scare me wake up," she listened to his breathing, there was none. She cradled him in her arms singing softly their favourite song they had played at their wedding, her voice faltering as she sang.

Linchman rode into Cotton Wood Plantation.

"Call your, Master; tell him Linchman is here to see him?" Tom hurried to Theodore's study.

"Good day to you, Sir," said Theodore.

"It is indeed a good day, Sir, for I have captured your missing slave and I look for my reward."

Linchman lifted Abel's head for Theodore to see, he was unconscious and bloodied.

"Tom, call Rufus and have Abel chained and put him in the stables, he is not to leave him, do you understand?" said Theodore.

"Yar, Mas'," replied Tom. Theodore paid Linchman and walked to the stables.

"Pour water over him," Theodore commanded Rufus. He poured a bucket of cold water over Abel's face and he regained consciousness. Theodore stood in front of him. "Why did you do it, Abel? Was I not fair in my treatment of you? I rewarded you for good work and you repay me by killing my daughter?"

"I am innocent, Master," replied Abel.

"As it says in the bible an 'eye for an eye' and a 'tooth for a tooth' you will pay with your life."

"Master I did not kill your daughter."

"There were witnesses you were seen, boy." Tomorrow you will hang.

Tom ran and found Beth to tell her that the bounty hunter had returned Abel. Beth so wanted to see Abel, but he was being guarded. Sebastian found Beth in her late mistress's bedchamber. She moved uneasily as he approached her. "We will hang Abel tomorrow," he said with a sneer across his face. He grabbed her hair and placed his mouth against her ear. "Remember what I said, I will kill you and your child, if you do not keep your mouth shut." He released her and pushed her to the floor.

Theodore tended his daughter's grave he was comforted just to be near her.

"My angel, I miss you so much, life for me is empty. I am tired and just want to join you and your mother." He knelt down at the foot of her grave he was inconsolable.

Beth was in a desperate state she went in search of Tom. "My dear friend, help me to see Abel once more?"

"You know I will help you, Beth," replied Tom. He knew that Rufus would be guarding the entrance to the stables. At midday, Kate would bring him a meal from the kitchen. This would be the best time for him to take Beth over to see Abel, since Rufus would be distracted. He took her to the back of the stables, through a small door. Tom put his finger to his lips telling her to be quiet. Beth followed him there was a split in the stable wall. Beth could see Abel with his hands chained behind his back. She rested her hands on Toms face and without saying anything, conveyed her thanks. Tom left Beth to talk to Abel alone. She placed her mouth up to the split in the stable wall and whispered "Abel, it is I Beth. I so want to hold you and tend your wounds. I will bring Will up to know his father was a great warrior and chief of his tribe. He will hold the name of Tukowunu with pride knowing the truth that you are innocent. I will tell him the stories of your homeland, as you told me. My love, every step you take tomorrow I will take with you, and when you take your last breathe I will be there holding you." The tears streamed down her face, being so close to him but so far away made the pain she felt inside unbearable. Abel whispered. "Be brave and hold your head high, you are a Chieftains wife."

"God bless you my, Husband," Beth replied. She took one last look at him then Abel turned in the direction of her voice. They looked into each other's eyes, transferring their love to one another. Then Abel turned back before Rufus noticed. Finding it hard to control her emotions Beth left.

All the slaves had to attend the hanging. It was eight in the morning a bright, cold day. Beth had not slept. She prayed for a miracle that would save her beloved Abel. She held Will tightly knowing her son would not grow up to see and know his wonderful father. Her whole body shook with despair at not being able to help him. She wrapped two shawls around her body so she would not be seen to shake she must be dignified as Abel wished. Beth walked with Tom to the top of the hill. Rufus and Gideon escorted Abel who had his hands chained behind his back. They dragged him towards the large single oak tree that had a rope hanging over one of the high branches. At the foot of the tree was a tethered horse.

Theodore and Sebastian followed closely behind them. Rufus and Gideon lifted Abel onto the horse and asked if he wanted a blind fold.

He replied "No." Beth held Abel's gaze with her head held high, her voice within her was begging God to help him. Theodore said to Abel, "Do you have anything to say?"

"God is my witness I am innocent, Master," replied Abel. He turned his head towards Beth.

"Goodbye my love be strong for the sake of our son," said Abel quietly to himself as he took his last look at Beth and his son. A silence descended.

"Continue," Theodore commanded.

Rufus hit the horse with his whip and the horse bolted leaving Abel hanging. As promised, Beth fixed her gaze on Abel transposing her thoughts of comfort and love to him in his hour of need. She felt faint but knew she must control her feeling as Able wanted. When his body had ceased writhing, they cut him down. Rufus checked that he was dead before pronouncing it to his Master.

Beth rushed towards Abel's body. Sebastian stopped her. She turned and looked into Theodore's eyes. "Allow her to bury her husband," he ordered. With that, he and Sebastian walked back down towards the plantation house.

Theodore could not understand why he did not feel any sense of satisfaction, he had just taken a man's life, but instead he felt guilty. As the commandment say you shall not kill and he had just done that. Was he indeed as guilty as the man who took his daughters life?

Theodore knew he must change his will. He had been putting it off since Emma's death.

I must change it in favour of Sebastian and make him heir to Cotton Wood Plantation.

The following day Theodore called his stepson into his study. "Sir, I wish to inform you I will be changing my will making you the sole heir of Cotton Wood Plantation.

Sebastian was delighted at the prospect of his future inheritance.

Peter and the other slaves carried Abel's body to the slave's church for a service and burial. Peter carved a cross for Abel's grave it bore the words—Chief Abel Tukowunu of the Manitou Tribe. Beth had her heart ripped out that day her beloved Abel died. In the midst of her grief, she had descended into a dark place within herself that even her son could not reach.

Chapter Six

Three years had passed since Abel's death. It was Christmas and Beth had made a wreath of fir cones and branches of ivy with bright red berries and placed it on his grave. It had been snowing and the red berries looked glorious lying in the dense white covering, it framed his wooden cross outlining his name. How she missed him.

"This is for you, Papa," said Will as he kissed his cross as he always did when they arrived. He was three now, he would soon have to help in the house when he turned four years. Beth always shared her thoughts with Abel at the graveside and encouraged Will to talk to him as if he were still alive.

There are rumours Abel that soon slaves will shall have our freedom. I heard it myself when the Master was telling Master Sebastian about it," she kissed his name. She told him how much she loved him, leaving their footprints in the snow as they left and walked back to the big house. She thought to herself how beautiful the scene was, God's wondrous hand at work. However, it hid such sadness for her and her son.

"Well, Persia, what a pretty name," said Sebastian to his new whore as she seductively removed her clothes to reveal her voluptuous body. Sebastian had gone further afield to find a whorehouse, hoping he was safe from Striker. This prostitute was different he thought she was clever and classy. Sebastian found he was visiting her more and more. He paid extra to the Madam to keep her strictly for him. She was on his wavelength, not prepared to stop at anything until she got what she wanted, and what she wanted was Sebastian.

He realized he could use Persia for she looked very much like Martha, Theodore's first wife. How long would he have to wait until he could get his hands on Cotton Wood Plantation was never far from his mind.

When he returned to his horse there was a letter pinned to his saddle saying. "Your days are numbered, pay up or we will find you."

"I need to get rid of my stepfather," he told Persia. "I would be able to pay off my debts with my inheritance from Cotton Wood Plantation and I think I have found a way," he told her.

Persia had fallen hard for Sebastian, so when he came up with a scheme to get her out of the whorehouse and living under the same roof as him, she jumped at it. She was prepared to do anything Sebastian wanted, just to be with him.

They had decided to set up an introduction with Theodore at Peter Riverdale's engagement ball. Persia would go as an acquaintance of Sebastian.

He spent hours familiarising her with information regarding Martha's virtues and Theodore's likes and dislikes. They rehearsed etiquette and dancing until she was convincing.

He bought her a dress that would keep Theodore's eyes on her all evening. It was velvet, sapphire blue in colour and clung to her curves. Her blonde hair was set in the style that Martha would have worn.

Now Sebastian needed to convince Theodore to go to Peter Riverdale's engagement party. He managed to convince him that this was what Emma would have wished.

Everyone stared at the beauty Sebastian had on his arm as he entered the ballroom. Many flocked to introduce themselves; everyone wanted to know who she was.

"Sebastian, who is this charming creature," said Judge Peabody looking Persia up and down.

"This is a friend of mine, who will be staying at Cotton Wood Plantation for a while. May I introduce Mistress Persia Lovell, from Chicago?" she recognised the Judge straight away as a visitor to a brothel she once worked in.

"It is a pleasure indeed to meet you" Persia replied.

He looked at her scrutinizing her features.

"Have we not met before, Madam?"

"Why, Sir, I would not have forgotten such a charming man as you."

The Judge looked flattered by her remark and pushed the thought away.

Sebastian took Persia's arm and walked her through the double doors onto the balcony where they could talk privately. Smiling and nodding their heads at the other guests as they passed.

Persia sighed with relief.

"That was close!" she said. Sebastian squeezed her arm tightly."

"We don't want anything to ruin our plan, what in the hell happened then?"

"Let go of my arm, you are hurting me and will leave a red mark."

Sebastian released his grip.

"Judge Peabody was a regular visitor to my friend Daniela when I worked in Madam Shari's, but I dealt with it—relax." Sebastian saw Theodore entering through the open doors to the ballroom.

"Time to go and catch our prey," he said to her.

Theodore was not in the mood for idle chitchat.

He wandered aimlessly round the room nodding his head to the neighbouring plantation owners. Theodore thought his heart would explode, there talking to Sebastian was a stunning woman in a dark blue gown that was the double of his beloved Martha.

"You must introduce me, Sebastian, to this beautiful lady," Theodore commanded as he smiled at Persia.

"May I introduce Persia Lovell. Persia, this is my stepfather Theodore Jackson, owner of Cotton Wood Plantation."

"It is a pleasure to meet you, Sir," Persia replied.

Theodore could not take his eyes away from Persia he felt intoxicated by her and did not leave her side all evening.

"You must come and stay at my home so I can show you Cotton Wood Plantation, my dear, how about next week. I will send a carriage for you."

"Theodore, I hope you don't mind but I have already invited Persia to stay while her father's away on business," Sebastian said interrupting. "So I could collect her as arranged?"

"That will be fine I look forward to your stay with us. I must insist you stay as long as you need to."

"Thank you, Sir; you are very kind my father will be happy that I am in safe hands while he is away."

Persia was in her element she loved her surroundings and truly felt she belonged in a grand house with servants to attend her every need.

She made sure she was with Theodore at every opportunity, working her charms on him, Sebastian was delighted.

One morning Theodore found her crying "What is wrong, my dear?" he asked her concerned.

"I have just received a letter telling me my father has been killed," she sobbed holding the letter. Sebastian watched from a distance. They had planned everything down to the last detail. The letter was very convincing. He watched as Theodore read it and then comforted Persia.

She is a good actress thought Sebastian he was pleased everything was going to plan.

Theodore was besotted with Persia and wanted her; he missed being part of a couple and felt lonely. His love for his first wife and soul mate Martha was holding him back.

"You look captivating this evening, my dear," Theodore said to Persia as he escorted her to the dining room for dinner. Theodore watched her across the table as the candle light flickered across her face. He was pleased Sebastian had gone into Charleston, for he liked it when he had Persia all to himself.

"I would like to show you the plantation tomorrow by horseback, you can ride my daughter's horse Star he is very safe to ride," Theodore's voice faltered.

"I would deem it an honour to ride your Daughters horse," Persia said as she placed her hand on his as an understanding of his feelings.

Persia's concern touched Theodore.

To think this could be mine thought Persia as Theodore showed her Cotton Wood Plantation the following day.

"May I come in?" said Theodore to Persia as she opened her bedchamber door.

"Please do," she replied.

"I need to visit Charleston for a few days, I wondered if you would care to accompany me?" said Theodore.

"I would love to," Persia replied."

"We can visit the theatre, would you like that?"

"I love the theatre, Theodore." Persia kissed him on the cheek.

"You have been so kind to me Theodore," Persia's voice quivered and then she started to feign tears.

"What is the matter, my dear?"

"I miss my father so much," she cried. Theodore took her in his arms to comfort her. Persia was hoping he would kiss her but he moved away. I have business to attend to in my study. I will see you at dinner," and left. Nothing she did to encourage intimacy seemed to work. Theodore still treated her with respect, things were not moving forward as quickly as she hoped.

He was aware that everyone at the theatre was looking at Persia she looked breathtakingly beautiful in her cerise coloured gown as she sat next to him in the balcony. Throughout their visit to his town house, Theodore had not made a sexual advance towards her, much to Persia's disappointment.

On her return to Cotton Wood Plantation Persia found a letter slipped under her door. Meet me at the ruins at three, Sebastian. Persia had missed him and got ready excitedly, in her riding outfit.

"Come here, you wanton women, now get down on your knees and do what you are good at." Sebastian said. The excitement of his plan to ensnare Theodore heightened his desire for her. Persia willingly agreed. "I want the works," he ordered. She loved it when he was masterful.

Theodore sat at his desk and looked at the portrait of Martha his first wife that hung on his study wall. His determination to hold on to her, the love of his life and mother of his child was placing a guard around his heart, stopping him from falling in love again.

Theodore spoke to the portrait of her "My dearest Martha, I have never loved any other women but you, but now I must let go for I am so lonely since you and Emma left me. You would like Persia she reminds me so much of you."

"My dear, come to the stables I have something to show you," said Theodore as he took her hand.

"This is your own horse, he is a thoroughbred called Bentley," he said pointing to a jet-black stallion that Samson was holding by its reins. Theodore had seen the stallion when he was last in Charleston and thought what a perfect gift for Persia

"Oh, Theodore, he is a handsome beast." Persia threw her arms around him. Theodore was delighted at her reaction.

Persia stroked the stallion.

"Now you can take him out whenever you wish, my dear."

"You are such a wonderful man," she said as she kissed him on the cheek. This would make her rendezvous to see Sebastian at the ruins much easier.

Persia was getting frustrated she had been at Cotton Wood Plantation six months now and Theodore had not made any sexual advances towards her. She felt she had given him all the right signals that she would welcome his attention that would ensnare him. Sebastian was getting impatient with her.

Persia knew she must try harder to get Theodore to make love to her. She told Sebastian to stay overnight in Charleston so that they could be alone. She wore her most seductive gown that showed her assets and sitting at dinner flirted with him.

It was a warm evening Theodore walked Persia out onto the veranda.

"Look, Theodore, a full moon." Persia lent against the railings staring upwards hoping he would kiss her.

"It is as beautiful as you are, my dear." Theodore struggled with his feelings, even though he had married again after his Martha had died. He only felt infatuation for his second wife Sophia, Sebastian mother. He had recognised that he needed a female influence around his daughter while she grew up. He now felt disloyal to Martha as he was falling in love with Persia.

Persia decided to use a different tactic. "Theodore, I have heard from my Aunt, she has returned from abroad and has offered me a home with her in California. I will be leaving in a couple of days."

The thought of her leaving filled Theodore with consternation, he must persuade Persia to stay.

He pushed a stray curl away from her eyes and looked longingly into them kissing her on the lips. He thought she tasted divine and without a word carried her upstairs to his bedchamber. He disrobed her and admired her shapely figure. Persia tried to tame her sexual experience and allowed Theodore to remain in charge. They lay in each other's arms. "Don't leave stay here at Cotton Wood Plantation," Theodore begged Persia.

Persia needed him to propose so she pushed the situation even further.

"My Aunt's my only next of kin now my father has died. She wishes me to join her.

I will write to my Aunt tomorrow, to tell her to expect my arrival in the next couple of days, she replied.

"I now need to return to my room as I'm in need of sleep Theodore, goodnight," she said as she kissed him. Persia prayed her gamble would work—or she would lose everything.

Theodore paced up and down in his study, he was distraught he must act quickly and convince her to stay, she was his and he was not going to let her go.

Theodore found Persia the next morning at the writing desk quill in her hand, he felt sure she was writing to her Aunt.

"Persia, can you spare a moment please?" he said.

"Certainly," she replied.

Theodore went down on one knee and said " Will you do me the great honour and marry me Persia?" he produced a ring box and opened it to reveal his mother's engagement ring. He looked hopefully into her eyes.

Persia threw her arms around him. "Yes, yes" she replied.

As he held her, Theodore thought he had found happiness again.

"Theodore, I love it!" said Persia admiring her engagement ring.

"It is a beautiful ring, for a beautiful woman, and the future Mistress of Cotton Wood Plantation. I will organise a party to celebrate our engagement," said Theodore. He kissed her and with a new spring in his step walked off to his study.

Yes! Yes! She had done it. She had trapped Theodore and now could feel the prize was within her grasp, Sebastian and Cotton Wood Plantation.

Tom had informed Beth that she would work in Persia's bedchamber. She was unkind to her unlike her previous mistress Emma.

"Beth, where are you?" shouted an inpatient Persia.

"Where is my yellow gown?" she questioned Beth.

"Mistress, you gave it to me to be cleaned yesterday."

Persia hit Beth across the face.

"How dare you be rude to me, I will inform your Master and have you whipped, now go and get my dress." Beth knew what was going on and felt sorry for Theodore.

Beth had seen Persia and Sebastian go hand in hand into the summerhouse. Tom had heard sounds from the attic and had gone to investigate only to see them rolling around on the floor in a passionate embrace.

Persia checked the coast was clear and knocked on Sebastian's bedchamber door hoping he would be there. She could not wait to tell him her good news.

"What are you doing, you are risking everything."

"I need to talk to you?" she said excitedly.

Exasperated Sebastian said, "Tell Theodore, you are going for a horse ride and I will meet you at the old ruins, now go quickly before we are seen."

Persia entered Theodore's study. "Theodore, I thought I might take Bentley out for a ride, it's such a lovely morning, do you mind?"

"Of course not, would you like me to accompany you?"

"No, you stay and plan a wonderful engagement party for me," Persia said as she kissed Theodore on the forehead. A contented Theodore smiled back at her.

Having reached the ruins, Persia dismounted her horse and ran to Sebastian.

"We have done it. Theodore has proposed to me, look," as she showed off her engagement ring.

He twirled her around and then they fell to the ground laughing. It was a warm summer's day.

"Well I think you deserve a gift for a job well done! Now come with me."

He took her hand and led her into the ruins. "Stand still," he ordered and covered her eyes with his cravat and tantalizingly removed her clothes.

Persia was in a heightened sexual state by the time he had removed the last piece of her clothing. She felt the sun on her nakedness. He was the best lover she had ever had. He quickly removed his clothes, and his ardour for her was evident. Sebastian ran his riding crop along the side of her face and down her neck to her breast. He slowly teased her following the contour of her breasts and Persia groaned with delight.

Sebastian followed the curve of her waist and moved it around to the back of her. "Bend over," he commanded. Persia leant over placing her hands against the walls of the ruins. Her body was on fire with desire.

Sebastian struck her cheeks in turn, Persia cried out in pleasure. Then he slid his riding crop in-between her legs and caressed her, and as she came to an orgasm, he pushed himself into her. She was in heaven her whole body was erupting with blasts of pleasure she did not want it to stop. Sebastian collapsed on the ground pulling her with him and they lay in each other's arms, their bodies entwined.

Every man present envied Theodore at the engagement party held at Cotton Wood Plantation. Persia looked stunning in a pink and crystal gown her hair had diamond clips holding it in place, with soft curls framing her face. Persia enjoyed being the centre of attention as Theodore introduced his future bride to his friends and neighbours. Theodore was in love and wanted everyone to meet the future Mrs Jackson.

Sebastian and his men were watching for Dr Garth Hogan to leave his surgery in Charleston. As he passed the alleyway, they were waiting. Sebastian pulled him in and held him against the wall out of sight of the street.

Sebastian stood inches from Garth's face, "I want my money?"

"I don't have it, give me more time, please I beg you?" Garth's voice quivered in fear.

"You have run out of time. Do you want me to divulge to your patients that you like men and frequent an establishment to satisfy your sexual needs, and then there is your wife."

"Please I will do anything, anything."

"There is a way you can pay off your debt to me."

"I will do it, tell me what I have to do?" Garth said desperately.

"I want you to supply me with a drug that would make you drowsy and unsteady on your feet."

"I cannot do that I would be struck off if I was caught." Sebastian was getting cross now and grabbed his collar twisting it making it difficult for Garth to breathe.

"I did not hear you?" he said.

"Ok, ok," Sebastian let go of his collar and he gasped for air.

"I will come to your surgery tomorrow to collect it," he said. Rufus and Gideon let go of Garth and he slid down the wall collapsing onto the ground, exhausted with fear.

The wedding was set for autumn after the harvest. The invitations went out and the chapel prepared. Beth helped her Mistress into her wedding gown. Persia then looked into the mirror, admired herself, and thought how close she was to her goal. Soon she would be Mistress of Cotton Wood Plantation and have Sebastian and the life she always dreamt.

Sebastian had to contain his pleasure when he stood in the chapel and heard the words, I now pronounce you man and wife. Not long now, until Cotton Wood Plantation would be his.

Persia played the dutiful wife but continued to meet Sebastian at their secret rendezvous at the old ruins near the river.

Sebastian informed Beth, "The Master has taken to his bed, close the shutters. You will see to his every need and *no* visitors now leave me," he said.

It had only been a month since the wedding and Theodore was bed ridden, he had rapidly deteriorated. When Beth helped him to the commode he would fall, he was unable to stand upright. Beth felt something was not right and voiced her opinion to Tom.

"Tom, the Mistress insists on feeding the Master herself. I have I seen from a crack in the door that she pour liquid from a brown bottle, that she takes out of her gown pocket and mixes it into the Master's food. I fear he is getting worse," said a concerned Beth.

"I heard Mas' Sebastian tell Mistress Persia that he had asked the doctor to call, "said Tom.

The next day Sebastian ordered Beth "Prepare the Master for the doctor?" She was relieved to hear that the doctor would call and therefore she put aside her niggling doubts.

That is very strange, a different doctor attending to the Master, why not his own Doctor Lloyd? Beth thought. She noticed at the bedside a brown parcel had changed hands and then the doctor had left.

Sebastian and Persia where now blatant in their lust for one another in the house, not worrying if the servants saw them.

Doctor Garth Hogan played out his role in line with Sebastian's wishes, giving him more of the mixture. Beth was confused perhaps she was reading too much into this, after all he was a respected doctor in Charleston.

Beth had her orders to collect some gowns from Charleston for Mistress Persia, as she approached the drapery she passed Doctor Lloyd.

"Beth, please pass on my regards to your Master, he must be in good health as I have not seen him since the wedding, and married life must suit him." He started to move away when Beth said hesitantly, "Sir he is bed ridden."

"Why have I not been called, I will call this afternoon please inform your Mistress."

"Please do not tell my Mistress I spoke to you, for I will be punished."

"Why, Beth, I know you have been a loyal and trusted slave to Theodore for many years, I am sure that is not true."

"It is not my place to talk out of turn but I fear for my master."

"Follow me Beth."

Doctor Lloyd took Beth to his surgery and sat her down in the office.

"Now tell me what concerns you?"

She told him what she had seen, and about Doctor Hogan's visit.

"Everything will be all right," Dr Lloyd, said reassuring her. "I will call tomorrow to see your Master." Beth prayed she could trust him.

"Can you tell your Mistress that Doctor Lloyd is here," he said to Tom as he gave him his gloves and hat as he entered the hallway.

"Tom bring Doctor Lloyd to me and then find Master Sebastian immediately and tell him I need him here." Persia was wondering why Theodore's doctor had called, she felt very nervous and needed Sebastian's support. She must keep calm. She smiled as he entered the drawing room.

"What a pleasant surprise, Doctor Lloyd," Persia said smiling warmly.

"Excuse my intrusion, Madam, but I was in the area and thought I would call in. I trust I have not come at an inconvenient time Mrs Jackson."

"Doctor Lloyd please call me Persia, unfortunately Theodore has ridden into Charleston he will be sorry to have missed you. May I get you some refreshment?"

"Doctor Lloyd," said Sebastian as he walked hastily into the drawing room.

Doctor Lloyd knew Sebastian was rotten through and through, just like his father.

"I was telling Doctor Lloyd that Theodore has ridden into Charleston." Persia desperately tried to put Sebastian in the picture.

"Well I have other calls to make, please, pass on my regards to Theodore, Good day to you."

As he left the drawing room, he went into the hallway where Tom was waiting with his hat and gloves. He suspected something was wrong. He quietly and discreetly said to Tom while putting his hat and gloves on.

"Tom, answer yes or no, is your Master ill in bed?"

"Yes," he replied nervously his eyes darting from side to side checking no one had seen him talk to the doctor; he then opened the front door for him to leave.

"What in the hell's going on, why did he call?" Persia was always scared of Sebastian when he was angry.

"Perhaps we are looking way too much into his visit." Persia said trying to defuse the situation.

Doctor Lloyd was very concerned about Theodore he was not only his patient but also a good friend. He knew Sebastian and the new Mrs Jackson must have been hiding something to call in another doctor and lie about him being ill.

Sebastian closed the drawing room door. "We must move things along, after you have given Theodore his Breakfast tomorrow morning, get him out of his bed with the help of Beth. Then dismiss her and walk him along the landing to the staircase. When you get close to the first step, then push him forwards and scream and act for your life as he falls down the stairs hopefully to his death, do you understand?"

"Yes," Persia paused, and thought, "I will say I was helping him exercise his legs and he lost his footing."

"Then we will call Doctor Hogan, he will write out a death certificate, then Cotton Wood Plantation will be mine."

"Ours, Sebastian," replied Persia correcting him, she was no fool the plantation would be in her name, and this was one sure way of keeping him.

Beth was distressed when she found out from Tom that Doctor Lloyd had left without seeing the Master. As usual, Persia turned up at Theodore's mealtime to feed him. Beth watched her through the crack in the door once again pour some into his food, and stirred it. She lifted him up and roughly shook him to wake him up. As Theodore mumbled, she pushed the food into his open mouth.

Sebastian would make sure he was out of the plantation house when Theodore fell down the stairs to his death, it would solely be Persia's fault. He knew Garth would keep his mouth shut; he had too much to lose. When the plan was successful, he would dispose of Persia, as she would be of no further use to him.

Beth watched Persia put the brown bottle back into her jewellery box in a cupboard in her bedchamber.

The following morning Persia called for Beth.

"Help me lift the Master out of bed," she said in her usual impatient tone.

"Mistress, the Master is too weak and unsteady to walk," she knew she should not have spoken, but she had to protect him.

"How dare you speak to me concerning my husband's well being, you will be severely punished for speaking out of turn. Now help me to the door, I need to give him some exercise."

She gestured to Beth. "You, can go now I need the Master's plate taken down to the kitchen and washed."

"Yes, Mistress," Beth replied.

Beth watched her stagger with Theodore along the landing it was far too close to the stairs, so Beth decided to stay where she was just in case it proved necessary.

There was a bang at the door. Tom opened it to see Doctor Lloyd. As the doctor walked into the hallway, he said to Tom, "Tell your Master Doctor Lloyd has called."

The doctor saw Persia struggling to hold up Theodore by the top step of the grand staircase and shouted. "My God woman, what are you doing?" as he rushed up the stairs and grabbed Theodore to steady him.

"Tom!" shouted the doctor take the Master's other arm!" and between them they led him into his bedchamber put him into bed.

"I was just giving my husband some exercise," said Persia trying to justify what she was doing.

"I thought, Madam, you said your husband was in Charleston yesterday?"

"Yes that is correct!" how dare he question me she thought and where was Sebastian when she needed him.

"Madam, your husband must have been ill for at least two weeks to be in this state!" Persia moved uncomfortably and fiddled nervously with her embroidered silk hanky feigning tears.

She sat down in a distressed state. "I am in shock please help my husband, doctor!"

Doctor Lloyd whispered in Tom's ear and he left the room.

Persia was feeling very anxious with no Sebastian by her side.

Tom came back with the sheriff and two of his men. The doctor had a word in the Sheriff's ear, he then ordered his two men to watch Persia.

"Why have you ordered your men to watch me?" demanded Persia. "How dare you come into my home and show me such disrespect."

"Madam, I believe you have lied to me concerning your husband's illness."

"Tom, and Beth, I need you to come with me."

Doctor Lloyd, the Sheriff, Beth and Tom, went to Theodore's study.

"Now, Beth tell the Sheriff what has been going on?" said Doctor Lloyd. "Do not be afraid we only want the truth," he said reassuringly.

"Sir, for the past two weeks the Mistress has been pouring liquid from a brown bottle into the Master's food, at each meal time. I only know because I watched from behind the crack in the door. The Master was not improving with the medicine but was getting worse. Tom and I needed to get help for him, that's why I spoke to you that day in Charleston."

"Is that correct, Tom?" said the Sherriff.

"Yes, Sir," replied Tom nervously.

"Beth, do you know where the brown bottle is?"

"Yes Sir."

"Please go and get it and bring it to me."

Doctor Lloyd examined it. "This is laudanum, do you know who prescribed this?"

"No, Sir, but a doctor did visit the Master."

"Thank you, you have both been very loyal to your Master."

Sebastian rode back from Charleston, to find a cart used by the sheriff to transport prisoners outside the plantation house, with several horses tethered nearby.

He knew the plan could go wrong so he had prepared a contingency his survival was paramount.

He confidently strode into the house.

"Oh, Sebastian!" cried Persia, who tried to move but was restrained by the two sheriffs men.

He knew he had to think quickly.

"What is going on here?" He said looking puzzled.

"Where have you been, Sir?" the Sheriff asked him.

"I've been Charleston."

"And what was your business there?"

"I visited a brothel, you can check!"

"I intend to," replied the Sheriff.

"You rat!" Persia said to Sebastian, as she showed her true colours.

"Are you aware of any medicine that has been given to your stepfather by his wife?"

"No Persia always saw to my stepfather, in fact she said he was her responsibly and she would see to him. I have been busy running the plantation for him. I thought he was on the mend."

"He is lying!" shouted Persia trying to save her own skin.

"Do you know how Mrs Jackson got the medicine she put in his food?"

"No, Sir, I was not aware she was giving him any medicine"

"Can't you see he is lying!" she sobbed, all her dreams came crashing down she was heading for one place and he was seeing to that—jail.

"I think you should check with Judge Peabody. He recognised Persia at a party held at Peter Riverdale's plantation, he knew her from working in a whorehouse that he frequented. I did not want to upset my stepfather until I had checked out this information. Then I would have informed him that she was a fraud." At this Persia spat at him.

"I think we have enough information, take her out and lock her in the cart," the Sheriff said to his men. "Sebastian you need to show how grateful you are to your loyal slaves, we could have lost Theodore!" Beth and Tom moved nervously.

"Beth, plenty of water and open the blinds and let fresh air in and I will be back tomorrow," said the doctor. Sebastian had to resist punishing Beth and Tom who were now under the protection of the Sheriff and the doctor. He would have to wait to get his revenge.

Chapter Seven

Doctor Lloyd directed Beth to stay and nurse her Master until he recovered. Sebastian continued to run the plantation. Things were not running smoothly as they had done when Theodore was in charge. It was not as prosperous for he was drowning his sorrows in drink and in ever spiralling gambling debts.

The Master had taken her beloved Abel away from her and a father for her son, but Beth knew he had suffered to, by losing his daughter. She felt compassion for him. Kate offered to look after Will for her, so she could stay and watch over the Master in case he needed her. She prayed for him to recover.

One morning he opened his eyes to see Beth sitting in the chair by his bed preparing to feed him soup. It was apparent to him that she had spent many nights nursing him, as she had a book and a shawl to keep her warm at night.

'Is that you, Beth?"

"Yes, Sir," replied Beth as she mopped his brow.

"How many days have I been ill?"

"You have been ill for over three weeks Master."

When Theodore was feeling better, Doctor Lloyd advised him that Beth had saved his life. Theodore thought Beth had set an example of true Christianity; he owed her a great debt of gratitude.

"Beth, where did you learn to read?" asked Theodore.

Beth was worried for the Master had noticed she had read the book left on his table. "I'm sorry," sir, but I could not resist reading the book."

"Beth, it is alright, now tell me where did you learn to read?"

"I had a tutor who taught me in my father's house."

"Where did you live?"

"In England, my father was a Duke. I learnt to play the piano and I often played in a musical group to entertain my father's friends. He recognised me as his own, and respected my mother and took me into his family." Beth wondered why the Master had asked her so many questions. After Beth had fed him his dinner, Theodore said

"Beth please take a book from the library and read it to me."

From then on Beth read to him every evening. Theodore recovered and started to take control of Cotton Wood Plantation.

"Beth, the mas' wishes to see you in his study, is yar in trouble?" Tom said concerned.

"No," she replied. She nervously knocked on his study door.

"Come in, Beth, please sit down, I would like you to take on the duties of teacher at Cotton Wood Plantation. By using your good, grasp of English and knowledge of literature you can teach the other slaves English and religious studies. I do not know if you are aware, but soon they will be free and they will need these skills to help them. You can have the use of the library, and you can use the room at the back of the church as your classroom. You will receive a sum of ten dollars a month for performing these duties. You will also be given an allowance to provide suitable clothing for you and your son, befitting the post of teacher."

Beth was stunned at the Masters suggestion. Theodore felt uneasy at the delay in her reply.

"Well Beth, what do you say to this new position?"

"Mast . . ." Theodore interrupted her. "Now you may address me as Mr Jackson if you accept the position. "Beth looked into his eyes and saw a more gentle side she had not seen before, it was as if she was seeing him for the first time.

"I would like to accept the post of teacher here at Cotton Wood Plantation, when would you like me to start Mr Jackson." she felt awkward not saying Master. Theodore realised this and smiled at Beth and she blushed in embarrassment.

"Straight away, your son can stay with you and help you with your teaching. We can help do Gods work together, Beth." His sincerity reached out to her and her heart raced, what an opportunity he was giving her to help her fellow slaves.

Theodore summoned his stepson to his study. "Sebastian, I have heard rumours of your gambling and drunkenness, the accounts that you were responsible for are in a complete mess. I will not tolerate this behaviour, you have brought dishonour to the family name," said Theodore.

"I am therefore reducing your allowance, Sir, until you prove to me that you have changed your ways. I had left the running of Cotton Wood plantation in your hands but you have disappointed me." Sebastian walked towards the study door, feeling the anger build inside him.

"Oh yes, I have also employed Beth to teach the slaves English, she will be using the room at the back of the Church, that's all." He said dismissing him.

I will have to remind that slave to keep her mouth shut, thought Sebastian, worried that Beth would now be privy to Theodore's ear in her new position as a teacher.

Beth told Kate her good news. "Kate, I am to teach reading and writing to the other slaves, it will be my full time duties," she said excitedly. "I am allowed to have Will with me." Kate's mouth dropped open. "Beth, why de Mas' give you this job?"

"He has heard that a bill is likely to be passed shortly in Britain for the abolition of slavery and this will surely follow here." Kate asked, "What dar mean by, how you say Ab . . . ?" Beth responded, "Abolition means freedom for slaves Kate?" The master will need to pay for help and an educated work force would be an advantage, it will also help the slaves looking for paid work, especially the young ones. He feels I have the necessary attributes to carry out this work. In other words a good grasp of the English language."

"Will yar take it, Beth?"

"Yes I have accepted his offer," looking straight into Kate's eyes she paused. "I have to consider my son, we will be given clothes and money each month, and I would be a fool to turn it down. I feel more than equipped to do the job."

"Well, I pity you with the likes of Rufus, Gideon and Lottie, who have always considered themselves to be in a higher position than the rest of us they will resent you telling them what to do. Rather you than me watch yar back girl."

"Would you watch over Will, I need to visit Abel's grave?"

"Yes," Kate said as she hugged her. Beth wanted to confide in Abel about the Masters kind offer, she would look for a sign from him telling her she was doing the right thing for her and their son.

Beth set about compiling a timetable so that everyone knew when they should attend classes; the hours of attendance, she then agreed with Theodore. All the slaves arrived. Beth was full of excitement she explained what was going to happen and there was a stunned silence. "I look forward to our first lesson," said Beth. No one replied, there was coldness from all of them—this hurt her deeply. As Peter left he did not acknowledge Beth, Lottie moaned under her breath as she barged passed. Tom just nodded his head at her, only Kate embraced her and the rest ignored her. Why could they not see how this could help them? When they had left the classroom, Beth buried her head in her hands and wept. Will clung to her skirt she picked him up and cuddled him for she knew in her heart, that the education of slaves would eventually benefit him as well. She set about ordering the books and items required for the lessons.

Beth could hear Lottie talking about her in the kitchen. "Who does she t'ink she is, she be a slave and will always be!"

That evening Theodore asked Beth if she would care to play the piano for him."

"Of course, Sir," Beth browsed through the music on the piano, placed her chosen piece on the stand, and began to play. The music floated around the room, Theodore got up from his seat and walked over to the piano and stood next to her, almost touching her. Beth's heart pounded and her hands became sweaty with nervousness. He was amazed at how accomplished she was. When she had finished the piece, she placed the lid down gently over the keys and thought to herself what a joy it was to play again. He took her hand and helped her up from the piano. Looking into her eye's he said, "Thank you, Beth, that was lovely, it was pleasant to hear music resounding throughout the house again."

"Sir, I have to attend to my son, please excuse me."

"Certainly, but please play for me again," she nodded and left the room. Beth was feeling more and more concerned at the way she felt in his presence.

Sebastian walked into the classroom at the back of the white chapel, and shut the door behind him. Beth turned she had been busy sorting the books for the first lesson. Now she felt fear as he walked towards her smiling. He grabbed her tearing her dress and tried to kiss her. She pushed him away throwing a chair in his path as she rushed for the door. He snatched at her hair and it tumbled down, he held on to it and pushed her to the ground in amongst the books.

As he tugged her hair he said, "Have you told anyone?"

"No," she screamed.

"You, will do my bidding, she could smell the liquor on his breath, he undid his belt with his other hand and his trousers fell around his ankles. Beth yelled with pain as he pulled her by the hair and said, "Put this in your mouth, you whore! He commanded."

Beth bit his thigh; he hit her hard across the face catching her skin with his ring.

Theodore had decided to call in on Beth to see how the lessons were progressing and to wish her well. As he crossed the path to the white chapel, he heard screaming, his walk changed to a run.

On entering the classroom, Theodore saw Sebastian hitting Beth, his attire around his ankles. He immediately leapt at Sebastian and wrenched him from Beth. Sebastian cowered under the ferocity of his attack, and then crumpled to the floor. Theodore lifted Beth up, covered her modesty and took her back to the big house. In his study, he laid her on the chaise longue and gently cleaned the blood from her mouth. She was in a state of shock, so he gave her a sip of brandy to revive her.

"It was fortuitous that I decided to visit your lesson today. I had a gift for you and wanted you to be able to use it at the lesson today. I dropped it when coming to your aid. I will retrieve it and give it to you tomorrow." Beth's shock had turned to tears.

"Would you like to go to your room now, Beth?"

"Yes, Sir," she said between her sobs. "My son will wonder where I am?"

"I will find him and send him up to you do not concern yourself. Is there anyone I can get to help you?"

"Could you have Kate sent to me please Sir," said Beth.

She touched his arm—"Thank you for your kindness, Sir." Theodore carried her up the stairs. He shouted for Tom to open the bedchamber door of the guestroom and laid her down gently on the soft bed. "Tom, fetch Kate and then find Will and bring him to his mother." Tom did not know what to think as Beth's clothes were torn and bloodied and she seemed very distressed.

"Mas' needs yar up stairs in the guest bedchamber, straight away."

"Wuh for Tom?" Kate asked. All went quiet in the kitchen Lottie loved gossip and eagerly awaited Tom's reply. Kate had never been upstairs before, her place was in the kitchen.

One thing that you need as a House Servant was to be discreet. "The Mas' orders you to assist Beth, now stop asking questions and follow me," said Tom in a superior voice. Kate tried to tidy herself up as she climbed the staircase behind Tom. She was conscious of her stained apron she pushed her loose hair into her mopped hat. He showed her into the guest bedchamber where Theodore was already waiting. "You are to attend to Mistress Beth until she recovers, and you must bring her meals to this room that will be your duties, do you understand Kate," said Theodore.

"Yes, Mas' "she replied.

"Now, my dear, anything you need Kate will get you." The door opened and Will ran to his mother climbing onto the bed to cuddle her.

"I will leave you now; if I may I will call on you after dinner to see how you are?"

"Thank you," replied Beth. Then Theodore left.

"Beth, what happened?" Kate asked as she helped her out of her blood stained dress. "Sebastian attacked me in the classroom he tried to force me to do an awful act," she sobbed in Kate's arms. "Mama, please do not cry." Will held onto his mother tightly while Beth composed herself. Kate tucked Beth into her bed and sorted her clothes. Kate's mouth dropped open as she surveyed the bedchamber.

"Wuh a room," she said as she lifted a gold handled hairbrush from the dressing table and felt it. A smile came to Beth's face, poor Kate this was a completely new world for her. She so valued her friendship.

Lottie was making up her own version of events to the kitchen menials when Tom entered the kitchen. "I think yar should keep your opinions to yourself," he said to Lottie as he passed through. "Yar get on with your work instead of gossiping." Lottie mumbled under her breath as she peeled vegetables on the large wooden table. Gideon will tell me everything I am sure, she thought to herself.

Theodore sent for Sebastian. "Come in," shouted Theodore. As Sebastian walked towards his desk, he knew he was in for it, as he held his bruised ribs. Theodore stood up and came face to face with his stepson. The sight of him triggered his anger, remembering what had happened to Beth. He grabbed him by the collar of his shirt and said. "If you ever touch Mistress Beth again I'll have you whipped and you will lose your inheritance. She is in my house as my guest. You will adhere to these rules while you live here, is that clear. I will expect you to apologise to Beth, and ask for her forgiveness. If you do not agree to do this then you can pack your belongings and return to your mother's house. I am sick and tired of your disobedience and your bullying ways. I will now deal with all matters concerning the slaves. You will concentrate on the growing and harvesting of my crops, you have until tomorrow to do as I ask. Now get out of my sight for you disgust me." Theodore said with his voice quivering with rage.

Theodore knocked on Beth's bedchamber door, Kate answered. He addressed Beth who was lying on the bed, "Good evening, Beth, how are you feeling?"

"Better thank you." He dismissed Kate, and then sat down beside her and produced a wrapped gift from behind his back. Beth opened it to find the most beautiful carved wooden pointing stick, for her to use in the classroom. Her hand glided over it.

"Thank you so much for your kind gift but I cannot accept it."

"May I ask why Beth?" she noticed the look of hurt on his face.

Although my husband is dead Sir, I still consider myself married." Theodore shifted uncomfortably in his chair.

"Well, please see it as a gift from your employer to help you in your new position as teacher," he replied. There was a knock on the door and Theodore irritated by the interruption shouted.

"Come in," Sebastian entered the room.

"Mistress Beth, I would like to ask for your forgiveness for my behaviour yesterday?" He tried to act contrite in front of Theodore, Beth felt uneasy.

"I accept you're apology." Theodore looked pleased.

"Well you had best get back to work, Sebastian," he said dismissing him.

The field slaves sat outside their cabins it was a hot clammy evening.

"Peter, I am surprised at Beth, I would never have thought she would ever have worked so closely with the Mas' after he had Abel hung," said Soul. "I loved Abel as a brother and I will never forgive her for betraying his memory, she is dead in my eyes," replied Peter.

Nothing for Peter was a good enough reason to work and live in the big house with the Mas' their enemy. The other field slaves muttered their agreement.

"Well I am grateful to Beth, because it means while I attend lessons, there is less time for my Mas' to hit me," said a grateful Lawrence.

Chapter Eight

Theodore had decided to hold a ball to celebrate the centenary of Cotton Wood Plantation. He had sent out invitations to his neighbours, friends, and acquaintances. He would purchase a special dress for Beth to wear so he could introduce her at the ball. He knew there would be some that would show their disapproval. He felt they needed to remember how they all came to him at some time for loans to save themselves and their plantations. This was his life and plantation and he would do as he pleased, he was answerable to no one.

"Tom, would you organise the decorations and Lottie the food and drink, there will be a bigger budget than normal as this is a special occasion for the plantation. Also, inform Kate that her position has been made permanent she would be working in Mistress Beth's bedchamber. Also, please find her the appropriate clothes and give her a servant's bedroom close to her mistress.

"Yes, Mas'," Tom replied.

Lottie was annoyed at losing Kate. "Wuh I do wid one less," she moaned as she shouted at her children who were fighting as usual.

Kate was so excited when Tom told her of her promotion. "This will be your bedroom and your new uniform, as he pointed at clean clothes hanging on the door."

"From today, Kate, you will always address Beth as Mistress is that clear, anything you are not sure of come to me. You must remember not to repeat anything you hear, or are told, to anyone, is that understood."

"Yes, Tom."

"Mister Tom to yar, girl," he said in an aloof manner, as he walked away. He thought of all the years he had worked here and she gets promotion just like that. His position in the big house was very important to him. As he saw it, Kate needed to know that he was still her superior within the household.

Kate felt very important now and could not stop smiling as she explored her new bedroom. It was so different to the cold and stark cabin she had shared with her parents near the cotton fields.

Beth sat at her dressing table brushing her hair when there was a knock at her bedchamber door; she opened it to find Kate beaming from ear to ear dressed in a uniform befitting a chambermaid.

"Mistress Beth, I am serving you from now on, Mas' orders!"

"I feel very uncomfortable, Kate, with this situation. I am so sorry to put you in this awful position, I would not have allowed it if I had known."

"Me will work hard," said Kate. "I get beat in de kitchen," her face fell. Beth wrapped her arms around her.

"If that's what you want Kate. It will be lovely having you close by me, my dear friend." Kate with a big smile on her face twirled around in her uniform.

Will had the adjoining room to Beth, Theodore had arranged for some toys to go to his room. She could hear him running round the room with excitement. Beth popped her head round his door; he was sitting on a rocking horse laughing. This was what she had dreamed of, to see her child so happy and to be able to give him these pleasures, now it was happening.

A large pink box lay on Beth's bed she opened it and inside was the most glorious pale yellow silk dress. On top was a note, Mistress Beth, please accept this gift and wear it when accompanying me to the Centennial Ball, Theodore. Beth held the gown against her and gazed at herself. It had crystal buttons on the bodice and delicate white lace framed the sleeves and neck.

Kate helped her get ready for the ball. There was a knock at Beth's door and Kate opened it. Beth smiled when she saw it was Theodore. His heart raced every time he saw her, he loved the way she tilted her head when he spoke to her, such an endearing trait he thought.

He knew he had chosen well for the soft yellow silk ball gown complemented her colouring.

Her soft curls framed her face emphasizing her large hypnotic, dark brown eyes. Theodore was besotted with her, God help anyone who showed her disrespect he felt very protective towards her now.

"Mistress Beth, it will be an honour to escort you tonight," he lifted her hand and kissed it, she blushed. "You may leave us," Theodore ordered Kate. He produced a black velvet box, "Open it Beth". Beth opened it and inside was an Emerald necklace and drop earrings. "Sir this is too generous."

"Don't you like them Beth?" He asked.

"They are exquisite," she replied. He took the necklace and fastened it around her neck, "There they were made for you!" He leant over and slowly kissed the nape of her neck. She closed her eyes at the touch of his soft lips caressing her. She was overwhelmed with pleasure.

Theodore left her side and walked towards the door, turning to face her, he said "May I have the pleasure of the first dance!" She opened her eyes, and looked at him through a veil of pleasure and smiled at him.

"Yes, Sir, it is yours" she replied. Theodore was well aware that his technique would have had this affect, and left her bedchamber with a trace of a smile.

He descended the grand staircase with a bounce in his step he was in love.

The carriages started to arrive, and Theodore welcomed his guests at the door. "Good evening Theodore," said Matthew Walton with his wife Susan on his arm, followed by brother's Lloyd and David Southgate with their wives, and Joseph and Joanna Riverdale. All fellow plantation owners in the area

"Thank you for coming to celebrate the centenary of Cotton Wood Plantation," said a proud Theodore. "If you agree could we meet in my study later this evening to discuss a matter of urgency?" Those present agreed to attend the meeting, besides none of them knew when they might need his financial assistance again.

"You men," said Julia, David's wife who was a gentile woman in her sixties, we are here to enjoy ourselves she laughed, pulling her husband through to the ballroom. Joanna Riverdale huddled up to her women friends.

"Where is she?" This slave Theodore has befriended," they all quietly wanted Theodore, especially Joanna. She knew him as a boy and always dreamt of marrying him when she grew up, but he only had eyes for Martha her friend.

The ballroom was full and the music began, Beth could hear it from upstairs, she was nervous. She took a last look at herself in the mirror and thought to herself, was she the same woman who had endured that terrible time on board The Camberley. Now she was on her own and was responsible for her son's future, she would do whatever she had to do to give him a better start in life. After all, he was the son of a chief. She heard a voice in her head; it was her beloved Abel saying—hold your head up high Beth.

Her ball gown was full and skirted the stairs as she came down. She raised her head and confidently walked into the ballroom all the guests eyes were on her. A woman dressed in cream and black shook her fan in disgust as Beth passed her and said to the group she was conversing with, "I will not socialize with a—SLAVE." She tugged at her husband's arm; his drinking glass fell and smashed as they left the ballroom. They scurried out in disgust. You could hear whispers emanating around the ballroom. Many women had to chastise their husbands for looking at Beth. The men thought how lucky Theodore was, and the women where envious of her having his attention, as well as their husbands.

Theodore turned around from the guest he was talking to, when he heard the smashed glass and was overwhelmed at how stunning Beth looked as she entered the ballroom. He needed to rescue her. He walked towards her daring anyone to say anything and held her gaze, trying to reassure her. Beth could only see him as he took her hand and escorted her to the centre of the ballroom he nodded to the orchestra to start playing a waltz. Beth picked up the hem of her ball gown nervously, knowing all eyes were on her, hoping she would remember how to dance, it had been a long time. She realised quickly that Theodore was an accomplished dancer she relaxed in his embrace. They were in a world of their own as they twirled and turned on the dance floor, slowly more couples joined them. She knew she was falling in love with him.

Late into the evening, Theodore gathered the other plantation owners in his study.

"Men, we need to think about protecting our land." As you are all aware, Robert E Lee has formed an army to protect the South, but he cannot be everywhere.

We need to be able to react quickly if there is an attack on any of our plantations, I would suggest that we maintain a strong force with men from each plantation and should the need arise we come to each others' aid. All in favour say aye. There was overwhelming agreement to Theodore's suggestion.

A group of wives approached Beth "Why, my dear, what a beautiful gown, where did you purchase it?" Joanna asked Beth with an insincere tone to her voice.

"I have no idea—it was a gift."

"How fortunate you are," Joanna replied looking, Beth up and down. She then walked away with a smirk on her face arm in arm with her women friends, laughing.

Beth moved out to the Garden feeling uncomfortable, she decided to go to her room away from prying eyes and unkind comments. The feeling engulfed her reminding her of her days growing up in England. How her stepbrother was so unkind to her because of her colour. She knew her father the Duke loved her, and he always treated her, the same as his other children.

She crept into Wills room he was fast asleep; she gently kissed him and pulled his bedding up around him. In a chair near his bed, Kate had fallen asleep, Beth smiled and shook her gently, and Kate stirred and opened her eyes. "Kate, you can go to your bed now, thank you for watching over Will for me"

"I will help you get out of your gown," she said sleepily.

"Thank you but I will be fine, go to your bed." Beth felt awkward having a servant especially, her dear friend. Beth went to her room and removed her gown.

She could hear the carriages leaving and the music subside, a knock at her door disturbed her, she put on her velvet robe and answered it; she hoped it would be him.

"Beth, I hope you are not in ill health. I was concerned when I could not find you in the ballroom." Theodore looked worried, had he pushed her too soon into the social world of his neighbours and friends.

"No, Sir, I am fine I wanted to I check on my son," she thought it best not to mention how cruel his friends wives had been to her.

"Mistress Beth, it was an honour to escort you this evening," he moved closer to her holding her gaze, her heartbeat quickened she so wanted him to kiss her. He placed a kiss on her cheek, he did not want to be too forward and frighten her away. She hoped he would be able to tell by her eyes that she wanted more. She moved closer to him. He traced his finger down the side of her face and ran it over her generous lips that sent tingles down her spine bringing her body alive. Her breasts heaved with excitement. He cupped her face in his hands and kissed her lips. Beth's body reacted to his touch. He removed her robe and unbuttoned her nightgown revealing her generous breasts, and lifted her onto the bed.

"Beth, I must have you," he said passionately.

"I'm yours," she said wantonly. He traced with his finger the curve of the side of her body from her breast down to her hips, "I love this shape," he said. Theodore caught sight of her back and the scars from her whipping. He washed her scars and her branding mark with his tears and asked for her forgiveness. She kissed his eyes and moved down his body caressing it with her lips.

His touch was gentle as he fondled her breasts, Beth moaned with pleasure as he entered her, their bodies moving in tune with one another. They both floated in the pleasure of the moment. They kissed and held each other, falling asleep in each other's arms.

Beth watched him as he lay sleeping. How could she love this man when she still loved Abel, but she did? Theodore opened his eye's "Good morning my love," he said as he smiled at her.

"How beautiful you look in the morning light," he said as he stroked her face. "I must return to my room, I do not want to compromise your reputation."

Kate helped her dress, chattering away about the gossip Lottie was talking about in the kitchen. Beth could not stop smiling she was so happy and in love.

As they ate breakfast, Theodore asked "Mistress Beth, I would like you to join me for a visit to Charleston, it would make me very happy."

"I would be delighted Sir," she replied smiling back at him.

Theodore left Beth in the drapers shop in Charleston while he attended to a business appointment. She enjoyed looking around the shop at the many colourful hats for sale. He had told her to buy one; there was so much choice. She decided on a cream satin hat with netting which draped across her eyes. The shop owner's wife whispered to her husband, the other women in the shop were staring and whispering between themselves. Beth felt increasingly uncomfortable. "I would like to purchase this hat please."

"That will be $40." the shopkeeper said bluntly. Beth handed him the money and he placed it in the till, while his wife placed the hat in a large round hatbox.

On the way back to the plantation in the horse and trap, Theodore said to Beth "May I see your purchase?" Beth showed him her new hat.

"You are very quiet, Beth, is there something wrong?"

"No everything is fine," she replied, trying to sound cheerful. Theodore was cross with himself for letting her go into the drapers shop on her own. He took her hand and kissed it.

He lifted up the box next to him and placed it on his lap. "Look what I have for Will," he said as he raised the cover. Inside was the most adorable puppy. "Oh Theodore, he will love it."

"That brought a smile back to your beautiful face." He wanted so much to make her happy.

Six months had passed, Beth was happy and in love.

"Kate, I am with child," Beth said as she stroked her tummy.

"Oh, Beth, does the Mas' know?"

"No not yet, I am going to tell him after dinner tonight. I hope he will be pleased."

"Of course he will," said Kate as she put her arms around Beth to reassure her. She dressed for dinner, hoping Theodore would be pleased with her news.

Theodore thought how radiant Beth looked at dinner. They adjourned to the sitting room; he reached out to hold her hand for he felt so blessed. She looked into his eyes, "Theodore I am with child." He lifted her up in the air with joy. "I could not be happier you have given me so much love and now an heir." He held her in his arms thanking God for the joy she had brought him.

Theodore wanted to legitimise the heir to Cotton Wood Plantation. He commissioned an engagement ring of diamonds and sapphires for Beth in Charleston. He had decided once the child was born they would get married and then he would change his will for the child to inherit Cotton Wood Plantation.

Two months later he collected Beth's ring, he sat in his study and admired it; he could not wait to give it to her. She was now eight months pregnant and finding it hard to walk.

Theodore knocked at Beth's bedchamber, Kate opened the door "How are you feeling, my dear?" said Theodore as he approached her bed.

"The heats getting to me but other than that well," she said as she fanned herself. Turning to Kate, he said, "Leave us?" When Kate had shut the door, Theodore took the ring box from his inside jacket pocket and opened it.

"This is for you, my dear, I would like you to be my wife and Mistress of Cotton Plantation, please say yes?" he said anxiously.

"It's gorgeous, Theodore; Yes I will marry you." Beth was so excited she held the ring up to look at it, the sun's rays from the window bounced off the gems. She looked at his face and said,

"Thank you for making me so happy. Will adores you and soon we will have our own child." Theodore kissed her.

He wanted the wedding to take place before the birth of their child, an intimate affair so he set about organising it. Theodore had bought a wedding gown for her. He had also arranged for the Minister to marry them in the Chapel on Cotton Wood Plantation.

Theodore had called Sebastian to his Study. "Sir, I do not want you anywhere near Beth, you are to stay in Charleston until after my wedding. I will then decide what to do with you and your future here at Cotton Wood Plantation, now gets out of my sight." Sebastian knew he had to be careful, how he hated that whore. He would wait and when the time was right, he would have Cotton Wood Plantation.

"I think an intimate wedding would be wise, my love, being in such a late stage of your pregnancy." Beth touched Theodore's face.

"You are so thoughtful all that matters to me is that we have a wedding day with the people that are the most important to us. They will be there to hear me say yes to the man I love." He held Beth and kissed her, feeling so fortunate to be getting married and having a family at his time of life.

He handed a box to Beth, she opened it and pulled out the most beautiful wedding gown she had ever seen, it was enlarged to accommodate her increasing size. It was white satin with gold threads woven through it. Crystal beads along the neckline and hem sparkled as they caught the light. Theodore could see that Beth was delighted.

"Beth, these were my mother's jewels. She would have loved you as I do, I would feel honoured if you would wear them at our wedding." He handed her a red velvet box, inside Beth found a diamond tiara, necklace and drop earrings." These are my wedding gifts to you."

"Thank you I know how precious they are to you having belonged to your mother, I will wear them with pride. But I do not have a gift for you."

"Beth, you have given me the greatest gift of all, your love and you carry the heir to Cotton Wood Plantation, I could not be happier. I will await you at the Chapel tomorrow." Kissing her on the cheek, he left the room.

It was her wedding day, Beth felt a niggling pain as she got out of bed but it went as fast as it came. She was so busy getting ready for her wedding that morning that she did not give it another thought.

Kate was excited, as she would be a bridesmaid. Beth gave her one of her dresses to wear and a bunch of pink roses to carry. She kept turning this way and that, loving the feeling of the dress as it swung back and forth.

Beth looked at her reflection in the mirror, how different she looked she was blooming with Theodore's child. She would always love Abel he had a special place in her heart. She now needed to move forward. What she felt for Theodore was a different love. She swore never to forget her past.

"Yar look lovely," said Kate as she handed Beth her bouquet of roses. Kate helped her down the grand staircase and they made their way to the white chapel near the house.

A beaming Kate walked down the aisle first. Followed by Beth who in the stillness of her mind thanked her God for the happiness he had brought her and her son, as she walked towards Theodore standing at the altar.

The Chapel looked magical, it glowed with many candles and the scent from the flowers filled the air. White roses entwined with pink ribbon hung down the walls. Beth thought Theodore looked so handsome in his royal blue velvet jacket, which matched his eyes.

To him she radiated beauty that came from carrying his child, he felt so protective towards her. Her face glowed with happiness as they locked eyes. When the Minister had married them he said to Theodore, "You may kiss the bride," Theodore whispered in Beth's ear "I love you, Mrs Jackson." Kate threw rice over them as they left the Chapel.

"My darling," he said cupping her face.

"I would like you to read this it is another of my wedding gifts to you." He handed a large envelope to Beth. She opened it; it was an official document stating that Theodore had given her and her son Will their freedom, dated August 1862 signed by Theodore Jackson, Cotton Wood Plantation. Beth grabbed the table near her to steady herself. Then the tears flowed down her face, this was what she had always dreamt of for her son, and now he would grow up a free man. She was overwhelmed, Beth looked at Theodore, "thank you, thank you, God bless you for your kindness to my son and I," she cried. Theodore carried her to her bedchamber and laid her on her bed.

"You must rest, my dear."

Drying her eye's she said to Theodore," Please sit down my love, I have something to tell you." He sat down on the chair next to her bed perplexed by her sudden seriousness.

"I am able to tell you this because I am now free and fear no more the consequences of imparting this truth to you. I was not able to before because my life and that of my son was threatened if I did so." She felt her heart beating hard as she recounted it to him

"I witnessed the murder of your daughter Emma by Sebastian. I could not help her as Rufus knocked me to the ground and held me there. Sebastian falsely accused Abel who was innocent. Abel made me swear, I would not endanger our son's life by trying to save his."

Theodore stunned by these revelations got up from his seat and went to the window there was silence. What if he does not believe me, she thought. He walked back to Beth's side and put his arms out to her and Beth clung to him. Can you forgive me my love?

"I also have to find forgiveness for what happened to Abel."

"What a burden to carry and pain you felt at seeing your husband hung when you knew he was innocent, leaving your son without a father."

Looking into her tearful eyes he said, "I swear to you, Beth, Abel's name will be vindicated and I will bring Will up as my own. I have to carry the weight of Abel's death on my conscience for the rest of my life. May God forgive me?" His head was reeling with what Beth had told him.

"I will see that those responsible will pay with their lives," how could he have been so betrayed by Sebastian?

A pain engulfed Beth, she knew the baby was coming and gripped the sheets. "Theodore feared the shock of the traumatic disclosure and the truth that Beth had carried for so long had brought on the birth."

"Kate, go and tell Tom to send Samson for the midwife and return quickly to see to Mistress Beth," he ordered. Beth's pains were now coming in quick succession. Theodore could hear her screaming in pain from his study, where he was anxiously pacing up and down. He put his head in his hands, thinking of the birth of Emma and the devastation of losing Martha, he could not bear to lose Beth.

"Now push, my lovely, I can see the head," said the midwife who was in her early forties, round faced and with a mouth of blackened teeth. Although she had delivered most of the children in the area, she liked her tipple and most nights you would find her drunk in the tavern. She supported the baby's head and shouted

"One more push, my lovely, and it will be here." Beth let out protracted agonising cry.

"It's a boy," shouted the midwife as she cut the cord, and wrapped the baby in a blanket and passed the child to Beth. Beth was shaking from exhaustion as she took hold of her son. He was white with blue eyes like Theodore's, Beth was grateful he looked healthy and strong, she hugged him and held him against her full breast to suckle. Kate started to cry when she saw Beth with her son. "Thank you Kate for your help, you are such a dear friend to me," she said as she reached her hand out to hers. "Could you go and get the Master, I would like him to meet his son."

"Of course," replied Kate.

Beth was examining every part of her newborn son, he is perfect, she thought. When she felt a sharp pain in her stomach and then another in quick succession, she shouted, "Kate come quickly, I need you." She came rushing back to the bedchamber.

"What's wrong, Missy?"

"Take my son quickly and lay him in his cradle, I have spasms of terrible pain," she cried as she could feel the next one coming. Beth was feeling the need to push now and felt a movement pass her thighs. I need you to check me because I can feel something happening. Kate pulled the blankets back to find a pool of blood and a black baby boy still attached to the umbilical cord lying lifeless. Kate started to cry.

"What do I do Missy?"

"Quickly cut the cord with my scissors on my dressing table and smack his bottom, he must cry to get air into his lungs," said an anxious Beth. Kate did as Beth said; her hands were trembling as she smacked its bottom, it cried and she wrapped the bloodied newborn baby in a sheet and passed him to his mother. "I have twins, Kate, you where wonderful my dearest friend," she said. Kate was so pleased with the faith that Beth had placed in her.

Beth beamed looking at her second baby he had more of her features but had his father's dimple in his chin. Theodore came to see Beth. I would like you to meet your sons." Beth was concerned at what Theodore's reaction would be, would he accept the black twin as his son. Even if he felt uncomfortable about seeing one twin was black he never let on to Beth. Theodore replied "Twins, we are doubly blessed and kissed them both. "My darling, you have given me the most wonderful gift, Twin sons who will inherit Cotton Wood Plantation, you have fulfilled my dream," and kissed her on the lips.

Kate watched the happy scene, and slipped quietly out of the bedchamber, leaving them to enjoy their special moment.

Chapter Nine

(On the outskirts of Charleston) 1862

⚜

The Corporal saluted the officer. "Sir we have carried out a reconnaissance and there is a large force of Union soldiers ahead in the woods and another on the ridge, it looks like an ambush Sir.

"How many are there Corporal?"

"I would say in the region of 200, Sir."

"Prepare the men for an attack."

I for one am not going to die in a futile attack on that ridge, thought Corporal Benson. He had good reason to hate the officer since four months ago he was one of only a few who survived the attack, which had cost the lives of 150 men from his company. He had lost many good men including his best friend in a similar ambush led by this officer.

"No, Sir, we will be slaughtered! We will be riding to our deaths," he replied.

The officer pulled out his pistol and pointed at the Corporal. "Put this man under arrest until I can deal with him later." The Corporal realising the enormity of the situation made for his horse and shouted for his men to follow. The officer fired his pistol in the direction of the Corporal; his shot missed. There was now a general stampede of men making for their horses. The enemy now knew where they were. The officer and the remainder of his men had to make their own decision in which direction they should take flight.

"We are with you, Corporal," said the group of eight deserters as they rested in a wooded copse.

The deserters had now been on the run for some time and had needed to scour the woods and countryside in search for food. They made camp most nights with their bellies empty.

"This is the last of the eggs and bread from our last raid men. You two go ahead and see what you can find? The Corporal ordered.

"Give it here," said a bedraggled soldier as he grabbed the remains of a whisky bottle from his pal.

"No it's my turn," they fought for the bottle, it spilt on the ground. A fight ensued, the corporal attempted to keep them apart. Every day it was becoming more and more difficult to control them.

They heard horses approaching there was a shout from the sentry. "The men are back."

"Corporal, there is a large plantation to the south, two miles away,"

"How many people did you see on the plantation?" the Corporal asked.

"I observed a white overseer and a large number of slaves working in the cotton fields and there is bound to be more men working in the outbuildings and in the main house."

The Corporal ran through the plan, to attack the plantation.

Beth went to Abel's grave to tell him that she had now cleared his name. She arranged the flowers on his grave as she spoke to him. My dearest Abel, Theodore is a kind man. Will loves him as I do; he has promised to look after us. He has given us our freedom. I hope you are happy for us, as she bent down and kissed the cross that bore his name.

As Beth sat in the drawing room, Theodore took her hand. "My dear, I will be going into Charleston this morning to see my Solicitor to change my will in favour of you and our twin sons who will eventually inherit Cotton Wood Plantation." Just then, Theodore heard the sound of gunfire from outside. Theodore could see through the window, smoke rising from the cotton fields. He saw Sebastian followed by Rufus and Gideon racing down the avenue towards the house on their horses.

Theodore shouted for Tom. "Take, Mistress Beth, the twins, Will and Kate to the bedchamber and lock the door and position yourself outside." He took from his desk drawer a handgun and gave it to Tom saying, "Guard them with your life." Tom would defend Beth to the death, for he loved her.

Theodore kissed Beth. "Go with Tom." Sebastian and his men ran through the front door.

"Sir, it looks like we are under attack by Confederate deserters, scavenging for food I would estimate there are about eight of them. I came across them on my return from Charleston. I think it is necessary that we give Rufus a gun to protect the cotton in the store shed and the horses."

Theodore, agreed, and quickly unlocked the gun cabinet in his office and handed out the rifles and bullets. "Rufus, place yourself at the window in the store shed so you can also protect the back of the house."

"We will need to send Samson to get help from the neighbouring plantation owners."

Theodore despised Sebastian, and he would pay with his life when this was over, but for now he needed him, his first concern was for the protection of his family and Cotton Wood Plantation.

"Sebastian, I want you to stay here and defend the front of the house. Gideon, take this rifle and defend the side of the house through the kitchen window, I will position myself at the back of the house on the veranda." After Theodore had left the room Sebastian took Rufus to one side "Rufus, I will reward you well with your freedom and a share in the plantation if you kill the Master from your position in the store shed, everyone will believe it was the deserters who killed him." Rufus did not think twice.

"Yes, mas'."

Rufus headed out the front door to the store shed; Sebastian locked the front door behind him.

Sebastian had seen the hold Beth had over Theodore, he thought it would not be long before she had told him the truth about Emma.

Lottie and her children hid behind the kitchen table and Gideon with a rifle in his hand knelt down by the window. "Get your head down and protect those little ones," shouted Gideon. Lottie held them close to her.

The deserters had dismounted from their horses and were desperately trying to reach the main house. They had planned to distract the occupants by concentrating their attack on the front of the house, while three of them slipped around the back. Two of them managed to reach the rear of the house while the third reached an upstairs window via the balcony. On the veranda at the rear of the house, Theodore was awaiting an opportunity to return fire and did not notice the two deserters behind him. Theodore hearing movement turned and fired, instantly killing one of the deserters, the other startled by the gunshot gave Theodore the opportunity to club him with his rifle butt. Only slightly disabled the deserter fired his pistol at Theodore wounding him in the thigh Theodore dropped to the floor of the veranda. Thinking Theodore had been killed, the deserter limped back to rejoin the main attack. Theodore having regained consciousness but in pain, realised he was now pinned down by the gunfire from the shed. Since he was unable to crawl to reach his rifle and losing blood, he decided, to remain where he was and reluctantly take no further part in the action. The third deserter having managed to get in an upstairs window, crept quietly along the corridor and found Tom with a gun at the front window with his back to him. The deserter was short of ammunition and decided to use his knife; he pulled it from its sheath and stabbed Tom in the back, Tom let out a groan and fell with a thud to the floor. He then tried the door, it was locked which made him even more interested.

He managed to kick the door in, to find a startled Beth and Kate huddled together protecting the children against the far wall of the bedchamber. He smiled and shut the door behind him.

"Well, my lovelies, what do we have here, a Mistress, and her maid, this is my lucky day."

"Who's going to be first, or shall I have you together," he laughed.

"I will start with you, Missy! "He grabbed Beth's arm. Kate pushed Will behind her for safety and swung at the deserter with a vase from the table. She missed him and he pushed her to the floor. Beth saw him go for his pistol and screamed "No, not Kate," she tried to shield her but the deserter kicked her out of the way. He aimed his pistol at Kate and fired. Looking down at her body on the floor, he said. "Now look what you have made me do, waste a bullet," he said with annoyance.

It had gone quiet, no sign of soldiers at the front of the house. Sebastian went in search of Gideon in the kitchen. He found him lying dead, with Lottie sobbing over his body with her children clinging on to her apron.

She looked up at Sebastian, but there was no sympathy for her. He heard gunfire coming from the back and passed a grieving Lottie and on opening the swing door found Theodore lying with a wound to his thigh, he was losing a lot of blood. He crouched down and moved along to him.

"Thank God you have come, Sebastian, I'm wounded, help me I'm pinned down by gun fire coming from the direction of the shed. We need to check on Beth and the children." Theodore put his hand out for Sebastian to help him.

Sebastian looked Theodore in the eyes with utter contempt.

"I have waited a long time for this moment," said Sebastian. "What do you mean by that?" Theodore tried to pull himself up, but he kicked him back down," he winced in pain.

"Look we can talk later, now help me inside," begged a breathless Theodore.

"You are going nowhere." Sebastian raised his rifle, and shot him in the chest. As he lay there bleeding he lent over him and said. "While you lie dying you can think of this. I will kill your whore, sell your bastards into slavery, and take over Cotton Wood Plantation. It should always have been mine." Callously he walked away.

With his last breath, Theodore called Beth's name as he lay dying on the veranda of his beloved Cotton Wood Plantation.

The sound of gunfire had now died down and Sebastian hearing the commotion upstairs went to investigate. "Get off her you, scum." Sebastian raised his gun and shot the deserter in the back.

Beth felt his body jerk and go limp on top of her and then the feel of his warm blood as it poured over her skin.

"Theodore's, dead I've put him out of his misery, he'd asked the wrong person for help," Sebastian smirked, "So you see there is no one to help you now," he said as he shut the door and locked it behind him.

Theodore dead, no, no, she could not get her head round it. Once more, she had lost a husband and her children were fatherless. She struggled to crawl out from under the deserter's heavy, body. Then she paused and straightened her body telling herself this is not the time to grieve. I am all the children have now and I must protect them at all cost. She rushed over to Will, who was cowering in the corner of the room crying, she grabbed him and held him tightly. She then knelt by Kate and realised that she was dead. "God bless you my dear friend." The sound of her babies crying broke through the shock that had taken hold of her. She went to their cots to placate them. She thanked God for keeping her children safe.

She now had time to consider Sebastian's admission and his future intent, I do not know if he will try to kill us as well. I must leave a record of his crimes or he will remain unpunished.

Beth quickly wrote in her journal and hid it behind the wooden cladding in her bedroom praying that one day someone would find it.

Sebastian was standing on the veranda by Theodore's body as Captain Peter Riverdale rode up with his troop.

"Sir, your slave Samson told me what was happening here, we heard the gun fire and came as fast as we could."

"Captain, Confederate deserters have killed my stepfather. They have taken my stepmother and two of her children hostage. I managed to save one twin but there were too many of them, they overwhelmed us." Sebastian acted heartbroken and broke down in tears, he felt sure he had fooled the Captain. They moved Theodore's body into his study and laid him on the chaises'-longue.

"We will search for the deserters; they must have retreated back into the woods as we arrived. Have no fear we will find them. As I recall this was exactly what Theodore was afraid of," said the Captain.

Sebastian watched as the column disappeared from sight.

Sebastian went to Theodore's study to search for money he found the drawers of his desk locked.

The keys must be still on him he thought, he felt through Theodore's pockets as he lay on the Chaises longue and located them in the inside pocket of his waist coat. He winced as his fingers touched Theodore's stiffening body.

There was enough cash in the desk drawers to pay off some of the debt he owed Captain Kelly and get him off his back. He had an idea that could neatly address both of his problems and would leave him a comparatively wealthy man. He would make an offer to Captain Kelly that would settle the rest of his debt, by taking Beth and her children to England on his cargo ship. He would be able to sell them in the slave market at Bristol, and make a considerable amount of money.

"Well, well" said Captain Kelly as he staggered to his chair after a good nights drinking in the Chain and Anchor alehouse, in Charleston. Sebastian outlined his proposal.

"That will indeed settle your debt and make me a profit, you've caught me in a good mood Sebastian," as he counted his money.

"I will deliver the goods to your ship tomorrow."

"Now don't be thinking of double crossing me or you will regret it," Captain Kelly said as he stroked his grey unruly beard with his sinewy hand.

"Sebastian raced back to Cotton Wood Plantation

"Here," he said as he threw a stained kitchen maids dress at Beth, also a grey cloak and stable clothes for Will for he needed them to look like servants. "Put these on," he ordered.

Then he picked up Malaki from his cot, gave him to Beth, reached in again to pick up a blanket, and handed it to her. Whether that was his compassion showing or guilt at what he was about to say to her next.

"The other twin stays here," he said matter-of-factly.

"No, Sebastian, I beg you," Beth cried. Rufus covered her mouth and dragged her from the room she fought him like a lioness fighting for her cubs. Will screamed "Mamma, Mamma," as he tried to help her, Sebastian held a hand over his mouth.

It was dark outside, Beth, and her children climbed onto the cart. Malaki was strapped to her chest and she wrapped her cloak around Will to protect him from the cold night air. As she watched, the lights of Cotton Wood Plantation disappear into the distance the pain in her heart increased. For it was taking her away from her dead husband who she had not even had the chance to grieve for and her son Isaac—would she ever see him again? Rufus sat with them to make sure they did not make a sound as Sebastian drove the cart to the harbour at Charleston.

As they drove along the dock, a fresh strong wind buffeted the ships up against the harbour wall. They could hear the sound of the sails flapping loosely in the wind and the chaffing of the ropes that secured them as they tightened and loosened with the swell of the sea. Beth now began to realise Sebastian's intentions was to get rid of her and her children completely. She had hoped she would never see a ship again after 'The Camberley.'

Sebastian found Captain Kelly's cargo ship, the 'Cotton trader' moored in the docks. Sebastian sent Rufus on board with Beth and her children, as he did not want anyone to see him.

As Sebastian drove away from the harbour he was ecstatic, he had done it. Theodore was dead and he was to inherit Cotton Wood Plantation that's if Theodore had not changed his will, but if he had then he would control it through Isaac. If he proved difficult or the will remained unchanged then he could easily get rid of him.

"I will see you are rewarded, Rufus, this visit to the docks must never be spoken of again, do you understand?" "Yes, Mas'," said Rufus.

Rufus was now the only one who knew the truth, he must eventually get rid of him, but until then he must maintain his loyalty.

A sailor that was drunk and reeked of gin shoved Beth into a small cabin, she heard him lock the door behind her. A faint light from a lantern, which stood on a table, cast its light over a stark room. There was a small wooden bed with a metal bedpan under it. The blankets were rough and filthy, but Beth was grateful for them, she knew it could always be worse. As soon as Will's head touched the grimy pillow, he instantly fell asleep. Beth sat on the edge of the bed and suckled Malaki. Her breasts were gorged with milk and as she fed him her other breast started to flow with milk since there was no Isaac to suckle. It ran down the inside of her dress making her feel uncomfortable. She felt bereaved as if her son Isaac was dead.

In despair, Beth held her children close to her and asked herself what would become of them as her eyelids felt heavy and darkness over took her.

"Well, look what we have here? So you are my special cargo," said the Captain, as he looked her up and down. Pretty he thought but not for him as he preferred boys.

"Scully, take her down to the galley, she will be working with Paddy on this voyage."

"Yes, Captain," replied the scrawny looking lad.

The ship the 'Cotton Trader' was an old and rusty hulk, its hold was full of cotton destined for the mills in England.

Will held onto his mother tightly as the sea was rough, the ship rolled from side to side as they made their way down the steps to the galley.

They walked into a hot steam filled galley, which was a delight after the coldness on the deck. A voice resonated from within, and a short thickset man emerged from the mist.

"To be sure what do we have here?" Paddy barked. He was a miserable looking man who's hair was lank and greasy, his stained clothes revealing his large stomach which overhung his belted trousers, he stood by the cooker shaking a saucepan in each hand.

"Captain, said they are to help you in the galley during this voyage."

"He does, does he?" The cook turned and looked at Beth. "Well you listen to everything I tell you, and do it quickly and we will get on fine. Lad, start that washing up," he said. He looked at Will and pointed to a large stack of dirty pans in a sink. "And you, what's your name?"

"Beth," she replied bracing herself against the wall to stop falling as the ship rolled in the rough seas.

"You start peeling those potatoes," he said as he indicated to a large pile in a bowl on the table.

After a busy day in the galley, Beth lay her weary head down with her children safely by her side. She thought how much worse it could have been and thanked God for their deliverance. Cuddling up to her children fell asleep.

Will woke her he was crying having fallen off the bed with the violent movement of the ship. They were in heavy seas. Beth held onto Will and Malaki, huddling on the floor of the cabin she wedged herself between the bed and the table waiting for the storm to dissipate.

Over the weeks, the cook mellowed and started to speak to her as an equal. Beth asked him where the ship was bound.

"England, I never go onshore for I lost my family when my bakery burnt down. I decided to take to the sea to forget my painful memories." Beth's heart went out to him.

Beth always remembered her mother saying to her that if you took everyone's problems and put them on a table everyone would have the same amount in one form or another. At least her children were well fed but then she worried as to what would happen to them once they had reached England? Her thoughts wandered to her family home in Somerset.

The English coast was now in sight.

"I'm sorry, Beth, but the Captain said you must be chained," said Scully. All the crew had become quite fond of her and her children during the trip.

Captain Kelly took her to his favourite tavern in Bristol Harbour, The Jolly Sailor on the Quay; he knew the slave market would be the next day. He paid for two rooms, one for him and another for Beth and the children. He ordered Scully to watch them closely.

It was hot and smelly above the pub and all she could hear was drunken sailors shouting and fighting all night.

Scully said "Time to go, missy," as he awoke Beth." They followed the Captain as he made his way to the slave market. It was busy but Captain Kelly found a good spot at the entrance to the market.

"Good quality slave, speaks English and still has years to breed, she comes with a young boy and baby, Good value," he cried to every passerby.

A physician called Dr Richardson was looking that day for a servant to help in his town house in Bristol.

"Sir, how much do you want for this slave?"

"280 guineas, very good value"

Dr Richardson was interested in the female but not the baby, the lad as he saw it could work in the kitchen. He considered his options. Captain Kelly did not want to lose this buyer so he decided to drop his price.

"Ok, Sir, to you, a special price 250 guineas, now that's a real bargain."

The Captain waited anxiously for his reply.

"You have a sale Sir."

The Legacy

The doctor passed over the money and took charge of Beth and her children.

"I think we can remove your chains now," he said, as he unlocked them and then handed the chains and key to Captain Kelly.

A carriage was awaiting him, Beth was told to climb in, the doctor sat opposite her and Will. Malaki slept soundly at his mother's chest held tightly by the shawl.

"What is your name?" he asked her.

"Beth Jackson."

"And what are your children's names?"

She gestured to each child, "Will and Malaki."

Doctor Philip Richardson was in his late fifties. He was stout man with very bushy grey eye brows, under a grey wig that lay comically tilted to one side of his head. His legs seemed stiff as he used the aid of the walking stick that he held in his right hand. It had a beautiful silver carved handle. The carriage came to a stop outside a town house in an affluent area of Bristol.

Black railings and steps leading up to a black front door with shiny brass fittings surrounded the outside of the house. A brass plate on the wall read 130 Lamont Avenue—Dr Richardson—Physician.

His driver opened the carriage door and Dr Richardson stepped out. "Wait here," he said to Beth.

A middle-aged man in a smart uniform opened the front door. "Good morning, Sir," he said standing tall as he held the door open.

"Thank you Lawson," the doctor said to the manservant as he took his coat and hat. "Would you see that Miss Partridge, is informed that we have a new house maid and kitchen boy, and to take them to the kitchen and give them some food. They are waiting in the carriage," the doctor said. He then used his walking stick to steady himself along the hallway.

"Yes, Sir," Lawson replied in a subservient manner.

"Follow me?" said a painfully thin woman dressed from head to toe in black with keys dangling from her belt. She had a high pitch voice and came across as having a superior manner.

She opened a small black gate and went down a flight of stairs.

"This is the servants entrance you will use it at all times."

❖ 109 ❖

Beth followed her into a large kitchen that had a number of saucepans boiling away on a large cooking range, the air smelt of apples and cinnamon.

"Mrs Cooper, find something for them to eat, when they have eaten show them to my office," said Miss Partridge and left.

Mrs Cooper was the cook, she was plump and rosy faced and had a cheerful disposition.

"Well, my dears, sit down and tuck into this," she placed a large bowl of hot vegetable soup in front of Beth and Will and a chunk of bread. They sat down at the end of a large table with ten chairs around it. Will bolted down his soup.

"Hold on laddie you will have a sore stomach if you eat it that quickly," she smiled.

"What about the babe would you like some mashed up food for it, my dear," she said to Beth as she cooed at Malaki touching his hand.

"I am still feeding him myself thank you."

Mrs Cooper knocked on Miss Partridge's door, a room off the kitchen

"Come in," replied Miss Partridge.

"Thank you, Mrs Cooper, shut the door behind you."

"What is your name?" she enquired looking directly at Beth, she sat tall and important behind her desk.

"Beth Jackson."

"She pointed at Will.

"Will and my baby's name is Malaki."

"What sort of work have you done before?"

"I have been a personal maid working in the bedchambers of a large household."

"Well here, I will require you to be a housemaid and when we have the doctor's sister staying or a female guest, you will be required to attend them in their bedchamber."

"Will can work in the kitchen and you will be allowed time during the day to see to your infant. "I run a tight regime downstairs, never cross me, remember that girl!" She got up and opened the door, the noise from the kitchen flooded into her office.

"Lilly!" she shouted over the noise.

"Yes Miss Partridge," said a flustered young girl dressed in a navy blue dress with a starched white apron and a hat that just held her thick red hair.

"Beth, is a new housemaid and will be working with you," dismissing Lilly she then turned her attention to the cook.

"Mrs Cooper," she shouted. The cook turned round with flour covering her hands exasperated at being disturbed while she rolled pastry on the large table in the middle of the kitchen. "Will can help in the kitchen, now get on with your work everyone," she said as she closed her office door.

"That woman," muttered Mrs Cooper.

"Laddie, come over here and fetch some coal for me, Molly show Will were the coal bunker is?"

"Follow me," Molly said. Molly was ten and pleased to have someone near her age in the kitchen, even if it was a boy.

Beth and her children settled into the tight routine.

Sunday they were to attend church at St Martin in the Field.

Miss Partridge said that Beth's son would be required to attend a Missionary school once a week, which fell on a Wednesday. He would go with Molly to prepare him for his first Communion.

Beth declined attending church on her day off as she felt God had deserted her, for this was between God and herself but she felt morally bound to send her son Will,

Beth was dusting in the doctor's library. She was unaware of the doctor's presence when she pulled out a book and started to read it.

"You like books Beth?" came a voice behind her.

Beth jumped, "Sorry . . . ," the doctor stopped her in midstream by raising his hand.

"Please take a book of your choice; it pleases me to see someone else enjoy the written word.

I will inform Miss Partridge that you have my permission to use the library regularly."

Beth read by candlelight in bed, what joy it was to be able to read the classics again.

The doctor approached the housekeeper as he had promised Beth.

"Is that wise, doctor, we would not want any of the books in the library to go missing."

"I believe her to be trustworthy and until I am proved wrong Beth will have access to my library, good morning Miss Partridge."

Who does she think she is, she has only been here a short while and the doctor allows her to take books from his library yet the doctor has never offered me that privilege.

Miss Partridge was an unmarried woman and lived for her position as Housekeeper; she thrived on the control she exercised over her menials. She always feared one day someone would come along who would take it from her—she feared Beth might be that person.

"Mama, mama" said an excited Will. I read from the bible to the group today at Communion class and Reverend Logan said how well I had read the passage. He asked me who had taught me, and I said you did Mama". Beth felt a pain shoot across her heart at hearing that name again.

Several nights she lay in bed thinking about Reverend Logan and the last time she had seen him as he tried to help her and her mother. Could it be the same man? No, it could not possibly be him, it would be such a coincidence, but she had to know!

The following week when Will was due to go to his Communion class, Beth gave him a note for Reverend Logan. Please don't forget Will, it is very important." Beth placed it into his pocket for safety.

Beth went about her duties anxious as to what the outcome of the note would be.

The doctor had never married he was too busy trying to gain recognition in his chosen field of medicine. He suffered from rheumatism in his legs, which had curtailed his career. He now lectured at the university.

He had written many papers as a heart surgeon and had them published. He and his sister Veronica were close, she frequently visited her brother with her husband Rupert who was also a leading heart surgeon, practicing in Bristol and London, and he had many aristocrats as his patients.

"Who is this new maid that attends to me, Phillip?" said Veronica to her brother as they sat around the dinner table.

"I bought Beth two months ago at the slave market, she has a young son and a baby and has settled down well, he replied".

"Well she seems to know how to serve and attend in the bedchamber."

"I am pleased to hear that," replied the doctor.

"I heard the doctor's sister praising Beth at dinner this evening," said Lawson to Miss Partridge as they sat alone in the kitchen, after all the servants had gone to bed. "Mark my words Mr Lawson, that one cannot be trusted, I am going to my bed now, good night," she said as she left the table.

"I cannot find my small silver container of perfume," said the doctor's sister, I know it was packed as I gave strict orders to Lucy my maid," she said to her husband as she searched for it.

She knew she would need it for their evenings out during their stay. "How annoying." she muttered to herself.

"Beth, have a search for my perfume while I am out, I know it is here somewhere," she said as she left the bedchamber.

Beth set about looking through the mistress's belonging's, she remembered using the silver container when her mistress had asked her to spray the perfume behind each ear just as she was getting ready to go out for the evening.

"Reverend Logan, my mother asked me to give this to you." Will said as he handed the note to him.

Reverend Logan took the note and started to open it just as two of the boys began to misbehave; distracted he placed the note down on a pew and went to resolve the situation. He did not give it another thought and when the lesson was finished, he locked the church and went home.

"Did you give the note to Reverend Logan, Will?"

"Yes Mama."

"Did he give you a reply?"

"No, mama," Will replied.

How silly was I to think it could possibly be him, she told herself and put it to the back of her mind.

It was Miss Partridge's afternoon off she visited a Pawnbrokers that she had passed many times on her way to church.

"How much money would you give me against this," as she produced the silver perfume bottle from her black cloth bag.

"I will offer you two guineas for the silver bottle," the pawnbroker replied.

"Very well," she said nervously, as she looked around her thankful she was the only one in the shop.

"You have a month to pay the money back or I will sell it," as he gave her the money and a ticket.

Miss Partridge waited until the servants had gone to church Sunday morning, feigning illness she said she would be in her room, instead she went into Beth's room and planted the pawn ticket under her mattress.

"Did you search for it, Beth?" the doctor's sister enquired.

"I have not been able to find it, Mistress," Beth replied, an annoyed Veronica recounted the incident to her brother.

"It must have been taken from my room, Philip, this is most upsetting."

"I am sure it is just mislaid," said the doctor trying to calm his sister.

"Miss Partridge, would you check everywhere for a silver bottle of perfume that belongs to my sister, it has been lost."

"Of course, doctor."

Following the search for the bottle Miss Partridge informed the doctor that she had not found it.

"Philip the bottle must have been stolen can we extend the search to the servant's quarters," insisted his sister.

"I cannot believe any of the servants would commit such a crime," the doctor replied.

"Mrs Partridge, please do as my sister requests?"

"I will carry it out immediately."

Miss Partridge started with all the other servants' rooms first and left Beth's room until last.

"Doctor, I have found this under Beth's Mattress," and handed the pawn ticket to him.

"I cannot believe this of Beth," the doctor was shocked. "I am sure we are mistaken."

"I can take it to the pawnbroker's shop named on the ticket and see if it is the stolen item?"

"Would you be kind enough to do that please, Miss Partridge, and report straight back to me on your return."

"Of course, doctor."

On her return, Miss Partridge placed the silver perfume bottle into the doctor's hand.

He called immediately for Beth. "I am very disappointed in you Beth, that you should steal from me, I had thought I had been kind to you."

"Sir, I have not stolen anything from you and have been grateful for your kindness to myself and my children, please believe me Sir, I am not guilty of this crime."

"But the evidence points to you, Beth, the pawn ticket was found under your mattress."

"I know of no pawn ticket Sir."

"I will not call a constable because you have two children but I must insist you leave my house forthwith."

"Lawson, get Beth's things together and show her the door."

As the door closed behind Beth the doctor felt down hearted, he really thought Beth had promise. He was usually a good judge of character but this time he was obviously wrong.

"Reverend Logan," called Mrs Stokes one of the parishioners who helped clean the church."

"I found this note addressed to you on a pew last week when I was cleaning and put it in my pocket until I saw you."

"Thank you, Mrs Stokes," as he took the letter, put it into his overcoat pocket, tipped his hat to her, and carried on walking through the churchyard to his house a few streets away.

He took off his coat.

"Reverend would you like a wee cup of tea?" said a petite woman with her greying hair tied up in a neat bun that complemented her neat appearance.

"That would be wonderful, Mrs Cameron." She lit the fire and went off to boil the kettle on the kitchen range. Mrs Cameron was his housekeeper, after interviewing many candidates for the position; he knew she was the one. She was warm and amiable and made the house feel homely.

Sitting down in his favourite seat by the fire, he had a sip of his hot drink, and then recalled the note. He got up, rummaged in his overcoat pocket, retrieved it, and sat down to read its contents.

When he finished reading the note it fell from his hand, he was in total shock. He picked it up and re-read it.

Could this be his Beth he lost all those years ago in Africa, but what about his beloved Eliza there was no mention of her.

He must meet with the woman he would know if it were Beth. He went back to the church to find Will's address.

130 Lamont Avenue, Doctor Philip Richardson, was the address in the church diary.

Reverend Logan told himself not to get his hopes up and quietly prayed for Gods help as he sat in a carriage headed for Lamont Avenue. His thoughts took him back to Africa and to that dreadful day, he lost Eliza and Beth, and how he had laid there unconscious until Missionaries found him and took him with them to the coast and back home to England.

Nervously he lifted the brass knocker and knocked several times.

"I would like to see Doctor Richardson please?"

"I will see if he is at home, Sir," replied Lawson. After a few minutes, he was back.

"Doctor Richardson, will see you, follow me."

Reverend Logan followed Lawson.

"Good morning I am Doctor Richardson."

"I hope you will not mind my intrusion, Sir, but I believe you have a servant named Beth and her son Will working for you?"

"Indeed I did, but a week ago. I put her out onto the streets with her children as she stole from me. I had been a fair master to her, Sir. I have lost the money I have invested in her and should have called a constable." Doctor Richardson thought he needed to justify his actions, in front of a man of the cloth who might think badly of him.

"Do you have anyone who worked closely with her, Sir, as I would like to ask them some questions concerning Beth?"

"I will enquire." said Doctor Richardson and left the room.

"This is Lilly who worked with Beth."

"Lilly, I want you to answer any questions Reverend Logan asks you, is that clear?"

"Yes, Sir," said a nervous Lilly.

"Did Beth talk about her past with you?"

"No, Sir," Lilly replied as she played nervously with the side of her dress.

"Did you see any distinguishing marks on her?"

"Yes, Sir, she had one on the inside of her wrist, it almost looked heart shaped and was red in colour," as she pointed to her wrist.

Reverend Logan was shocked and steadied himself by grabbing the nearest armchair. "Are you feeling unwell, Sir?" asked Doctor Richardson.

"Please may I sit down?" Reverend Logan said.

"Please do, Sir," the doctor helped him into the armchair.

"Lilly, go and ask Lawson to bring me my doctor's bag and then get a tray of tea?"

"Yes, Sir," a relieved Lilly left the drawing room.

Lawson brought the doctors bag through and Doctor Richardson took out the bottle of smelling salts from it and wafted it under Reverend Logan's nose.

"Now take deep breaths, Sir."

The Reverend composed himself.

"Sir, do you have any idea where Beth and her children might have gone?"

"No I do not. Pray tell me why you have come to my house to enquire about a disgraced maid." The doctor wanted to know more. Lilly poured the tea as Reverend Logan explained briefly how Beth and her mother were enslaved and how he had feared they were dead.

"You see Beth, would never steal, her faith was too strong and she abided by the church's teachings." Doctor Richardson turned to his butler.

"Lawson, when Miss Partridge found the pawn ticket in Beth's room, can you recall that day?"

"It was Sunday, Sir, and Beth was searching the bedchamber for Mistress Veronica's silver perfume bottle. I went to church as usual with Will, Lilly, Molly, Mrs Cooper and Alfred. Miss Partridge was poorly and was too ill to leave her bed. I know that I was cross with myself forgetting my change for the collection box, so I told Mrs Cooper to carry on to the church. She was told to take responsibility for those attending church from this household while I rushed back to get the change from my room. I thought it strange that Miss Partridge was dressed and came out of Beth's room, as her bedroom is off the sitting room next to her office. I had been under the impression she was too ill to get out of bed. We started work when we returned and Miss Partridge was then in bed. When Lilly took her some lunch, she said she was too ill to eat it. Beth had not found the missing bottle and Mistress Veronica was upset at its disappearance."

"Thank you Lawson," said the doctor.

"Have you thought to ask at the Pawnbrokers for the description of the person who brought the silver bottle in?" asked the Reverend.

"Lawson, please go to the Pawnbrokers and make enquiries and inform me directly."

"Yes Sir." Lawson promptly set of for the Pawnbrokers.

"I must go and search for Beth, and her children. They have spent many nights outside and it is bitterly cold, I fear for their safety," the Reverend said as he got up from the armchair. "Thank you for your help, Sir."

"If it is any comfort, Reverend, I felt Beth was different and believed in her."

Reverend nodded his head in agreement.

The Reverend asked himself, where would he I go. What would I do to get food and shelter for my children? The Reverend decided to check the docks area, perhaps she would seek out a position in the kitchen of one of the many alehouses dotted along the harbour. They always need help catering for the number of sailors frequenting such a busy port.

"Driver, take me to the harbour."

He went from Tavern to Tavern asking if a woman had been asking for a job in the kitchens that had a baby and young lad with her. Finally, at the last but one tavern he found the owner attempting to serve a bar full of jostling sailors eager to spend their pay on getting drunk in the shortest possible time. The noise was deafening. The Reverend had to shout above the cacophony of noise.

"She only lasted one evening she was no good to me her children kept getting in the way, so I told her to go."

It was getting dark and Reverend Logan feared for them, as the light was fading and snow was falling again. He knew that he was running out of time.

He scoured the alleyways and stairwells looking for places where they could gain some protection from the harsh weather.

He came to the market square where a group of people were huddled around a pile of rotten fruit and vegetables it was a prime place to scavenge for food. He heard crying coming from inside a doorway. There he found crouched, a shadowy figure of a woman in a grey hooded cloak, which clung to her body with the thick coating of snow. When he got closer to her, he could also see it was covering her children.

He removed her hood, as he did so she retreated further into the doorway to get away from him. Her wet hair stuck to her face, all he could see were her eyes they were sunken in desperation, her whole body shook uncontrollably with the cold.

"I beg you leave us alone," she cried trying to protect her children with her body. "I have nothing of value," she said in a weak, weary voice.

The Reverend took her wrist she struggled but she had no strength left to fight. He turned it over to reveal a red heart shaped birthmark. "Beth, Beth," he cried. "Praise be to God, I have found you," he sighed with relief. Will recognising him said "Reverend Logan have you come to help my Mama?" he said through chattering teeth.

"Yes, Will, you are coming home with me." The Reverend said his voice breaking with emotion.

In despair, Beth recognised a familiar voice.

"Have you come for us, Reverend," she said, for in her mind she was in a peaceful place now—she was ready to meet her maker.

"Beth, Beth," the Reverend cried. "It's Reverend Logan I'm here you are safe, my child."

She touched his face-it was not an apparition as she thought, for she felt tears on his face.

"Is that truly you Reverend?" Beth said as she searched his face for recognition.

"Yes Beth it is." He held her tightly and heard Beth say. "Thanks be to God you have come for us," and then she buried her head in his chest with exhaustion.

"Come let's get you and the children into my carriage and get you home, warmed and fed." He carried Beth as Will held his little brothers hand holding onto the Reverends coattail as they walked to the waiting carriage.

Will snuggled into the Reverend who stretched his arm out and around him, as they travelled back to his house. Beth through weary eyes kept blinking to be sure it was Reverend Logan, she was now able to let go and drifted off to sleep.

"Driver, please stop at 130 Lamont Avenue," said Reverend Logan.

The Reverend climbed out of the carriage and knocked the door.

"Please inform Doctor Richardson, that Beth and her children have been found and are staying with me 233 Dunbar Street. I would appreciate a visit from him to check they are well."

"Yes, Sir." replied Lawson.

In the carriage on the way, back to the Reverends house Beth fell asleep with exhaustion with Malaki in her arms.

Will clung tightly to Reverend Logan in the carriage.

"I am so hungry." he said and started to cry.

"Well, Will, as soon as we get to my house and get you dry you will have some food, I promise you," as he reassured him with a hug.

"My wee darlings come in and stand near the fire and we will get you out of those wet clothes," said Mrs Cameron. Once they were dry, they sat down by the fire with blankets wrapped around their laps. The Reverend was able to relax, they were with him and safe from harm, his beloved Eliza's daughter and her family were now under his protection, he vowed that he would keep them safe with the help of God.

"Here we are a warming bowl of stew," said a beaming rosy faced Mrs Cameron. She was a mother hen and loved having someone to look after she was in her element.

"I will feed the wee bairn, I have softened some stew for its wee mouth, you go on and enjoy your food, miss," she said to Beth as she fed and interacted with Malaki.

Will sat contented once he had a full stomach.

"Come on, wee lad, let's put you to bed." Mrs Cameron held Malaki in one arm and waited for Will to say goodnight.

"Good night, Mamma," he said as he kissed her on the cheek.

"Good night, my son," Beth said to Will. "Don't forget your prayers you have a lot to be thankful for," she then kissed Malaki.

"Good night, Reverend Logan, thank you for finding us." Will said looking up at him hugging his legs as he stood in front of the fire. He kissed Will on the head and Mrs Cameron took Will's hand and climbed the stairs.

Silence fell, and the shadows of the lanterns danced around the room.

Beth had to approach a question she knew that must be upper most in the Reverends mind.

"Reverend Logan, you must want to know what happened to my Mother."

He nodded as he smoked his pipe. Little did Beth know how desperately he wanted to know what had befallen her? Inside his heart was breaking that she was not here.

Beth recounted the sadness of her Mother's death on the forced march to the harbour in Africa. After her tale, he sat silently and then said, "I will have a service in Eliza's memory. If you don't mind I will retire, we can talk some more tomorrow. Good night, Beth." He kissed her forehead and left the room. She knew he needed to be able to grieve for her Mother.

She watched the flames dart back and forth through the logs and in silence thanked her God for saving them. She could not bear the thought of what would have happened to her and her children if Reverend Logan had not found them. Now here she was sitting by his fire in his home with her children safely in bed with full stomachs. Beth felt blessed and her eyes grew heavy. "Come on, my dear, I have warmed your bed," said Mrs Cameron as she gently woke Beth. "Thank you so much for your kindness to myself and my children." Mrs Cameron smiled and putting her arm round her helped her up the stairs.

Chapter Ten

Rupert, Veronica's husband sat in his leather armchair puffing on his cigar as he faced Doctor Richardson. "Philip, I have a patient the Duchess of Pendragon who lives in Somerset. She has a heart problem, which runs in the family, her mother and brother both died young. I wondered if you would journey to see her next week with me, she is bed ridden at present. I would value your professional opinion old chap." Rupert said as they dined at their men's club."

"Rupert, of course I would be delighted to."

"Duchess, I have brought my learned colleague with me Doctor Richardson."

"Thank you for coming all this way to see me but please call me Charlotte," said the Duchess.

"My life is very limited now doctor as any exertion leaves me with pains in my chest."

"You say your mother and your brother died early and you are the only surviving child?"

"Yes but I do have a half sister on my father's side who went to Africa and never returned, we presumed she died out there, her name was Beth."

Could it be! Doctor Richardson thought.

"Duchess, can you recall if she had a heart shaped birth mark on her wrist?"

"Yes, Sir, indeed there was. How did you know for my father the Duke and Beth were the only ones to have those birth marks?"

"I have indeed met your sister Beth she lives with her children in Bristol with Reverend Logan."

"Praise be to God, can this be true?"

"Yes, I have seen her birth mark; please do not get over excited Madam."

"Beth is next in line to be Duchess of Pendragon when I die as I have no children. Sir, you do not know what joy you have brought me this day."

Charlotte handed the doctor a hand written letter, embossed with the family coat of arms in red wax, the front addressed to Bethany Pendragon.

"Oh please, doctor, would you deliver a letter to my sister for me I would be most grateful."

Over breakfast, Reverend Logan said, "Will, would you like to come and help me at the church today?

"Yes please, Sir."

Beth watched with contentment as they walked through the back garden and out through the picket gate. Will eagerly listened to Reverend Logan as Beth had done so many years ago. She could not stop smiling.

There was a knock at the front door, she heard Mrs Cameron open it.

"May I see Beth, please?"

"Who shall I say is calling?"

"Doctor Richardson."

"Doctor Richardson has called for you, Beth."

"Please show him in Mrs Cameron."

Beth thought the doctor's general demeanour seemed uneasy.

"Beth I wish to apologise to you. I wrongly accused you of stealing when it was my housekeeper, please accept my humble apologies," his face was flushed with embarrassment.

"Sir, I accept your apology."

"Thank you for I would never have forgiven myself if you and your children had come to any harm through my actions." He seemed to relax and took a letter from his coat pocket.

"I have a letter for you Beth."

"I called to check that you and your children are in good health."

"That is very kind of you, Doctor Richardson, but we are all well, thank you, Sir."

"I met your sister the Duchess of Pendragon Hall."

"My sister, Charlotte," Beth said anxiously wanting to know more.

"I'm afraid she is very unwell she has a hereditary heart condition that both her mother and Brother died from. Your sister has asked me to deliver this letter to you."

Beth took it from him and saw the address was in her full title.

"Thank you." Beth struggled to contain her delight.

"I must take my leave, please pass my regards to Reverend Logan."

"I will, Sir, and thank you for bringing me news of my sister." She guided him to the front door. "You are most welcome and I sincerely wish you and your children a happy future, for you so deserve it," said Doctor Richardson as he tipped his hat.

Beth sat by the log fire and pulled her shawl around her. She turned the letter over to see the family seal, her heart fluttered as she ran her hands over it she opened it quickly.

Beth, I could not contain my joy at hearing that you were alive, praise be to God. Doctor Richardson has given me some news of you. I have missed you so much. Please come home I cannot wait to meet my nephews. Please tell Reverend Logan his old home, The Vicarage awaits him as Reverend of Pendragon, should he wish to avail himself of this position. I excitedly await your arrival your ever-loving sister. Charlotte. Beth's tears made the ink on the letter run. She held the letter close to her chest. She now felt she truly belonged, and would be able to bring her children up in Pendragon Hall. She would never forget Abel, Theodore, and her past and swore she would get her son Isaac back with her where he belonged. Finally, she was going home and realized that her God had not forsaken her but had been walking by her side.

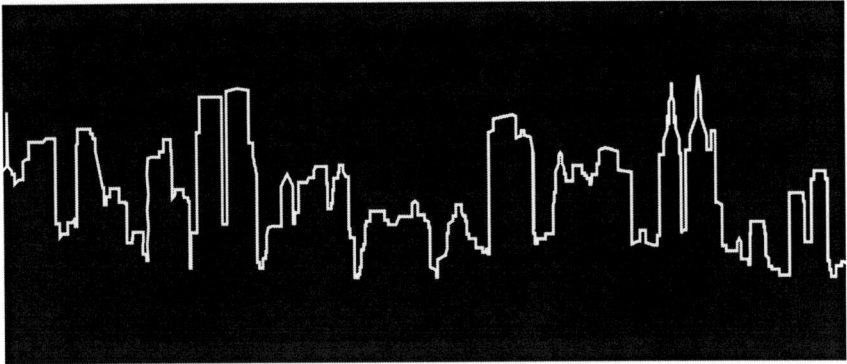

Chapter Eleven

(The fall 2008)

❧

E bony rushed out of J.F.K airport. She grabbed a yellow cab. "Long island please?" she said to the cab driver, her chest tightened with anxiety, she prayed she would be in time Not long now, she thought as she caught sight of the beach house.

"Thank you," she said as she practically threw the fare at the cab driver and fumbled in her handbag for the house key.

"Where is she?" she said abruptly to the nurse who was on the phone. She stopped her conversation, turned to Ebony, and said, "Your mother . . ." Ebony did not wait for her to finish.

"Mum," she shouted as she rushed through the house. She found her sitting in her favourite rocking chair on the veranda that overlooked the beach she so loved.

"Mum, I came as soon as I could," she said breathlessly, and knelt down by her side. She had her eyes closed and her face turned away from her. Ebony touched her hand—it was cold. Then she noticed her mouth was blue. A feeling of dread and a realization swept over her. Ebony shook her mother as she shouted, "Nurse: Nurse!"

"I tried to tell you, your mother passed away three hours ago, I am so sorry."

"No! No, she cannot have, Mum, mum," she cried as she continued to shake her mother's body hoping she would wake up. Ebony was in shock, her brain could not take in the fact her mother was dead.

She was too late. She had gone. She had not been there at her mother's end to say goodbye. Ebony cried broken-heartedly.

The nurse raised Ebony up and put an arm around her then guided her to the bedroom and said, "I have called your sister Elizabeth, why don't you go and lie down."

When she awoke for a few seconds, it did not register immediately that her mother was gone. She remembered the mornings when she had lived at home, she would wander into the kitchen and her mother would say, "Sweetheart would you like a warm bagel and omelette," Ebony's favourite breakfast but this was no ordinary morning—her mother was dead.

She found a note from her sister Elizabeth lying on the kitchen table.

I Thought I would leave you to sleep, will be back later. I am sorting out the funeral arrangements. Elizabeth.

It was eerily quiet as she walked around the beach house. She wandered into her mother's study, there lying on her desk was a large writing pad. She looked closer it read Family Tree.

Ebony then noticed the name Cotton Wood Plantation circled and the names Abel and Beth Tukowunu.—SLAVES jumped off the paper.

Ebony Marshall was unaware that her mother had been compiling her family tree. Guilt flooded her thoughts. She had been so busy with her career and helping with the Presidential campaign in the election office. She had forgotten about how lonely her mother was, and realised how selfish she had been.

She had been adopted and given a wonderful life, she had let her mother down. Ebony picked up a photograph of her mother and said, "I promise to finish your family tree for you mum." As she hugged her mother's picture, she felt the warmth of her mother's presence and the feel of her arms around her. The waft of her favourite perfume, 'Beautiful' filled the room. "Mum, oh mum, why did you have to leave me," she cried. Her whole body shook with emotion and grief as she tried to come to terms with her loss.

Ebony was getting more and more stressed as she waited for the traffic lights to change, she was running late for work and she had a meeting at ten. She looked at her watch anxiously. Her thoughts wandered to her biological parents, who were they? She always felt she would have hurt her adopted parent's feelings if she had asked too many questions. Now they had passed away she could search for them. Perhaps there might be some documents relating to her adoption at the beach house. There was a sound of a car horn from the driver behind her telling her the lights had changed

She came out of her daydream and put her foot down. She had been working for Houghton, Druitt and Sons, a well-respected company. They had held their position as one of the top ten surgical equipment manufactures for the past twelve years. As she alighted from the lift on her floor, Fay from admin called out "Good morning Ebony I was so sorry to hear about your mother." Thank you Fay," Ebony said in a touching way after feeling guilty thinking unkind thoughts about her. Fay was a pencil thin woman in her thirties, who looked as if she had not eaten for days; she always made Ebony feel fat but did have a kind heart.

Ebony entered her new office she noticed her new title on the door, Overseas Sales Director.

At last she had made it, she had worked her way up through the company. There had been fierce competition especially from Isabel who now was working in the London office. Thank goodness, she would not have to see her face at work for a while. She had an enviable figure with legs that went on forever she was the archetypical man-eater. She was well aware of the way she attracted men. They fell around her acting stupidly and their age did not seem to matter. To Ebony, this was so shallow; she did not need a man to make her feel good about herself.

Ebony had just celebrated her twenty-eighth birthday and Laura her best friend and some of her other girlfriends from work had gone to a spa in down town Manhattan for a pampering weekend. She was constantly battling with her weight, though she had curves in the right places. She also had curly hair, which she had given up trying to straighten, as it took too long. Her best feature she felt was her large dark brown eyes that people always remarked on. She was from African American descent and proud of her heritage. She was helping with the campaign to get the Democratic candidate into the White House.

That is where she had met Daniel he managed the campaign office. A much-focused individual who made you feel you could achieve anything if you put your mind to it. He was easy to be with and made her feel special. Ebony always thought his voice was so sexy to listen to, and what he could do in the bedroom was amazing. He was divorced and had a grown up son. She did not want a heavy relationship. They had started seeing each other shortly after the office had been set up for the election. They were both of Afro American decent and both had demanding jobs. She came from a long line of Activists and desperately wanted to do her bit for the cause.

Laura McEwen Ebony's P.A put her arms around her. "How are you?" she asked. "You look tired you should have had longer off work." She was a wonderful P.A and her best friend. When the position had become available, she had told Laura to apply for it. She needed someone to watch her back and Laura was the one to do that. Both of them knew that the confidences they shared with one another were safe.

Laura was thirty and married to Doug, a Plastic surgeon who had his own private clinic in Manhattan. They had a son Harvey and one granddaughter called Jennifer who Laura and Doug adored.

"We all thought your mother's funeral was lovely, Ebony, with so many friends and beautiful flowers. I have been worried about you. I tried to ring you several time last night but only got your answer machine," said Laura looking concerned.

"I'm fine just feeling a bit sensitive."

"Laura, please place in my diary that I will be away next week, I need to clear Mum's house and canvass for the election."

"You do too much for the party your mother would want you to take care of yourself."

"This is important to me replied Ebony we all have to do our part to insure that we have our first Black American President in office." Laura knew how strong minded she could be and did not try to persuade her any more.

Ebony went into her office and shut the door. She usually had an open door policy but it was her first day back at work and she still felt fragile, she needed her privacy.

On her desk were a bunch of yellow roses in a beautiful vase, pinned to the ribbon was a message, love from all at Houghton, Druitt and Sons.

Ebony was so touched she fired up her laptop and sent a thank you e-mail to all departments. As she opened her mail, she found a condolence card with a small keepsake card inside it fell out onto her desk. Ebony picked it up and read it. The tears flowed down her cheeks, what beautiful words and how typically thoughtful it was of Daniel, her boyfriend.

Ebony had grown up at her adopted parent's beach house on Long island. Although they had houses in London and Chicago, and could have had a home in Manhattan closer to the family business Jessica her mother insisted their home be the beach house for she loved it. Her father Robert would often crash at his apartment near his office rather than drive home through the traffic in Manhattan.

Her father had died from a heart attack several years ago and there was only her mother and sister Elizabeth, who they rarely saw.

The following evening she decided to sort through her mother's things at the beach house. All the memories came flooding back. She had bags of things to go to the charity shop and sacks of rubbish to be disposed of. As she came across photographs she wished to keep, she put them into her large box for items to take with her.

She walked into her mother's bedroom her dressing gown hung on her bedroom door and her slippers were still by her bed. It was as if she was in the house and that she would reappear at any moment. I miss you so much Mum, Ebony cried.

As a child, her mother Jessica always said a walk along the beach would clear away the cobwebs and would make you feel better. This was her solution to any problem and it always worked.

Ebony kicked at the sand beneath her feet, the sea breeze blew through her hair as her tears rolled uncontrollably down her face. She remembered the smell of cooking that came from the kitchen and the joy they felt from tasting her first attempt at a cake recipe. They would sit on the veranda eating it warm from the oven. There was now only Elizabeth and herself whom she had not seen since the funeral, they were never close.

Ebony's stepsister Elizabeth was the only child of Robert and Jessica, she wanted for nothing. Her mother Jessica fought to keep her feet on the ground but Elizabeth was a daddies' girl. She was intelligent and very beautiful, never short of admirers. Jessica often felt shut out by the closeness of the relationship her daughter had shared with her father. Jessica and Robert tried for another child, but it never happened.

Chapter Twelve

It was a hot balmy evening and Robert was working late as usual. Elizabeth had jetted off to London with her latest beau. Robert was hardly at home busy with building his business so Jessica had spent most of her married life alone. She was always trying something different. This month it was learning yoga. She had just finished her workout, Jessica went into the kitchen, and poured herself a long, cool drink. She decided to go and sit on the veranda to take advantage of the breeze coming off the sea. She heard a knock on the front door of the house. She shouted,

"I'm just coming." When she got there, no one was in sight so she checked around the driveway.

She returned to the veranda, sat in her rocking chair on hearing a noise coming from the steps leading from the beach, went to investigate. There on the last step was a brown, leather bag; she picked it up, it felt heavy. Jessica sat down on the step and pulled the zip back.

"Oh, my lord, what do we have here," she lifted out a baby. A message pinned to its clothes said, my name is Ebony and the baby started to cry.

"Oh, sweetheart," Jessica said trying to warm the little thing in her arms. Holding the baby securely, she went down onto the beach to see if she could find who had left it, but the beach was deserted.

As Robert walked through the door briefcase in his hand, Jessica said. "Robert, look what was abandoned on the house steps tonight?" She beamed as she cuddled the little one.

She now had time to notice that the baby had a light skin and her facial features were Afro-American.

"Have you rung the Sheriff's office?" Robert said in a non-fazed manner.

"No, I just needed to talk to you. It appears that someone has abandoned her here. Perhaps we could keep her, adopt her, what do you think? She eagerly awaited his reply.

"She is not ours to take, now ring Sheriff Gardner."

"I have not asked you for much during our married life. I have supported you, brought up Elizabeth, and looked after our home. Neither of you need me anymore my life's empty. I am telling you now I want to adopt this little one."

"But you are too old to be its adopted mother. How will it feel when you take it to kindergarten and school you will be a grandmothers age, now see sense women."

"Now I have had a tiring day at work and I need a whisky." Robert poured himself a drink and sat down in his comfortable chair, as far as he was concerned the discussion was over.

The next moment Jessica stood before him with her coat on, baby in one arm and a bag in her other hand.

"I have had time to consider this, we could give this child a good home where it would be loved, but if you are not prepared to do this for me then I have no other choice but to leave. I will struggle to bring her up on my own." Robert sat there dumbfounded at the sudden change in his fortunes; suddenly from nowhere his wife was leaving with an unknown baby.

He had not seen Jessica's spirit for a very long time.

"Well I can see how strongly you feel, would you really leave me?" he put on a sad face taking her bag out of her hand. He cupped her face in his hands.

"Darling if it means that much to you, we will find out what we need to do from my Lawyer—ok?" He kissed her beaming face and looked down at the baby, "She is rather cute," he said and embraced Jessica and gazed at this potential new addition to the family.

Elizabeth was a Director in her father's business learning the ropes, which would allow her to be able to take over from him one day. Robert could not have been prouder of her. She was a natural in the business world and he enjoyed running the company with her. When Ebony was old enough to start work, Jessica approached her husband about her joining the company. Elisabeth did not intend to let her into the family business. It was her birthright, as far as she was concerned Ebony was not family and made it very clear to her father how she felt. He would not do anything that would upset his princess.

"Are you feeling alright dad you look awfully pale?" Asked Elizabeth concerned.

"I'm fine," Robert said as he continued with the contract on his desk.

"Can we meet for lunch dad? It's on me, say one o'clock at Perkins restaurant?" Robert nodded at her as she left his office. Elizabeth was just about to leave at twelve thirty to meet her father when the phone rang. "Good Moring Elizabeth Marshall speaking."

"It's April," she sounded distressed. "It is your father he has collapsed. I think it is his heart. The Ambulance . . . Elizabeth did not wait for her father's P.A to finish, she dropped the phone and rushed to his office.

Elizabeth rang from the hospital. "Mother, come quickly dad has had a heart attack."

With a shaky hand, Jessica left a message for Ebony on her mobile to meet her at the hospital.

By the time Ebony got there, her adopted father had passed away. Elizabeth could not stop crying as she tried to pull her mother away from her husband's dead body. It was the first time Ebony had seen Elizabeth show any emotion. She kissed her father, wept, and then led her mother out of the room.

Ebony owed so much to Robert. She went up to his bedside leant over and kissed his cheek, and thanked him for taking her into his family. She left the room and helped Elizabeth support her mother back to her car.

It was a quiet, sombre journey back to the beach house. Her mother stared out of the car window deep in thought. Elizabeth now had controlled her tears and was driving her car in a robotic manner. Ebony's thoughts wandered back to her childhood. She knew she was never that close to her adopted father but he was always kind to her, she felt that he tolerated her mainly to please his wife. He was seventy-eight when he died; the stress of the business had finally caught up with him

Elizabeth inherited her father's business and houses in London and Chicago and an apartment in New York. Ebony inherited her father's apartment in Manhattan.

Ebony and her mother had been inseparable since his death, helping each other through the pain of their loss.

"We will lean on each other," she said to Ebony giving her one of her wonderful hugs. They strolled along the beach, as they had done so many times. Mother adored the beach she said it was because she was born in March and was a Piscean, a water sign. They would laugh as they walked arm in arm. As a child, she would search for pebbles that had holes through because her mother said they would bring luck to the finder. Ebony would then add them to her collection hanging on the veranda.

Her adopted mother had left the beach house to Ebony for she knew she loved it, as she did.

Ebony was emotionally exhausted she pushed herself to continue sorting through her mother's paper work. It would feel strange this precious beach house now belonging to her. She put the box of things she wanted to keep of her mother's into the car and drove back to her apartment.

Ebony settled down in her apartment and at her desk looked through the box of documents and photos she had brought back with her.

She opened up the folder marked 'Important documents. Ebony so hoped she might find her adoption papers—nothing surely there should be something. She was devastated, who was she? Ebony had never felt so lonely.

She opened the first document it was her adopted mother's birth certificate nineteen thirty five. There in a see through protective cover a cut out from a newspaper. The headline read Martin Luther King led mass protests against discriminatory practise in Birmingham. In the photo of the crowd, a face circled. Ebony looked with a magnifying glass and yes, it was her adopted mother, Jessica. She remembered her telling her about the Civil Rights March on Washington where he delivered his famous speech.

She noticed a very yellow coloured document. Ebony unfolded it to find it was Soul Tukowunu's death certificate, Jessica's father, death caused by severe trauma to body, verdict misadventure. Mother never spoke about her parents; Ebony thought that this was strange. She knew her mother grew up with her father's brother Tom and his wife Maize, and by all accounts had a happy childhood. The next death certificate read Lilly Tukowunu, Jessica's mother, cause of death— haemorrhaging, baby still born. She noticed they all died on the same day.

Ebony typed into her laptop the date on their death certificates.

Chicago 18th November 1940. What had happened to them? She needed to know.

In the Chicago News for that date, the headline read, more trouble hits the streets of our city. Ebony read on. Since early light black, men and women had been queuing for many hours for jobs. A fight ensued between the blacks and the white youths, some of the white youths wielded baseball bats. Many blacks were injured. Soul and Lilly Tukowunu lost their lives leaving a young daughter. The Mayors son will appear in court for his involvement in the attack. The Mayor's office gave us a statement. The coloureds waiting in the queue outside the factory early that morning started the fight and the youths had to defend themselves.

That has to be my adopted mother's parents and Jessica was their daughter. She could not believe what she had just read. That was why she went to live with her Aunt Maize and Uncle Tom, who worked for the Marshall's in New York.

Jessica's Aunt and Uncle lived in a small wooden house in the grounds of Falcombe Heights. Tom worked as a grounds man and

Maize was a cook in the big house. Jessica loved that time of her life it was carefree. Robert Marshall and his elder brother Gordon were home in the school holidays. She was a friend of Robert who she really liked as he was kind and fun and called her Jess. His brother Gordon did not want to know her, he treated her as if she was beneath him. She did not care as long as Robert was there she was happy. The years rolled on and both boys went to Harvard. Jessica was heartbroken she and Robert had become very close.

"Girl," her Uncle said. "You mustn't be getting any ideas about Robert Marshall, he is destined for bigger things than you, so get those ideas out of your head," he patted her arm in affection.

Jessica worked in the local library she was stacking books when a familiar voice broke into her thoughts.

"Good morning Jess,"

"How lovely to see you, Robert," Jessica's heart was racing at the sight of him, how she had missed him.

"Can I pick you up and take you for a spin in my new car, what time do you finish work?"

"Two o'clock," Jessica replied, noticing everyone looking at them, and feeling wonderful that she should be the one to get his full attention. She checked her hair and put some fresh lipstick on. Looking in her compact mirror she saw a beautiful women, she wanted Robert and she was determined to have him.

They drove to a beauty spot. "Gee I have missed you," Robert said as he gently stroked Jessica's neck. She was melting inside with his touch. She had played out in her dreams how it would feel to make love to Robert so many times, and perhaps this would be it. He put down the hood of his sports car and pulled the lever on the seat Jessica was sitting in and lent forward. He kissed her fully on the lips and undid her silk blouse.

She was now floating on another level; the intensity of his touch was almost more than she could bear. "I have always loved you since we were children, Jess, I so want you," Robert said desperately as he caressed her breasts. Jessica replied breathlessly. "I have always been yours." He was a considerate lover thinking of her, trying to please her. Robert thought her body was amazing, voluptuous and curved all in the right places. They met euphorically at the same time, holding on to each other, trying to make the moment last as long as they could. Jessica had not felt happier. He pledged his love and commitment to her.

They met regularly. Robert would collect Jessica from work and take her to the lane by the river. Where they would make love and spend hours in each other's arms planning their future together.

Robert knew that because of this prejudicial age his family would not consider inter-racial marriage acceptable.

Richard Marshall looked at his son Robert disapprovingly. "You are not listening to me, son, it is out of the question. You are meeting Loraine Douglas; she is the heiress to the Douglas estate in New England and is a perfect match for you. She will be arriving with her parents on Sunday and I will be expecting you to entertain her during her visit. The subject is closed, his father said dismissing him from his study. There was no way he could ever marry someone he did not love. Jessica owned his mind, body, and soul—she would be his wife.

"Mr Marshall would like to see you in his study at two," said Maize to her husband when he popped into the kitchen of the big house for his lunch.

"What would that be about, Tom?" said his wife concerned.

"I have a fair idea of what it is about if I am right I will tell you tonight when we get home." They did not want the other servants to know their business.

"Tom, I want to make it quite clear that my son Robert will be marrying someone of his own class and race. I want this friendship to stop forthwith between Jessica and Robert. Do I make myself clear because if not, you will lose your job and home, you will be dismissed," Richard Marshall said in a forceful manner.

"I understand, Sir," said Tom.

"You may return to your work." He said dismissing Tom curtly.

Jessica was at a loss to know why Robert had not called. She hoped she had not come across too keen? Then on the way to work, he pulled his car up and said, "Hello sorry, but we have had important guests staying and I have had to fulfil my duties and entertain them."

"Say you will let me pick you up after work, Jess," he said with a pleading look.

"Of course I will, "she leant into the car and kissed him on the cheek, which pleased him and Robert drove off.

"Where are you going?" asked Jessica's uncle.

"To meet Robert," she replied as she buttoned her coat up in the hallway.

"No you are not, you are forbidden to see him again." Tom found it hard to stop her from seeing Robert he knew how much she liked him but he had to be firm or he would lose his livelihood and their home.

"I am going you cannot stop me," she said defiantly." Tom barred the door Jessica looked at Maize whom she always had gone to if she could not get her own way with her uncle.

"Tell him how unreasonable he is being, Auntie," she pleaded with her.

"Jessica, you need to know that you're Uncle was called to Mr Marshall's study yesterday and told that your relationship with Robert must end. He has plans for his son to marry someone of his own class and race. If this does not happen then your Uncle and I will lose our jobs and home, do you now understand?"

Jessica was stunned from what her Aunt had said there was so much to take in. Did Robert know, why did he not tell her? She thought they were close and shared everything. Of course, she had no choice she owed everything to her Uncle and Aunt for taking her in after her parents died. How would she cope without Robert, the love of her life?

Robert had to see Jess to find out why she did not turn up. He waited outside the library for her to finish work at two. Jessica spotted him in his car she called on all her willpower to walk past him.

"Hey, Jess, hold up, have I done something to offend you?" asked Robert as he caught up with her. "Ask your father, using my Uncle and Aunt telling them that they would lose their job's and home if I did not stop seeing you, it is totally abhorrent." Jessica said as she walked away.

"Father, how could you do that to Tom and Maize? These two loyal workers have been with the family for years. I will marry Jessica and you cannot stop me," he said to his father in a defiant tone.

"If you do not follow my wishes I will stop your allowance and you will no longer be a son of mine, is she worth being penniless and homeless for?" said his father. Robert knew he would go through with his threat to sack Jessica's Uncle and Aunt and make them homeless if he did not marry Loraine Douglas.

This was a choice from hell for them both. Now he knew why she had not turned up, his father had won.

Six months later Robert was engaged to Loraine Douglas. Their engagement noted in the New York Times.

Unbeknown to him Jessica was six months pregnant. At least having Roberts baby meant she had a part of him, and this thought helped her get through each day. After the initial shock, Tom and Maize were quietly excited at the thought of having a baby in the house. It had always been a disappointment in their marriage, that they never had children. Jessica coped with the sneers and whispers at work, but she did not care. As she saw it, it was a wonderful gift from the man she so loved.

Robert often drove through the town hoping for a glimpse of her. He could not believe it when on this occasion he noticed her walking along the road. He slowed down so he could acknowledge her. As he came level with her, he saw she was pregnant. His first reaction was disbelief, then shock. He did not know what to do, so he kept driving.

Jessica always thought he would see she was carrying his child, and he would whisk her up in his arms and tell her all would be well and that he would look after her and the baby. It broke her heart when she saw him drive away. Robert pulled up at the beauty spot they always came to, and sat letting what he had seen sink in.

His father had a stroke and died, the family were in shock. Robert was busy comforting his mother and organising the funeral. While Gordon the heir to Falcombe Heights took over and ran the estate and the family business.

Roberts's father had left him a generous yearly allowance. A company in Manhattan that Robert had helped set up. The Beach house on Long island also houses in Chicago and London. Now he could marry and support Jessica.

"Gordon, I have broken my engagement to Loraine as I will be marrying Jess who is carrying my child." Gordon was angry with him that he would blacken the family name.

"You are no brother of mine if you marry beneath you and to a black woman, what are you thinking of Robert? Come to your senses man. Have her on the side, and if you have to keep the bastard keep it hidden. That is acceptable. I tell you now if you do not marry Loraine and you associate yourself with this coloured trollop, and its offspring then I want nothing more to do with you. You will not be welcome at Falcombe Heights anymore," Gordon said in a forthright manner for he now was head of the family.

"I will marry Jess she is the only woman for me. I'm saddened brother; you feel that way I will move out today."

Jessica opened the door to find a smiling Robert. She tried to shut it, but he put his foot in the way. "Listen to me—please, Jess!" He explained what had happened, on the wooden veranda went down on one knee and pulled a ring box from his pocket.

"Jess, would you do me the great honour of being my wife?"

"If you are marrying me because of the baby, there is no need I can manage with the help of my Aunt and Uncle," said Jessica praying he would not give up on her so easily.

"Jess, I have loved you from the first time we met on my father's estate all those years ago. If you feel the same way, please say yes?" He waited anxiously for her answer. Jessica twiddled with a strand of her long hair as she always did when contemplating something.

Then she threw her arms around him, "Robert, I have always loved you, YES, I will marry you." she was concerned about their different social standing but felt their love would overcome that. Three months later Elizabeth was born to the delight of her parents.

Chapter Thirteen

E bony was busy helping in the campaign office. "This is Ben, he will be helping you, Daniel asked if you could show him the ropes and give him an idea of what happens here," said Joe.

"Nice to meet you, Ben, this is a very exciting job making bill boards you will be covered in glue, you will find it everywhere when you get home tonight" she laughed.

Ben liked Ebony's warm personality. "What line of work are you in?" Ben asked her.

"I am an Overseas Sales Director for Houghton Druitt and Sons. I love my job, and you?"

Ebony liked the guy. She guessed his age at being in his late twenties, he was black with his wild hair tied back and had penetrating brown eyes and a strong jaw line, she wondered whether he was a model with his good looks.

"I am a dress designer in New York, something I always wanted to do.

"How fascinating, Ben, I will know who to come to for that special dress."

Ebony was printing leaflets at the campaign head quarters and Ben and Joe were packing them in three bags. "Fancy a coffee afterwards, you two, pounding the streets we will need it," joked Ebony.

"Ok," Joe and Ben replied.

"Let's see who distributes their leaflets the fastest and the one who takes the longest, pays for the coffees, agreed?" Ebony replied playfully. "Let's go, have your money ready you two." Ebony laughed as she threw her heavy bag of leaflets over her shoulder. They left the election office chatting and laughing. As she raced along Brooklyn Avenue to the first building to post her leaflet, she thought what two lovely lads Joe and Ben were, very dedicated to helping the campaign. She was very fond of Joe he was the brother she never had. He was at college studying business and law and was destined to join his father's Company when he had qualified. He was the offspring of Matthew Houghton who was the son of her Boss.

Ebony called a meeting of her sales team. Sitting on the corner of the large table in the meeting room, she said. "Guys I need you to push the sales forward in Spain and Italy; we are losing business to our competitors Newton, Greg and Sons." She felt she had a great team.

"Steve, I am leaving you with the Chinese market, get me those extra sales." If anyone could do it, it was Steve. He was her sales manager a natural salesperson and was destined to go far in the company. He was great with his team, who loved him. He always came up with the goods. He was smart, good-looking and likeable; his customers loved him, especially the women. The remaining members of the team were Tess, Jonathan and Joanna. Tess was very ambitious and tough, she had her eye on his position. She was gay and fought for their rights, she was difficult sometimes but Steve managed to control her, she was in charge of the Italian market. Jonathan moved with promoted and joined them from the U.K. office. He was very polite and had been very successful in the British market. Joanna was pretty and bubbly with long blonde hair; she was very popular with the male customers. She used her female charms to get the sales. "Joanna, I want you to give the German market to Jonathan and focus on Spain," said Ebony. She had expected Joanna to complain but she did not say a word, there was such rivalry between her and Jonathan. "Keep up the good work. I will be concentrating on new business in Japan. I will be flying out tomorrow for a week. If you need me, ring me on my mobile," Ebony said as she packed her briefcase. She waved saying. "Bye guys have a good day."

She left the meeting for home. She had preparations to make before her visit to Japan the next day. Ebony set her projector alarm clock for six am and lay back on her bed staring at the red number eleven projected onto her ceiling. She snuggled down under her duvet her thoughts turning to her disappointment in not finding any adoption papers. As soon as she had finished Jessica's family tree she would start her search for her biological parents.

Ebony settled down in her seat on the plane. She had purchased enough magazines and with meals and movies on board, the time would pass quickly. She did hope the person who would occupy the seat next to her would not be chatty or snore. She opened her magazine and started to read an article when a bag hurtled through the air and landed on the seat next to her. She carried on reading hoping she would not have to acknowledge them.

"Hi I'm Matthew Houghton." She looked up at him and forced a smile.

"It was a last minute decision of my father's for me to accompany you; he thought it would be good for me to see how the Japanese market works. I promise I'm not here to spy on you," he laughed. Ebony felt annoyed that John Houghton had sent his son to watch over her. Matthew pulled out a paper and started to read. Thank goodness for that she thought, she so hated having to make small talk.

"Fancy meeting for dinner, Ebony," he asked her at the check in desk at the hotel.

"No thank you I need to catch up on some work and go over the agenda before tomorrow."

"Well a drink then about nine I'll meet you at the bar, I will not take no for an answer," with that he followed the bellhop to the lift.

Ebony did not feel in the mood to have dinner with Matthew. She would much rather have a hot bath and eat her dinner in her room, but he was the boss's son!

She made an effort with her appearance although she felt tired, she found him at the bar chatting up a busty raven-haired women.

He acknowledged her with a smile, turned to the woman, and said. "My wife is here now I must go, it was a pleasure meeting you," and took Ebony's arm saying. "Darling what would you like to drink?" as they walked away and sat down at a table. "You timed that just right, she was trying to get her nails into me, sorry about the wife thing," he smiled. You could not help but like him, she thought.

"I must warn you, that the Japanese are very formal and ritualized. Greetings are of extreme importance to them. I have a beautifully gift wrapped present for them, as that is very important." Ebony said to Matthew. "Just follow me tomorrow."

He was impressed with this woman she had obviously done her homework.

Ebony was pleased with how the meeting was progressing. Matthew just took a back seat at the meeting, which was a relief to her. It was difficult to tell if they would buy or not because of the nature of their culture, their expression never gave anything away.

The next morning in her hotel room as she was getting ready to go down for breakfast, she received a phone call from Seito the sales Manager with a massive order. She was thrilled; her hard work had paid off. Ebony told Matthew her good news when she joined him for breakfast.

"What wonderful news!" he said. "Why don't we have a tour of Tokyo we could do with some chill out time. We or rather you deserve it. What an excellent result in gaining our first sales in Japan." Not giving Ebony a chance to reply Matthew took out his mobile and said, "I must tell my father, the good news." With that, he got up, wandered over to the buffet bar, and began talking on his mobile. He returned to the table with a smile. "My, father's, delighted at the news and sends his congratulations to you, now let's have breakfast, I am ravenous. So do we have a date?"

"Yes I would love to explore this city." She thought he was a bit presumptuous calling it a date.

There was a knock on her hotel room door, darn she thought, as she hopped to open it with one shoe on. It was Matthew whom she thought looked rather nice in his casual clothes, this was the first time she had ever seen him in anything other than a suit. "Please come in," she felt self-conscious of the clothes scattered all over her bed.

Matthew produced a wrapped gift and handed it to her. "This is for you, to say thank you for putting up with me."

Ebony opened it to find inside the most exquisite Japanese black lacquered fan. She opened it up and put it in front of her face so that her eyes were only visible and looked over it flirtatiously

"Thank you kind Sir," she said.

"Has anyone told you what beautiful eyes you have," Matthew replied. What was she doing flirting with him like this? She decided she ought to behave professionally.

"I have emails to answer and phone calls to make before we go, so I must get on." She tried to show him the door, feeling embarrassed.

"You know what they say all work and no play makes, Ebony, a dull girl," she could not help but laugh. "Now that's better, be ready in ten minutes. I will book a cab and will meet you in the lobby."

As soon as he left, she delved into her suitcase to find her new pretty, pink dress that she knew she looked good in and put it on. Then she piled her hair on top of her head and secured it with a silver ornate clip, some strands fell forward softening her look. She put on her pearl earrings and pleased with her appearance picked up her bag and locked the hotel door. Just as she went to press the lift button, she remembered she had left her fan behind in the room. She could not go without his lovely gift, so she rushed back to get it.

Chapter Fourteen

⸙

"Tokyo Tower please," said Matthew to the cab driver. "Ebony, you will enjoy this," he said as he sat down next to her in the back of the cab. "It's the highest self supporting steel tower in the world and has spectacular views from the observatory, I hope you like heights? I thought we would check it out. I need to pick up a gift for my son so I thought we could go afterwards on the Tokyo metro. It is supposed to be one of the fastest commuter transit systems and find a shopping mall and restaurant for dinner, What do you say?"

"Sounds great," she replied as she tried to take in the sights of the city through the cab window.

The view from the tower was amazing. Matthew draped a casual arm over her shoulder in the lift going up to the observatory platform, as if it was the most natural thing to do. She felt so relaxed in his company that she really did not mind. If she was honest with herself, she loved his body close to hers. A well-dressed sea of people moved orderly onto the trains, the station was immaculate. The trains were smart and clean and everything was larger than life, but so many people! With Matthew, she joined the throng; they moved en masse onto the train. As the doors closed, Ebony felt concerned, I hope the journey will be quick she thought. They were soon at their stop. The doors of the train suddenly opened behind her. With the weight of passengers, trying to get off, she lost her balance falling onto the platform. All she saw were feet and legs. The next thing she knew was Matthew's hands grabbing her and lifting her up. He held onto her and edged himself through the throng to the street. "Are you alright? Are you hurt anywhere?" he said worriedly.

"My left ankle's painful," she tried to put weight on her foot, the pain was excruciating. Matthew supported her then sat her on a seat while he hailed a cab. "Please take us to The Royal Hotel." He laid Ebony down on a sofa in the reception area of the hotel. "I won't be a moment," he said as he went to the reception desk. Ebony observed him as he stood and spoke to the hotel receptionist. Matthew had an air of authority about him. He was tall, slim with curly short dark brown hair and strong features. You would not say he was handsome but he had charisma and a sense of humour, which she loved in a man and he was great company. "A doctor will be here soon," he said trying to make her comfortable.

"Matthew, if you can help me to my room I will be fine after resting my ankle." Ebony said feeling embarrassed at her clumsiness.

"I insist your ankle should be looked at, now can I get you a coffee, something to eat?" Matthew said fussing over her. "No thank you." Her leg was throbbing and was swelling by the minute; perhaps he was right to get it checked out.

A doctor appeared and examined her.

"You will need to rest that ankle you badly bruised it when you fell. I will give you painkillers and an anti-inflammatory cream to rub on the area. It will be at least a week before you can put any weight on it," said the doctor. Matthew produced a wheel chair and took her up in the lift to her room.

"I will have to get into work there is so much to do, I can always use crutches," Ebony said.

"No way young lady will you please do as the doctor ordered?" replied Matthew.

He ordered Ebony to have the week off work. He said he would be checking up on her. She secretly hoped he would, she really enjoyed his company.

The next day Ebony looked through her mother's documents relating to her family tree. She found a black tube against the wall in the study. She opened it to find the family tree already partly drawn. Ebony unrolled it and laid it on the dining room table securing it at each corner to stop it rolling back. There were the names of Abel and Beth Tukowunu the founders of the family and in capitals printed by their names SLAVES. This was where she would continue her research. She looked again at the writing pad on her mother's desk with the reference to Cotton Wood Plantation. Underneath she had written near Charleston, South Carolina U.S.A. She typed it into her laptop. Up came Cotton Wood Plantation, Charleston. Theodore Jackson who had died during the Civil War defending his Plantation had owned it.

Were Abel and Beth his slaves? Ebony asked herself. This gripped her imagination she needed to know more. Her mobile rang; she did not recognise the number. "Ebony Marshall," she said

"How's, our wounded soldier, doing?" It was Matthew's voice. She smiled instantly.

"On the mend thank you," she replied.

"Why don't you let me take you for a drive, a break would do you good. We need to look after our top sales person!"

"Actually I would like that; I am going stir crazy stuck in doors."

"Good I will collect you at 4 pm."

"You will need my address," she said.

"I already have it from personnel, I am after all the boss's son," he laughed.

"We'll that won't do you any good as I am not at my flat, I am at my house on Long Island. So being the boss's son did not help you."

"You were supposed to be resting that foot, how did you manage, you should have called me and I would have helped you."

Please don't fuss, I'm a big girl and managed with my crutches and a kind cab driver."

She gave him the directions and hung up.

Ebony hobbled around tidying up deciding to leave the family tree on the dining room table to continue working on it later and closed the door. She changed into a long skirt. Only one shoe fitted her so she placed a flip-flop on her swollen foot. She opened the door to Matthew. "What a wonderful house you have right on the beach."

"It was my mother's she has recently died and left it to me." What was she doing telling him everything about herself, she was not usually that forward with her personal life. She knew she was falling for him. She told herself he was just a business colleague; she knew she was deluding herself. "I am sorry, Ebony, I did not know, please accept my condolences."

"So you didn't contribute to my lovely flowers from everyone at work then," she said as she looked at him." I repay my secretary at the end of the month for any incidental cost, so I'm sure I did."

"Matthew, it's ok, you have a business to run you can't be expected to know about the little things. I was only teasing," she said when she noticed he looked embarrassed.

He was annoyed with himself. Ebony must be devastated at the loss of her mother. He caught sight of her flip-flop, and smiled. She took her crutches and Matthew helped her into his car.

Matthew drove her to a lovely Italian restaurant down by the harbour. There was a cooling breeze. The temperature had been in the thirties that day so it was very welcome. The candles on the table fluttered gently and the lights around the quay reflected in the water. He made her laugh so much her sides ached. When he looked over the table at her, he had the most wonderful twinkle in his eyes that just drew her in. Ebony felt very content, one of those good feel moments; she had not had one of them in a long time.

"I've had a lovely time thank you," she said as they drew up outside her beach house. "Would you like to come in for a coffee, Matthew?" She was feeling awkward, worried he might think she was to forward.

"Thank you, I would," he replied. They talked for ages she found him so amusing and interesting. He suddenly became serious. "I know I can trust you, Ebony, not to repeat this. However, someone in our company is spying for our competitors, Newton, Greg and Son's. We really do not need this as we are having financial problems because of the state of the economy we may have to let staff go. It is vital we grow the business in the next quarter. "Ebony could not believe what she was hearing. She was touched to think he could trust her enough to confide in her.

"You know, Matthew, I will do everything I can to get more sales for the company. I cannot imagine a member of staff being so disloyal."

"Well it is late, I must go."

"Thank you once again, I have really enjoyed your company, she said. Matthew leaned forward and kissed her on her lips; it sent a tingle coursing through her body.

"I'll go before I get told off," he smiled that smile that made Ebony's legs go weak at the knees.

She could not sleep her ankle was throbbing. Her thoughts turned to Matthew. What was happening was the boss's son really making a pass at—her? In the end she decided to get up, she put on her dressing gown and hobbled out onto the veranda. It was a warm and beautiful night there was a full moon casting its reflection on the sea and the stars sparkled in the night sky. She sat down in the rocking chair and looked out to sea.

The gentle sound of the wind chime hanging from the roof of the veranda broke the silence.

Her mind wandered to her biological parents. What did they look like? What jobs did they do? Where did they live and why did they not want her? So many questions, she needed answers. She had always felt there was something missing from her life and an ache and emptiness she carried around inside her.

The doctor gave her the all clear and she returned to work.

Ebony went as usual from work to the Campaign office and settled down at the computer. "Where have you been, Ebony, I have missed you? Ben was asking after you, I think he has a crush on you," sniggered Joe as he put his arm around her.

"Don't be silly, Joe, he's a nice guy, and anyway I have been away on business I injured my foot while I was away, but its fine now." she said, touched by his concern.

"Well not long now to voting day, it's going to be close. I know we can do it and make the dream a reality." Joe said enthusiastically. She thought what a great kid he was so dedicated to the cause. She thought it best not to mention meeting his father.

Ebony had found a name and number written down, under things to do list in her mother's black file box. She picked up her mobile and rang the number.

"Tom Igwe, speaking."

"Hello my names Ebony Marshall, my mother had your name and mobile number written down in a file where she kept papers relating to research on her family tree. Her maiden name was Jessica Tukowunu. I wondered if you have received any correspondence from her."

"Indeed I did we helped each other in the search for our ancestors, please pass on my regards to her?" Ebony felt a lump in her throat and her emotion stir.

She composed herself and said, "I am afraid she passed away two weeks ago."

"I am so sorry to hear that, we had many interesting conversations on the phone. Please accept my condolences. I hope you are continuing the family tree as she was so passionate about it."

"That is why I am ringing, Mr Igwe."

"Well I am glad you decided to. I came across a name that could be of some help in your search, just hold a moment while I find my papers."

The name is Abena Kalejaiye she is the local historian in Charleston, here is her mobile number.

"Thanks" Ebony said as she wrote it down.

"Now keep in touch, if there is anything else I can do I would be only too happy to help."

"Thank you so much you have been very kind, I will definitely complete the family tree in mother's memory, good bye."

What a lovely man she thought as she placed her mobile down on the table

Ebony decided to take holiday leave for a few days before things got hectic in the campaign office, and flew to South Carolina. I will visit Charleston and arrange to meet Abena Kalejaiye and find Cotton Wood Plantation, she thought.

Chapter Fifteen

E bony had booked a room in the Holiday Inn in Charleston near the harbour. Her thoughts went to Abel and Beth, they could have been one of the many slaves that would have disembarked from the slave ships and sold in the regular slave markets. She shuddered at the conditions they would have had to endure.

She had booked a hire car to travel around easily. She would be able to visit Cotton Wood Plantation and search for the graves of Abel and Beth.

From her hotel room Ebony rang the historian. "Could I please speak to, Abena Kalejaiye," she asked.

"Whose calling," said a female voice, in a sharp tone on the other end of the phone?

"Ebony Marshall," replied Ebony

"What do you want with her?" The woman replied in a defensive manner. Ebony felt uncomfortable.

"Tom Igwe gave me your name and number. I believe you could help me with some names, as I am researching my mother's family tree."

"I am sorry," her voice softened but I have had some intimidating phone calls since I have been giving my time to the election campaign."

A woman after her own heart Ebony thought, standing up for what she believes in and persecuted for it, sadly times do not change, Ebony thought.

"Would you like to call around tomorrow, my address is 119 Mangrove drive, say at noon?"

"Yes, I will see you then." Ebony thanked her.

The next morning she went in search for Abena's address.

She knocked at her door. It was a typical South Carolina house; the sun's rays had caused the paint to peel. On the veranda stood an old, faded brown leather armchair and a swing seat, which creaked as it, moved in the slight breeze. Ebony was looking forward to getting out of the sun, which beat down fiercely. A young black girl with her hair tied in plaits and wearing a blue cotton dress opened the door and a female voice shouted out from inside. "Tammy ask their name?"

"Missy, what's your name?" the girl said in an enquiring manner.

"Miss Ebony Marshall."

"Come in, come in, I have been expecting you," shouted the women from inside the house. She introduced herself as Abena Kalejaiye. She was red faced, rotund, and sat with one leg under her on a well-worn sofa; she fanned herself as she greeted Ebony. "Tammy go get missy a cold glass of lemonade." The young girl returned with a long glass of cooling lemonade, which Ebony sipped thankfully. The sound of the ceiling fan creaked as it turned, but the relief from it was welcome.

"Tom gave me some information about your family name. I have managed to find some information that you will find interesting, regarding your ancestors in these parts in the 1800's. Ebony excitedly looked at the books and paperwork placed in front of her. Abena picked up a tatty looking book in her plump hand from the table. "This church register is dated 1810-1880 from the slave's church at Cotton Wood Plantation. My ancestor Samson and Grace Kalejaiye kept this church register, it has been passed down through the family." Abena had marked a particular page and handed it to her. "Look here is the names of Abel Tukowunu who married Beth.

There was also an entry regarding the birth of a son Will." Ebony felt emotional at the evidence of her adopted mother's ancestors lying in front of her, Abena turned the page. "You need to see this?" she pointed to a page and there written was Abel Tukowunu who had died in the year 1859 hung for killing Mistress Emma Jackson. Ebony could not believe what she saw. The euphoria she had first felt had now turned to shock. She thanked Abena for her help and left.

She sat in her air-conditioned car stunned at the information that she had uncovered. It was not what she had wanted to see, but she was glad her mother had not discovered these facts.

She just wanted to go home but she felt it was imperative that she visit Cotton Wood Plantation.

Ebony stopped and looked at her map it should be around the next corner. She first noticed a 'For Sale' sign alongside a large carved wooden sign bearing the name 'Cotton Wood Plantation,' at an entrance to an avenue of Oak trees. Her heart started to beat rapidly. Then she saw a large imposing house it was everything and more than she expected it to be. She excitedly drove down the avenue towards it. As she approached, she saw a derelict three-storey building, with large white pillars either side of an impressive front door. The white paintwork was peeling. There was a white wooden quaint chapel to the far side of the house, also an array of outbuildings on the other side. She surveyed the scene and could still make out where the cotton fields had been.

She reached back and found the flowers she had brought to place on Abel's and Beth's graves if she was fortunate to find them. She walked around the house. The windows were shuttered and doors locked she was disappointed that she could not see in. Ebony wandered around to the back of the house and found two large buildings, one was a large shed and the other stables, which faced each other, a forecourt, lay between them. In the distance were cabins set around a square with a post in the centre and a small hut. She then caught sight of a larger wooden building in the distance on the outskirts of the plantation. It might be the slave church and if it is it will have a graveyard next to it, she thought. Ebony's heart leapt in her chest, would she find Able and Beth?

The grass was tall but you could still see wooden crosses peeking through. The graveyard was surrounded by wooden picket fence with a little entry gate. It was difficult to open because of the tall grass. She was so close now and felt very excited. Ebony pushed the grass out of the way to read each cross, she knew that there was a story of pain and suffering to every name she found. As she removed the weeds from the next cross, there it was Chief Abel Tukowunu of the Manitou tribe, in large bold letters still clear to the eye. "I have found him," her emotions took over and she sobbed uncontrollable touching his cross. Ebony stood there in the stillness and talked to Abel. "If only you could tell me what happened that day that so cruelly took your life leaving Beth and Will." She then placed her flowers on his grave. "These are from your descendant Jessica Tukowunu who died before she could do it herself. Ebony immediately decided she would complete this trail and dig deeper for any more information surrounding Emma Jackson's death.

She continued to look for Beth and Will, but they were not there. Ebony walked back to the Plantation house and visited the white wooden chapel, behind it she hoped was the family graveyard. It was very grand the head stones were marble or granite and either engraved in gold or silver lettering with surrounding ornate railings. This was a stark contrast to the slave's graves.

Then Ebony saw an angel carved out of granite towering over what appeared to be the family plot. In gold lettering, one head stone read Emma Martha Jackson aged 21 years died 1859 beloved only daughter to Theodore and Martha Jackson, rest in peace my angel your mother will watch over you now. It was next to her mother's grave. Martha Jackson.

So where was Theodore? Ebony continued her search amongst the long overgrown graveyard. She came across a grave with a plain simple head stone visible through the long grass. It bore the name Theodore Jackson who died defending his estate in 1863 during the Civil War. How she despised this man for what he stood for, the hardship and suffering his slaves had endured because of his greed.

Ebony had a lot to think about on the flight home, she knew one thing her heart was saying, buy Cotton Wood Plantation.

"Fancy lunch?" Matthew said peering round Ebony's office door. He had missed her.

"That would be lovely but I just have to finish this important e-mail, take a seat I won't be long." With a gesture of her hand, pointed to the cream leather sofa at the other end of her office. He sat down and looking round he noticed some leaflets on her coffee table and picked one up to read.

"I cannot understand anyone who would want to give a moment of their time to this," said Matthew in a mocking tone. Ebony looked up from her laptop to see Matthew reading the campaign leaflets that she would be shortly distributing. She could feel her temperature rising, and thought how dare he come into her office and pass an opinion on her personal matters. Ebony looked directly at him

"Firstly the leaflets are not a waste of time people need to be well informed as to the Democratic candidate that will be standing. Secondly, I did not ask for your opinion, we obviously see thing differently." She went to her office door and held it open, Matthew got up

"Ebony, I did not mean to be rude, please forgive me?" he said as he passed her and walked out of the office.

I did not deal with that very well, he told himself. I knew she had strong cultural beliefs and would want to be involved in the election campaign, he thought as he returned to his office.

Perhaps she was right that they did see things differently.

Matthew went back to his office kicking himself for his silly remark, picked up his phone, and ordered some flowers for Ebony to say sorry. He needed a break and thought he would ask his son Joe if he would like a trip away.

At dinner that evening, Matthew put it to his son. "I thought we could plan a holiday and spend some quality time together son, you don't have college, what do you say, Joe?"

"Sorry, dad, but I'm needed at the campaign office."

"Holding on to your heritage will not help you in the business world. It is better to let go, now forget this nonsense."

"I cannot believe you said that, dad, I am proud to be African American and I am doing my bit to help elect the first Black American President." Joe said as he got up from the dinner table leaving his half-eaten meal and slammed the dining room door behind him.

How could he expect his son to understand? Matthew's father had sent him to boarding school when he was eight. He remembered the headmaster informing him that his mother had died. He had seen very little of her growing up all he could remember was her English accent. His parents did not have time for him. They were both white but he was born coloured. Although his skin colour was light, it was never discussed. His father was always busy building his empire, having no time for him and his mother drank heavily. Matthew hated boarding school. One of the Captains of his dorm bullied him, making him wear a collar around his neck. He called him nigger boy to the amusement of the other boarders; in the Captains opinion, his skin colour made him second-class. He had nightmares for years afterwards. Matthew had tried to distance himself from his heritage because of those experiences.

As Ebony lay soaking in the bath, she thought about Matthew. How could she have a relationship with someone who did not respect her beliefs? She had developed feelings for him and felt disappointed that he could be so dismissive of her background and culture.

"Good morning, Ebony," Laura said as she walked into her office. "Who's the admirer?" There on her coffee table lay a large bouquet of pink roses with a matching bow. Ebony opened the card. Sorry, please be my friend, as I do not have many. Matthew had drawn a sad face at the bottom of the card. He always had the ability to make her smile.

Chapter Sixteen

❦

They had all worked hard towards the big day, Election Day it was finally here. Ebony had voted first thing. She had never seen such a turnout of people voting. People across the country had been queuing for hours. She was so hopeful. Ebony, Joe and Ben watched the results come in together. "All we need is another two points to get 270 college votes to win" said Joe, as they watched the large screen set out for the campaign team. There would be food and drink, as this would go on into the early hours of the morning. Excitement was building at 4 am on the 5th of November the Democratic Candidate passed the necessary 270 college votes and finished with 349.

Their dream had now been realised. This was truly a historical moment and she felt privileged to be there, to see America's first black President elected. The three of them hugged each other, the crowd screamed with joy when the announcement came. They watched on the large screen as the new President gave his acceptance speech. Then his family joined him on the platform. Everyone in the packed hall was screaming or crying with joy, waving their flags, this was the first family of America. Daniel brought over a bottle of champagne to celebrate. He had not been able to see Ebony as he was so busy, but now they could make up for lost time. They drank three bottles. Joe took a digital photograph of the team and then one of Daniel and Ebony after all this was an historical moment in time.

Daniel and Ebony ended up at his flat very drunk and on a high. They grabbed at each other's clothes pulling them off and ended up having frantic sex, it was over quickly and they fell asleep until Ebony awoke to Daniels snoring. She carefully climbed out of his bed so as not to wake him and crept around the room trying to find her clothes.

Ebony returned to her apartment and took some headache pills for her thumping headache, and visited her adopted mother's grave. She wanted to tell her the good news that they now had America's first black President. How she wished she had been with her to share that historical moment. She bought several copies of the daily newspapers that morning for a keepsake

So that she could show her children one day that she had been present and had witnessed this momentous time in American history.

The next day at work Isabel was all over Matthew like a rash in the corner of the meeting room. I didn't know she was back, damn she thought. He seemed to love the attention he was getting from her. Ebony could not wait to leave. Oh no, he is coming my way thought Ebony, as Matthew stood in front of her.

"Ebony I need to see you. I will call into your office at 3 o'clock—if that is convenient?" said Matthew looking her directly in the eyes.

"I am afraid I will not be there, I have another meeting scheduled. Sorry I must leave I have a conference call," said Ebony looking at her watch. Does he really think that every woman falls at his feet, well this one does not, she said to herself as she walked out through the door.

Ebony knew that Isabel and Matthew had a fling two years ago, as it was common knowledge. However, before she went to the U.K office she was seeing Robert Druitt who was too nice for her. There were rumours she was two timing him with someone else but no one knew who that could be. Could it have been Matthew?

She ploughed through her e-mails and one jumped out at her. Mrs Rose Nantukie. She clicked on her name. It read Abena

Kalejaiye asked me for help in tracing some of your ancestors. I do have some information that might be helpful to you. Ebony clicked on the attachment. It showed a legal document stating Beth and Will Tukowunu received their freedom by Theodore Jackson. Wow! Thought Ebony, Theodore was not such a bad person after all. She could not wait to go home to add this information to the family tree.

Ebony prepared for her business trip to Japan. Seito, Ebony's opposite number had collected her from the airport and taken her for a meal. He had just said good night and dropped her back at her hotel. Ebony's feet hurt and she was tired, she kicked off her high heels and climbed on the hotel bed. Her mobile rang; damn she thought it is in my handbag. She got off the bed and fetched it and by the time, she found her mobile it had stopped. Typical she thought and laid it on her bedside table. Then it rang again. "Hi it's Matthew, I am sorry to ring you so late but I need the contract for Castle Health Care in Barcelona—it's urgent. I rang Steve to see if he had it but he said it was with you. When will you be back?" He sounded impatient Ebony thought.

"Not until Friday." Ebony replied.

"That's too late." he said.

"Matthew, there is a spare key in a glass jar under the veranda, please use it. The paper work is in a folder marked Castle in the top desk draw in the study. The study is a door off the hallway just put the key back please."

His voice softened and said. "Thank you, have a good trip and no travelling on commuter trains," he laughed. She smiled as she laid back on the bed thinking about him.

Matthew found the spare key as she had said under the veranda. He opened the door and worked his way up the hallway, opening each door leading from it. He entered the dining room to see a large rolled out sheet of paper held down at the corners. A family tree how interesting he thought. This must have taken her many hours of work, to gather all the information needed to put the family tree together, he was impressed.

He could not resist looking at it and the more he looked at it the more interesting it became. Matthew entered a bedroom in search of the study. He noticed a photo in a silver frame on a bedside cabinet of Ebony with a man, who had his arm around her, she looked very happy. He shut the door he did not realise she was already seeing someone. The next door was the study and as she promised, the file was in the drawer. He sat down at her desk, opened it to review the contract. He picked up a paper clip, bent it open, and ran it through his nails, something he always did when concentrating. His mind wandered, the problem was Ebony, he had fallen in love with her and now he had a rival. What am I to do he asked himself as he ran the paper clip along his nail.

As Ebony returned to her office after her trip to Japan she heard Laura say. "Well what do you think of that," to someone on her phone.

"I must go," and hung up when she saw Ebony. "The phone lines are hot with gossip this morning," said Laura.

"What are you talking about?" said Ebony, as she started up her laptop.

"Isabel has been fired." Ebony looked up from checking her e-mails.

"Are you sure?"

"Yes Fay rang me she had an e-mail it has been sent to all heads of staff, you should have one?" Ebony scrolled down her unopened e-mails and there were many. She opened the e-mail from HR. It read Isabel Leyton has had her contract terminated due to improper conduct.

"What does improper conduct mean? I will find out?" said Laura as she went back to her office and immediately picked up the phone.

"Don't blame Laura; she was busy making a phone call, so I let myself in, said Mathew. "Could I have a few minutes of your time?"

"You're the boss," said Ebony coldly.

"I just popped in to give you back the Castle contract, thank you for allowing me into your home to retrieve it. It was an important piece of information that I needed to expose the spy in our company. I expect you have heard about Isabel."

"Yes I read my e-mail."

"She was the mole. She had been passing details of our impending contract deals to our competitors, apparently, Isabel was having a fling with the managing director, and they of course got in before we could and took the business. James Druitt tried to cover for her because although she had broken off their engagement he still loved her and sent her to the U.K office out of the way. His father is furious with him, how blind love is," Matthew replied." Ebony could not believe the news, why did she need to do that when she appeared to have everything going for her. It appears she had it all wrong, thinking Matthew fancied her.

"I thought you were seeing her?" she said to him.

"Why did you think that?"

"Well you appeared very cosy the other day in the meeting room." Matthew laughed.

"I have been out with her before and that was enough believe me. He looked at his watch and said. "Well I have to attend a meeting, good morning," and hurriedly left. Ebony felt Matthew was very businesslike with her, not his usual relaxed self. What did she expect when she was so off with him over her leaflets? She missed his warm and friendly manner, perhaps the fact he is the bosses son will come between them.

Matthew picked up the newspaper it was full of the election of the First Black American President. His eye caught a picture of Joe, Ebony and others with the unknown man he had seen in the picture at Ebony's home. It said Daniel Lloyd and his team at The Democratic election Headquarters, down town celebrating. Well what did he expect; she would have more in common with him. He did not realise Joe knew Ebony. He had never mentioned her but why would he after all he had not shown any interest in his sons pursuits.

His divorce from Joe's mother had been an acrimonious one and very hard on his son. Senita Joe's mother married shortly after their divorce to an oil magnet and moved to Arabia. Joe did not want to go, so reluctantly she agreed he would live with Matthew. He thought how distant he had become from his son. He must make more effort to show interest in his pursuits. He took the cutting from the newspaper and took it to the photographers to have it enlarged and framed as a gift for Joe. He hoped this would help bridge the gap between them.

Joe found a wrapped gift on the kitchen table. "What is this?" He said as he read the gift tag. Son, something to remind you of all the hard work you put into helping the cause, love dad.

It was the picture taken at the campaign office. That was cool of dad to do that Joe thought and took it into his bedroom and placed it on his bookcase.

John Houghton looked at his son. "So, Matthew, what is your opinion of Ebony Marshall's work, her trial period is up and I need to confirm her position as Director of Overseas Sales?"

"I was very impressed with her dad," Matthew replied. "Hard working, does her research, I think she is a very valuable member of staff."

"Thank you for your opinion son."

As Matthew walked out of his father's office, he stopped and said.

"Dad I will drop in and collect the family photograph albums from you, if that is alright." Joe keeps asking about his relations so I thought I would show him the albums."

Matthew had recognised a familiar name from the family tree at Ebony's house and needed to investigate it.

"Hi Daniel, can we meet tonight, say eight at the Italian restaurant near the campaign office?" said Ebony.

"Sure, see you there" he replied.

Ebony did not know how to tell Daniel that their relationship was over. He was a lovely man but not right for her. She sat nervously waiting for him. Daniel kissed her on the cheek and sat down at the table, and perused the menu and said. "Why don't we go away for the weekend we both deserve a rest, it will be lovely just spending time together. Daniel said as he leaned forward to kiss her. Ebony turned her head away.

"I am sorry, Daniel, but there is no future for us. I never meant to mislead you." Ebony looked into his sad eyes. "I owe you the truth, you are a very special person and I am very fond of you, but I do not love you. There is the right person out there for you, but it is not me."

"I guess I knew you felt that way but hoped I was wrong. I envy the man you do fall in love with, Ebony." Daniel kissed her cheek, and left the restaurant.

Ebony felt so sorry for him he was such a nice person. She took her front door keys out of her pocket and let herself in.

Ebony pressed the red flashing light on the answer phone, and then took her shoes off.

"Ebony, its Laura, could you fill in and sign a holiday form for me for two weeks leave." Laura's voice started to break. There was silence then crying, and then the phone went dead. Ebony was worried, she found Laura's home telephone number on her mobile and rang her. No answer so Ebony left her a message. "Please take whatever time you need, I will sort everything out at work, and I will call round tomorrow to see you." Ebony put down the phone; she was very concerned as this was totally out of character for Laura.

Ebony knocked on Laura's door, when she opened it she looked tired and her eyes were red and swollen from crying. She hugged Ebony tightly and started to cry. "I am sorry I just can't stop crying, Jennifer my Granddaughter has disappeared," her voice broke and she sobbed uncontrollably. Ebony helped her to the sofa and sitting next to her, handed her a tissue from her bag, and said "Now tell me all about it, everything?"

"She was going to her friend's house for a sleep over after cheer leader practice at her college, something she had done many times before, but this time she did not arrive. We informed the Sheriff but they do not seem to be taking it seriously. The officer said do not worry Jennifer would be home soon, she would probably be meeting up with a boy she does not want you to know about.

Her parents are heartbroken. Harvey and Doug are out searching for Jennifer and her mother is staying by the phone as the police recommended. I know I should be strong for them but this is so out of character, she is such a sensible girl. She would never go anywhere without her parents' permission. She has been missing for three days now," said Laura as she started to cry again.

"Look at me." Ebony said to her firmly. "Dry your eyes and find a recent photo of Jenifer and I will get hundreds of photos copied, and we will get them distributed. Now go and get that photograph," said Ebony lifting her up from the sofa and reassuring her with a hug.

Ebony knew Jennifer's parents Harvey and Maria well. She knew Harvey would be holding it together for Maria, and was not surprised to hear that Harvey and Doug had been out there searching for the last two days, as Jenifer was their world. Ebony sat at her desk and designed the poster with Jennifer's photograph and the relevant phone numbers to ring. "I need these in a hurry," she said to Jane, manager of the company print room. "Of course, they will be ready by this afternoon "she replied.

Ebony, Laura and friends set about distributing Jennifer's photograph. They attached them to walls, trees and on people's mailboxes, and in the areas that she had frequented. They soon ran out of posters, a quick call to Jane and she had more printed. Her staff brought them to Ebony with a note from Jane. Need any more just give me another call, anything for Laura; our heart goes out to her. Love Jane.

Chapter Seventeen

✦

Ebony looked at her bank statement; her inheritance had now gone into her bank account. It was a lot of money—now what should she do with it? She sat down at her breakfast bar in her kitchen and sipped her green tea. Should she be sensible and invest it, she thought. Then a crazy idea flashed through her mind, what about buying Cotton Wood Plantation. She could renovate it and make it a conference centre or keep it, investing in property was sound, she told herself. Ebony searched on the internet and found Rushmore and Cooper a real-estate office in Charleston.

Ebony called them," Good morning, could you tell me if Cotton Wood Plantation is still on the market?" asked Ebony to a property sales adviser.

"Yes it is, we have had some interest but no firm offers yet. My name is Cindy, would you like a viewing?" she said.

"Yes please the name is, Ebony Marshall. Would it be possible to view it next week?"

"Ten o'clock next Monday is convenient." Cindy replied."

"That's fine, I will meet you there," said Ebony.

Ebony cleared her diary, took a week's leave, and booked her flight to South Carolina. Ebony booked into the Sheraton Hotel in Charleston and hired a car.

The ornate wooden door of the Plantation house creaked as Cindy from the Real estate office opened it. She was slender with a prim and proper attitude, her glasses sat neatly on her pale insipid face, which matched her pale grey suit. The daylight hit the most stunning staircase. The hallway was large with high ornate ceilings. Ebony wandered into a room to the left, it appeared to be a study, while Cindy gabbled on. Ebony brushed the dirt and dust from the beautifully carved wooden door and pushed the gold coloured doorknob. Against the window was an exquisite desk and chair, where she imagined Theodore Jackson had sat and looked down the avenue of trees. There was a wall of bookshelves on the far wall. Hanging down over the shuttered window were heavy drapes, dust and dirt covered them due to many years of neglect. They must have been vibrant gold colour brocade, as the light from the open study door reflected off the curtains and caught the golden strands. Everything was dusty and worn but even so, it astounded her. The stories these walls could tell if they could only speak, she thought. Cindy accompanied the tour with some background history as they toured the house.

Ebony followed Cindy up the grand staircase. "Be careful watch your footing, some steps are insecure." she said. Along the landing were doors leading to eight large bedrooms with stunning four-poster beds. Four of the bedrooms had windows looking out to the front of the house and a view of the tree lined avenue. Further, along the landing were some steps that led to another floor with four small rooms with no windows. "This would have been the servant's bedrooms," said Cindy. Ebony entered the rooms, they were all dark and oppressive with little furniture and she felt very uncomfortable. "I must get out of here," said Ebony to Cindy. They moved down stairs.

"Let me show you the ballroom," said Cindy with an excitement in her voice. This room was enormous with windows running along one side of the room with what must have been thick brocade curtains that touched the wooden flooring. Looking closely at the curtains they appeared to have been crimson and gold, but were now faded. Hanging from the ceiling was the most exquisite crystal chandelier that was dull and dirty. Against the far wall stood a grand long table with seating for thirty people, and a large marble fireplace where an ornate gold mirror hung.

"You can imagine the wonderful balls that must have been held here," Cindy said. She then took Ebony across the hallway to the kitchen.

There was a large fireplace and a range at one end and a massive wooden table in the middle of the kitchen. There were many cupboards around the walls. A door led to a wooden veranda at the back of the house. "Let me show you the grounds, Miss Marshall, this way."

Cindy held the kitchen door and Ebony walked onto the wooden veranda, the door swung back and forwards until it slowly closed. "Miss Marshall, watch for the broken and missing boards," said Cindy. Ebony noticed a man hanging around the back of the house.

"Seb Pike get off this property," Cindy shouted at a lone figure loitering by the Veranda. "I have told you before you are trespassing, now do as I say or I will tell your mother?"

With that, a black scruffy young man shuffled off down the avenue.

"He is always hanging around his grandfather James Pike currently owns Cotton Wood Plantation and has asked us to sell it for him. There are rumours circulating that he has to pay his debtors. It is a shame as it has been in the family many years. Seb's grandfather disowned Seb's mother when she married a coloured man when he was born. The family is well-known around these parts."

"How sad" replied Ebony?

Cindy unlocked the stable doors and the large store shed in the yard, for Ebony to view. Then she walked a distance from the plantation house.

"This you will find interesting, these are the original wooden cabins the field slaves would have lived in, and they are now in a bad state of repair. That rotten post standing over there was for the punishment of the slaves, it was the whipping post." Ebony felt a knotted feeling in her stomach as she walked into the first cabin. "I don't like this at all," she said to Cindy. She saw the small basic square wooden structure with one small window. It had three wooden beds, three chairs, and a wooden table against the far wall. She could feel the presence of those that had occupied the cabin, they were whispering in her ear. Ebony felt dizzy and became unsure on her feet, as if they might not hold her. "I feel unwell," she said as she grabbed the foot of the bed nearest her to steady herself. She heard a voice, as if it was far away. "Miss Marshall are you feeling alright? Cindy took hold of her and sat her down on one of the chairs, and produced a bottle of water from her bag. "Here have a sip?" Ebony drank the water.

"Thank you, Cindy," she said as she passed the bottle back to her.

"No please keep it I should not have kept you out for so long, the humidity is high today. Let me take you back to my office and you can rest up in the air conditioning."

"I would just like to see the slave church before we go—please?"

"Yes of course, but then I must insist we return to my office and you can cool down."

As they walked to the slave's church Ebony asked Cindy. "Can I have a few minutes on my own in the church and then we can go?" Ebony gave a pleading look at Cindy; she nodded and unlocked the church door. Ebony touched the walls as she entered and looked around. She felt the wooden pews where so many slaves had sat in worship and said their prayers. Kneeling down she looked up at the crudely made cross, that must have been carved with love by one of the slaves, and closed her eyes. "Dear God you witnessed the cruelty done to these people and heard them praying. I am sure they are with you in the kingdom of heaven. Please accept my prayer for the safety of America's first black President; it has been a long time coming. Please bless all those that are enslaved today." She felt humbled and at one with those that had attended the church all those years ago.

Cindy pointed the air conditioning vent towards Ebony as she sat in the front of her car, the engine started and the cold air hit her face and body, the pleasure of the cooling air was a joy. She relaxed oblivious to Cindy rambling on. She had one focus she must acquire Cotton Wood Plantation. There was a definite connection between her and that place, and she must own it.

As Ebony relaxed in the air-conditioned office, savouring her cold drink of diet coca-cola, she made her offer. "I would like to make an offer of the full asking price for the purchase of Cotton Wood Plantation Cindy?"

"That's great I will contact my client and get back to you. Are you feeling better now?"

"Yes thank you, I just want to check you have my mobile number?" Cindy checked her paper work. "Yes we do, as soon as I have a reply from our client I will contact you." They said goodbye and Ebony returned to her hotel.

"Mr Pike, its Cindy from Rushmore and Cooper I have just received an e-mail offering the full asking price from Houghton and sons in Manhattan. Also Miss Marshall has offered the full asking price this morning," said Cindy feeling pleased with herself at the commission she would earn from the sale.

"Cindy, please enquire if any of the parties are willing to increase their offer. I will accept the highest bid."

Matthew was absorbed in the photo album he had borrowed from his father when Joe came into the lounge.

"Dad what photos are these?" he said as he leaned over his father's shoulder to look at them.

"They are your grandparents. I never had time to look at them before it is very interesting. I thought I might check out our family tree." Joe was surprised at his father showing interest in their ancestors it pleased him. He felt as if they were building bridges having something in common. "Well I will help with some research," said Joe.

Matthew's mobile rang, "Mr Houghton, this is Thomas from Rushmore and Cooper's in Charleston. We have had another full asking price offer for Cotton Wood Plantation, would you like to up your offer?"

"Yes I would like to offer more please let me know from the owner what would be enough to secure the property, thank you Thomas." Matthew had decided he must have Cotton Wood Plantation and would pay whatever he needed to get it. Joe's voice broke through his thoughts.

"Dad, I would like to invite a friend of mine home for dinner one evening?"

"Sure, son, you know you can have as many friends as you want round."

"It's, my girl friend Sara; I would like her to meet you." Matthew ruffled Joe's hair in fun.

"My son, is growing up, you kept that quiet I look forward to meeting her."

Joe was in love, every waking moment was of Sara, she was the one!

They had so much in common, their love of music in particular. Her father was a preacher in the African American church and her mother and father both helped at the election office down town, where they had first met.

He had been seeing her for a year, he so wanted to get her an engagement ring. He wanted to show her his commitment as Sara would be going to College in the fall for a year. He would start working for his grandfathers company and when Sara had gained her accountancy qualifications, they would get married. They had spent many hours planning their future together.

Joe had spent some time preparing a meal for her, he wanted it to go well it was important that his father approved of her and that Sara liked his father. The answer phone was flashing, Joe pressed play—Son I will be a little late but please start your meal and I will be back as soon as the meeting finishes. Well that is a good start to the evening, how many times had that happened to him in his life. The time's he had missed his part in a school play or his solo performance in a concert. This was a very important evening for him and yet again, he felt those pangs of disappointment at being let down by his father.

Sara snuggled up to Joe on the sofa; he was showing her the family photo album. "I am so nervous I do hope your father will like me."

"Sara, he will love you as I do," replied Joe reassuring her with a kiss.

Matthew kept trying Ebony's mobile number with no success. He loved her with an intensity he had never felt before, why will she not answer his phone calls. He grabbed his brief case and car keys and headed for the lift. His mobile rang "Mr Matthew Houghton?"

"Yes speaking" Matthew replied.

"It is Thomas from Rushmore and Cooper. You will be pleased to know your offer has been accepted for the purchase of Cotton Wood Plantation."

"Thank you so much," said Matthew, he could not stop smiling as he drove home.

As Matthew rushed through the front door, he called out. "Sorry I am late." He entered the dining room to find them eating. Joe jumped up from the table. "Dad I would like to introduce, Sara." Matthew tried to control his facial expressions as he looked at Sara, he had no idea that his son would bring home a black girl. He knew his son would be watching him carefully.

"I am pleased to meet you Sara." Joe touched Sara's hand to reassure her. Matthew could tell his son had fallen hard for this girl, but this was not what he had mapped out for him for the future. He would one day own the family business and there was no place for a black girl bringing his grandchildren into the family. Matthew knew he would have to deal with the situation carefully—perhaps it might fizzle out, he hoped.

Matthew sat in his study checking his e-mails when the house phone rang, "Mr Houghton speaking."

"Your diamond ring is ready for collection, Sir."

"I think you have the wrong number," said Matthew.

"Mr Joe Houghton, that's the name and phone number left on the order form to ring when it was ready for collection." Matthew gathered his thoughts.

"Thank you, yes." He placed the phone down and put his head in his hands.

At dinner, Matthew approached Joe about the engagement ring.

"Son, there was a message for you to collect a diamond ring from Benedict the jewellers in town. "Joe did not know what to say to his father. He was hoping to tell his dad his intentions once he had proposed to Sara.

"Dad, I love her and we plan to marry once Sara has her qualifications in a couple of years."

"Son, you are far too young, you have all of your life ahead of you to be thinking of engagement and marriage, trust me I know."

"Are you sure, it is not because she is an African American, dad? "Matthew went quiet.

"I will be honest with you, son, we need to shake off our heritage and be proud to be white as that's where we need to be to be placed in the upper echelons of the business world"

"I knew you could not have changed, dad, well I am proud to be African American and I am going to get engaged and married to Sara, I do not want or need your approval."

"You will do as I ask or you can leave and lose my financial support." Matthew shouted losing his temper. "I will prove you wrong, dad, I will move out tomorrow." Joe slammed the front door behind him.

Matthew felt down hearted after his row with his son and decided he would take leave and go to South Carolina and organise the restoration of Cotton Wood Plantation. He was looking forward to seeing his investment.

The next morning at work Matthew went to see his father.

"Dad, I'm taking some time off, I need a break. I have bought a property in Charleston South Carolina it is a good opportunity, we can use the building as a hotel with an adjoining golf complex, plus a conference centre. It's beautiful, I'll show you when I have it restored. It is special dad, all will be explained when it is completed and I take you to see it."

"Well I have a meeting planned next week to inform staff that we are now the sole owners, I would have liked you present, son?"

"Dad I really need this break."

"Ok son if you must."

Mathew landed and collected his rental car at the airport and went to the Realtors in Charleston to collect the keys for Cotton Wood Plantation.

"Here are the keys, Mr Houghton, may I ask what you intend to do with it?"

"Restore the house and out buildings."

"That is good to hear as Cotton Wood Plantation has played such a big part in this area's history for centuries."

"Do you have the names of builders I could contact? I need them to be reliable as I will have to leave them to get on with the work while I am absent," said Matthew. He observed the name badge of the man he was speaking to in the office . . . ah, Thomas, we spoke on the phone."

"Here we are, Sir, this is the number of my brother he owns a large building company, your property will be safe in his hands," Matthew smiled and said "Thank you, good day."

As Matthew sat in his hotel bedroom, his thoughts returned to Joe, he gave him another call, why was not he returning his calls. Matthew felt unhappy everything was going wrong in his life.

Matthew was looking forward to seeing Cotton Wood Plantation, as he had bought it from pictures on the internet.

Wow! Thought Matthew as he drove down the avenue of oak tree and caught the first sight of the plantation house.

Larry the builder, Thomas's brother was waiting for him outside the house. They toured the front of the building when a voice interrupted their conversation.

"Mr Houghton?"

"Yes." Matthew turned round and faced a black, spotty, scruffy young man.

"My name is Seb Pike; Cotton Wood Plantation has been in our family for centuries. It should be my mother's after my grandfather dies, but he wants' nothing to do with us. I need money for my mother's medical bills; I think you rightly owe my mother." Seb was high from drugs, which he took to take away the pain of the situation he found himself in."

"Son, you best leave or I will call the sheriff," said Matthew, but he quietly felt sorry for the boy."

"Mr Houghton," interrupted Larry, "I'll take care of him he is always hanging around here as it was his grandfather's house. He isn't right in the head everyone in Charleston tolerates Seb for the sake of Rebecca his mother, who is terminally ill." He took hold of Seb and escorted him up the avenue.

Ebony returned to work after her trip to see Cotton Wood Plantation.

"You have a meeting with John Houghton at 10am in the board room, and Laura's on line one for you, shall I put her through?" asked Julie standing in for Laura while she was on leave. "Yes please Julie and I don't want to be disturbed." Hello Laura how are things?"

"Ebony, I wanted you to know the sheriff has had a tip off. Apparently someone recognised the pictures we distributed of Jennifer she has been seen in the docks area," said Laura, excitedly.

They are searching the area; we are just praying we can get her home safely."

"Well that sounds positive," said Ebony. "I have to rush I have a meeting at ten, Laura, please let me know if there are any further developments." and put the phone down.

She grabbed her file and pressed the lift for floor twelve, the doors opened and she met Elaine from marketing. "I wonder what this meeting is about, I hope it doesn't take too long because I have a plane to catch at one o'clock. Good trip to South Carolina?" she said to Ebony. "No not really, the property I wanted someone else got there first."

"Never mind these things are meant for a reason," Elaine replied. Ebony did not want to talk about her private business too much, as lovely as Elaine was she was inclined to gossip.

All the other heads of departments sat around the boardroom table, Ebony joined them, no sooner had she sat down than John Houghton entered. "I will get straight to the point; I have bought Mr Druitt's shares in the business. As I am sure, you are aware Mr Druitt is in poor health, and wishes to retire. You will receive new-headed stationery in a few days. Keep the good work up everyone." With that, he got up and left the room.

"Well he has been ill for months what with his chemotherapy he needs to rest," said Cary from payroll. Ebony had always liked Mr Druitt he was the opposite of John Houghton a gentle spoken man, kind and always stopped to speak to her, showing interest in her work—she would miss him.

He was protective of his son Hugh, who was withdrawn and did not like to socialise, in all the years she had worked there he had never spoken to her; he just stayed in his office. Unlike Matthew who liked to be actively involved in the work place. He was always the life and soul of a party everyone loved him including her. Those smiles of his melted her heart in seconds. She was finding it difficult to keep her feelings in check, it would not work she told herself, they were worlds apart. Her mobile rang it was Matthew calling. Does he not get the message, she thought as she turned her phone off. She had not answered any of his phone calls or looked at any of his text messages for days, and she must not weaken.

Why will she not answer my call's said a frustrated Matthew as he sat in a cab on the way home from the airport. Perhaps he might see her tomorrow at work, if she will talk to him.

Josie was busy with a visitor when she noticed Hugh Druitt pass through reception. She thought that he was probably getting some items from his office as he had a box in his arms. Hugh took the lift to the top floor to John Houghton's office and passed his secretary Betsey's room, she was too busy with a phone call to notice him. He opened John's door, he was sitting at his desk dealing with paperwork. He looked up with a surprised look on his face, "Good morning Hugh, I was not expecting to see you today." Hugh shut the door behind him and moved closer to John's desk, not saying anything. John felt uneasy.

"Look I am busy perhaps we could schedule a meeting for another day, I will call Betsy to arrange a time for a chat." Hugh placed the box on John's desk.

"There is a bomb inside this box," John could hear the ticking.

"Call your son in here—Now!" said Hugh. John's hands were sweating as he picked up the phone. "Betsey, call my son to my office—immediately!" Hugh drew a gun from his pocket, and pointing it at John said, "Move over there into the corner away from the door." John did as he was told. Matthew entered his dad's office. "Oh my God what's going on, dad? He said seeing Hugh with a gun pointed at his father." Matthew's heart was pounding in his chest.

"Shut the door," said Hugh in a firm voice.

"He has a bomb in that box, Matthew," said his father as sweat ran down his flushed face. Matthew had to think quickly. Hugh's voice quivered as he spoke. "You always thought you were better than me, well who's in control now? You treated my father as a second-class partner, and you just dismissed his input into the company. And when he was ill you trod all over him to get the company for yourself."

Hugh shook nervously and shifted uneasily from one foot to the other.

"I lost the woman I loved because of this company and now I am going to lose my father while you sit in your ivory tower and sip champagne to celebrate your success and our loss. Well there will be no winners here today. You and your staff will die together here in the next . . .

Hugh looked at his watch. Matthew dived for the gun, a scuffle ensued and the gun went off. Matthew's father fell to the ground grabbing his stomach. Hugh ran for the door, Matthew gripped him by his jacket, threw him to the floor and pinned him down. Betsey heard the gun shot and rushed through the office door, Matthew shouted to her. "Get security, call an ambulance for my father and evacuate the building," he shouted at her. Betsey stood on the spot dazed.

"Move: woman!" Matthew commanded. At this point Hugh capitulated and just laid there in the foetal position crying.

The cold wind chilled their bones as the Staff waited outside for clearance to re-enter the building. Ebony asked Jane if she knew what was happening. "Well, Susan from the mailroom was on the top floor making deliveries, when security rushed passed her into Mr Houghton's office. Betsey was distressed and there was a mention of a gun apparently, Matthew Houghton tackled the gunman.

"Oh my God was Matthew injured!" Ebony was beside herself with worry. "Apparently John Houghton has been shot." Jane said as she joined the conversation.

Her first thought was to be with Matthew, but then decided he had enough to deal with, he would ring her if he needed her.

Matthew left a message on his son's mobile; telling him his grandfather was in the city hospital and that he would meet him there.

"Mr Houghton," the nurse called out, and escorted him to the surgeon's office. "Please sit down; I believe you are Mr Houghton's son?"

"Yes,"-replied Matthew.

"Your father is gravely ill you must prepare yourself, he may not pull through. The next twenty four hours will be critical, he is in intensive care." There was a knock on the door, it was a nurse accompanied by Joe. "Your son, I believe."

"I will have to go, but please use my office for a few minutes if you would like to," said the surgeon, Matthew thanked him.

"Dad, what happened?" Matthew explained. Joe sat stunned "Granddad will pull through—won't he, dad?" looking at his father for reassurance. Matthew put his arm round him.

"The next twenty four hours will be critical if he is to pull through son, please come home I really could do with your support right now." Joe looked at his father's face he had never seen him look so lost. "You know I will."

Matthew lay on his bed he could not hold back the tears any longer, they poured down his face. His thoughts went to the things he had never said to his father. It was a different generation; his father had never shown him the affection he needed. He would have given anything, if only he had hugged him when he left home for boarding school. His father's driver would place his cases down next to him, and then he would shake his hand and drive away. He felt abandoned and unloved. His mother never visited him because she was ill, that is what his father told him, but he knew it was because she was always drunk. She found it difficult to live with a cold man incapable of emotion, and who was obsessed with power and success. He often heard her crying. His father was not the type to marry, but he needed an heir. Matthew swore he would never make that mistake with his son.

Chapter Eighteen

"Ebony, its Matthew I expect you heard through work that my father is seriously ill in hospital. I really would appreciate a call from you." He hoped she would reply he needed to feel her arms around him right now. Oh, dad you must make it. I still need you and always will, Matthew said. He was not religious, but he put his hands together and prayed for his father's recovery, since he did not know what else to do. If only he could tell him, how much he loved him.

Matthew and Joe drove in silence to the hospital immersed in their own thoughts. Matthew was so glad his son was with him.

"Could you please tell me how my father John Houghton is?" The nurse looked on her screen.

"If you take a seat, Sir, I will get Doctor Fuller to see you." They paced up and down the corridor, how Matthew hated hospitals at least his father had private care, the best money could buy.

"Good morning, Mr Houghton, your father has had a difficult night. We managed to stabilise him, he is not out of the woods yet, we will obviously ring you if things change for the worse.

"Nurse, please would you show Mr Houghton and his son to Mr Houghton's senior's bed side. "Matthew and Joe gowned up."

"Here are some swabs to dip in water to freshen your grandfather's mouth, replace the oxygen facemask when you have done it," said the nurse handing the bowl to Joe.

His Grandfather looked so lifeless and vulnerable. Joe had always seen him as strong and invincible, this frail old man could not be his grandfather. Matthew saw his father connected up to a life support machine. There were tubes everywhere, bleepers and monitors lit up. He laid there still, not a flicker, just the noise of the machines keeping him alive. Matthew moved to the side of his bed, while Joe went to the other. His father's breathing was laboured, Matthew could see how his son was trying to hold it together. Matthew took hold of his father's hand "Dad, its Matthew and Joe, now draw on that strong will of yours, fight we need you." Matthew choked as the emotion swelled up inside him. Joe had never seen his father speak to his granddad so intimately before.

"Granddad its Joe, I need you to get better so you can teach me all you know about your business, so you can be proud of me when I work beside you and dad." Each word was broken with emotion. Joe held his hand stroking it, remembering how his granddad showed him a softness he did not show his father. Joe removed his facemask and took the cloth from the bowl to cool his grandfather's face. Matthew took a swab, dipped it in the water, and carefully wiped around his mouth. As the water ran down his throat his father swallowed, which gave them hope, as at least he was responding. They had hoped for a response, a flicker of the eye, anything that said he was still alive.

"Son, go and get yourself a coffee, you need a break."

"Ok I won't be long, would you like one?"

"No" Matthew replied, Joe shut the door behind him. Matthew needed time alone with his father. Matthew knew that his father was in his seventies; he did not want to lose him. When he recovers, I need to spend time with him, get to know him better he thought. Mathew leaned closer, hoping his father might hear him. "Dad I know you were unable to tell me you loved me. You showed it by working long hours building a business for me to inherit. I need you to know how much I love you. Please let me know you hear me, please," he said desperately.

"I love you, dad," he said as he stroked his face. Matthew was heartbroken he was not ready to lose his father. They had years ahead to work together and enjoy the rewards of his hard work.

Matthew jumped to the noise of the loud buzzer on the monitor. Then the lights started to flash continuously, Matthew saw his father's body jerk. The nurse rushed in followed by Dr Fuller, who started resuscitation while the nurse connected him to the cardiac machine. Matthew stood in the corner of the room as they tried to resuscitate him but he was gone. It was as if he was outside his body watching his father leave him again, as he did at boarding school all those years ago. "Dad I need you please, you can't die," begged Matthew.

The ride home was silent both dealing with the shock. Matthew put his arm around his son, Joe sobbed into his father's shoulder. When they got back to their apartment Mathew said, "I am going to my room son, I need to be alone." He checked his messages and was pleased to see one from Ebony. He opened it up as he climbed onto his bed. "I am here for you ring me." Matthew found his mobile and rang her. "Ebony, I am so pleased you left a message, my father has just passed away and I am lost, "said a broken-hearted Matthew.

"Oh Matthew, I am so sorry, believe me I understand how you are feeling right now."

"I have been so foolish and stubborn, can we meet and talk the issue through," he said. There was silence. "You have a lot going on at the moment Matthew, with the loss of your father, the funeral, helping your son and the business, we can talk later"

"Ebony, please come to the funeral my father thought very highly of you."

"If you want me to, I will be there," she hesitated but I think we should give each other space for a while, you have the business to see to now and you need a clear head," she paused . . . Ok?"

Matthew's heart sunk at her negative response.

"If that is what you want," he replied.

"I think it would be best," said Ebony. She put her mobile down on the kitchen table, she was shaking, she could have taken advantage of Matthew's vulnerability, but she loved him too much. He would need to concentrate on the family business now he was the owner. It was a big responsibility. She wanted him to want her when he was in control and certain of his feelings. Moreover, she needed to know that he was one hundred percent sure that he wanted her.

It was early February, there was a chill in the air, Matthew, and Joe put on their warm over coats and settled down in the limousine to go to the church. A car was collecting Matthew's ex-wife from the airport and she would join the cortege from the office.

Senita, Matthew's ex-wife climbed into the limousine, kissed her son and placed her hand on Matthews shoulder. "I was sorry to hear about your father's death Matthew, please accept my condolences." He nodded and continued to look out of the car window, he did not wish to talk to her, especially today.

All the staff lined up outside the office building, to pay their respects. Ebony watched the burial service keeping at the back of the mourners. This stunning woman stood next to Matthew and Joe, it had to be his ex-wife. She was elegant with long, flowing, dark hair. Ebony felt very frumpy against her, it was probably best that they were cooling things down between them. She was not in the same league as his ex.

She loved him and needed to let him go to be able to marry someone in his world.

Matthew spotted her in the crowd of mourners. "Ebony, thank you for coming," he looked into her deep brown eyes wanting so much to hold her tight. Ebony's heart leapt at the sight of him, I must be strong and not weaken, she told herself. "I said I would come."

"Please meet me we need to talk about our future."

"There cannot be any future now you have a family business to run which will take all your time and energy. You do not need any distractions and I cannot do the friend thing, so it is best we avoid each other at work. I will look for another position; it's for the best, Matthew." He watched her walk away. The pain was unbearable, another person deserting him he thought."

Chapter Nineteen

⚜

T he phone rang waking Ebony. She fumbled for her mobile phone as she squinted to look at the time on her projector clock, which was showing 5 am in bold red numbers on her ceiling.

"Ebony Marshall, speaking." she said in a sleepy voice.

"Ebony, Jennifer has been found," said an excited Laura." The sheriff has just rung me to say she was found in a warehouse at the docks."

"What wonderful news."

"Apparently she was being held with a group of children ready for transport by ship to countries well known for child trafficking. The sheriff is questioning the group. Thank God, she is unharmed. I am sorry it's so early but you did say to let you know if there was any news," said an elated Laura.

"I am so pleased you did, I will let everyone at work know. Rest now and we'll speak soon, God bless." Placing her mobile down, she rolled over into her favourite sleeping position and thought how the outcome could have been so different.

There was a phone call for Mathew from John Sacks Solicitors. "Matthew there will be a reading of your fathers Will at 10 am tomorrow in my office." and the phone went dead. Matthew thought his father's choice of solicitor was strange as John Sacks was always abrupt and had little in the way of people skills.

The next day Matthew and Joe sat in the reception of John Sacks Solicitors. Gloria the receptionist placed her hand on Matthews shoulder and said, "I was so very sad to hear that your dear father had passed away." Gloria was in her mid sixties and always had a warm smile particularly for Matthew's father; everyone thought she had a soft spot for him. Matthew gave her a peck on the cheek as she showed them into Mr Sack's office. As far as he was concerned, Gloria was the best asset the business had. John Sacks looked over his glasses and said. "We will commence the reading of the Will as soon as everyone is present." Joe looked at his father and whispered. "What does he mean dad who else would be coming?" Matthew looked at his son and shrugged his shoulders. The door flung open and in came an African American male in his late forties, with a confident stance and said "My meeting overran, have I missed anything?" and sat down next to Matthew.

"Sir, I do not like my time wasted, the reading was scheduled for 10 and you are late," said Mr Sacks angrily. John Sacks unfolded the Will in front of him and started to read it. "I leave my classic car collection and a yearly allowance to my grandson Joseph Houghton. To my son Matthew Houghton I leave my apartments in London and Manhattan also the businesses in London and New York that he helped me set up, also an annual sum of half a million dollars. The remainder of my estate, the family business and my personal fortune go to my eldest son Lucas Houghton.

Matthew stood up "This cannot be right, I am the only son."

Mr Sacks interceded, "I was present when your father wrote his Will and I have a copy of his eldest son's birth certificate. I have paid regularly into an account for Lucas Houghton since his birth for his upbringing and education. There is no doubt this is your elder brother, replied John Sacks.

"Well bro it's great to finally meet you," said Lucas putting his hand out to shake Matthew's. He was astounded at this revelation and found it hard to comprehend; he was in shock and needed a drink. Propping up the bar in the Damnson club down town, Matthew drowned his sorrows. Why did his father do this to him? He had spent all his life, thinking he was the only child when in fact he had a brother. He was now going to lose his father's business that he had always thought was his to inherit and pass onto his son. He would have to concentrate his efforts on what was left of his business empire. The world that he thought was his had evaporated in an instant in favour of Lucas, he drank to block out his loss.

Six months had passed since Ebony had seen Matthew. She had busied herself travelling on business and had sold her flat. She was now living at the beach house, which gave her comfort. Ebony thought it would be easier if she left Houghton and Son, and applied for senior positions in many high profile companies.

She answered a call on her mobile "Cindy, how nice to hear from you."

"I have some interesting properties that I thought you might be interested in."

"No Cindy I only wanted Cotton Wood Plantation, I just could not find the extra money to secure it," replied Ebony.

"I am so sorry you missed out on buying it. The new owners are restoring the plantation house; it must be costing a small fortune. I was in the area and had a peek."

"Well I am pleased it is being saved, thank you once again for your help, Cindy." Ebony was green with envy at someone else living in Cotton Wood Plantation.

She clicked on a red-flagged e-mail. Please attend the yearly directors meeting in Florida 1-8th June. This was always an opportunity for the directors to let their hair down. Last year it was in Vegas, although they had to consider the company's performance over the year they still had fun, and stayed in the best hotels.

Her heart was not in it, she would make an excuse. Ebony sent her reply to personnel. In her messages that afternoon was an e-mail from Henry head of H.R. Please note all directors will attend the yearly meeting on 1-8th June. Damn thought Ebony.

All discussion seemed to centre on the Directors yearly meeting. All Jane head of accounts talked about was what she was going to buy to wear for the trip. The last thing Ebony wanted was to spend a week confined to a hotel conference room with Matthew. It would be too painful.

An urgent e-mail flashed on Ebony's laptop, she was busy finishing replies to the markets. She clicked on the message. The hotel for the yearly Directors meeting has been over booked. We have now booked The Royal Hotel Charleston South Carolina the dates remain unchanged.

Ebony did a double take. "Laura, would you please check this message is correct?"

"Yes it is I heard Glenda and Lloyd in contracts discussing it at lunch time in the canteen."

On the aircraft heading for South Carolina, Ebony was fortunate to have an empty seat next to her and was able to stretch out and relax. The two seats either side of the aisle where empty, which was great, a quiet trip ahead for her she thought. She settled down and started to read the new novel she had purchased in the airport. "Is it good?" enquired a tall black, handsome man. He sat down in one of the seats on the opposite side of the aisle. She blushed at the way he made her feel by his presence. "I will tell you at the end of the flight," she replied coolly. She buried her head in her book ending the conversation.

Ebony thought she might have a refreshing bath before the pre-meeting dinner. It was a lovely hotel, not as hot as when she was here last, thank goodness she thought. She recalled how she had been overcome by the heat when she last viewed Cotton Wood Plantation. Her heart sank as she thought how close she had been in buying the property and how easily it could have been hers!

Chapter Twenty

Transport was organised for the Directors to go to their meeting. Ebony went to reception to find that they had already left the building. She checked her paper work, which clearly said nine thirty. She looked at her watch, which said nine twenty she was early. What is going on?

"Madam" said the receptionist and pointed at the clock in the foyer that clearly said nine forty five. "You have just missed it, let me get you a cab," she said as she picked up the desk phone. Ebony's watch obviously needed a new battery. Feeling foolish, she waited for the cab.

She got in, it was a beautiful morning, and she sat reading her notes, she was so engrossed in them, that she did not realise she had reached her destination. "Maim, we are here! Ebony said Wow! How different this looks, it was a derelict building last time that I saw it. "Yes," said the cab driver, it had been derelict for years and has now been renovated to become a conference centre." Ebony looked up to see her beloved Cotton Wood Plantation, how beautiful she now looked. It brought tears to her eyes. She sat in a state of shock. Why would they hold the meeting here, it is too much of a coincidence? She thanked the driver, stood, and looked up at the building. Her eyes ran over the front of the house she felt such a strong attachment to it. She entered the front door.

"Hello, Ebony, where did you get to?" You are the last one to arrive, said Carol from HR.

"Everyone's having a tour of the plantation if you hurry you can catch them."

"I'll stay here and read through my notes, thanks," she did not feel like explaining why she had missed the transport.

"Well there is coffee in the Ballroom help yourself, I won't keep you company I'm off to view the plantation with the rest of them," Carol said as she shut the door behind her.

Ebony's body tingled with excitement as she toured the house, the care and detail given to every aspect showed someone else loved this house as much as she did.

She stood for a while savouring the beauty of the grand staircase and the crystal chandelier hanging from the hallway ceiling. It sparkled with the sun's rays that flooded through the windows. Her eyes caught the heavy oak carved door of the study, how well she remembered rubbing her hand over the layers of dust to look at its exquisite carvings. How beautiful the door looked now. Ebony took hold of the ornate door handle and turned it in anticipation she was not disappointed. The sun shone through the windows onto the cleaned and restored writing desk still in its original position. The walls had dark wood cladding half way up and finished in flocked golden wallpaper.

Carol found Ebony and said, "They are on their way back from the tour of the plantation, and you can join them in the conference room." Ebony followed her and took her seat at the conference table in the ballroom. The other Directors joined her. Ebony was glancing around the beautifully restored room when in walked a woman in her late forties. She was a red head, obviously tinted Ebony observed, with a skirt she considered was far too short for a woman of her age. She sat down next to an empty chair at the head of the table. Then in followed a man she recognised as the person on the plane. He smiled and introduced himself as Lucas Houghton, President of Houghton and Son. Silence fell in the room. Murmurs of "Where was Matthew?" and "Where did this other son come from?" passed around the room. Ebony now knew why Matthew was not here.

Lucas managed to charm everyone and at coffee break, there was a real buzz of excitement from the Directors. A hand on her shoulder made her jump she turned to find Lucas Houghton.

"Ebony, I hear from HR you are about to leave us, we cannot have that, we need high achievers to push the business forward. Jane my PA will ring you to arrange a meeting to see if we can entice you to stay with the company." She felt everyone's eyes on her as she blushed, flattered by his attention.

The phone rang in Ebony's hotel room, she stepped out of her bath, and by the time she managed to get a towel around her, the phone had stopped ringing. "Blast," she said. She could see that someone had left a message by the flashing red light. She pressed the button to find it was Jane, Lucas's PA. "Mr Houghton, would like to meet you this evening eight thirty in the Study of Cotton Wood Plantation, a car will collect you." the phone went dead. The cheek of it she thought. Well Ebony concluded he still paid her wages, so with mixed feelings she got ready.

The smart business dress or the feminine flowery dress, she changed several times.

Don't be silly she told herself, he would not be interested in her. So she put on her smart business dress and tied her hair up, wishing she had time to have washed it.

Ebony knocked on the study door she was feeling very nervous. She was cross with herself for feeling this way. For goodness sake, she told herself she hardly knew the man. A voice replied, "Come in." Lucas was sitting at the desk by the window working on some papers in front of him. Ebony thought how rude it was of him to use someone else's desk. "Ebony, how good of you to come I won't be a moment," and carried on with the paper work. How dare he make me wait she thought? Her eyes ran over the room she marvelled at the transformation of the study.

"Come let me show you this amazing house," he said pointing to the door to the hallway. Ebony wanted to tell him to go to hell but curiosity won, so she followed him. As she climbed the grand staircase she felt the velvet feel of the banisters, quite different from the last time she walked upstairs with Cindy. Lucas showed her one of the bedrooms. "This wooden cladding revealed some interesting artefacts in this bedroom when the house was renovated," said Lucas. He rolled out a canvas, Ebony's eyes lit up when she saw a portrait of a young African American woman. She had beautiful dark brown eyes and held a baby in each arm. The babies were about the same size that suggested they were twins. At her feet sat, a boy aged about six years old cuddling a dog. What struck Ebony was that one baby was white and the other black. "There was a journal also. "Whoever it was wanted to keep them out of someone else's hands no doubt, and they succeeded," said Lucas. If only she could get her hands on the journal it could fill in some of her unanswered questions thought Ebony.

As he showed her the rest of the house, Ebony was amazed at how beautiful the building was. Lucas touched her arm. "I have a table booked in Charleston you must be hungry? I know I am." Without a reply, he opened the front door and a chauffeur was holding the car door for her, Ebony had no option but to get in.

Chapter Twenty-One

Lucas turned intently and said "Well to business. I am looking for a competent individual to act as Chief Executive for Overseas Business. I believe you have had a great deal of experience in this area and would be the ideal candidate. I have read your personal file and with your knowledge and experience, you could drive my business forward. There would be a larger office, a new car of your choice and a generous salary with bonuses. "What do you say?" Ebony was overwhelmed at his offer he certainly knew how to make a woman feel good.

"Well I need time to think this through."

"Take your time, Ebony; I will contact you when I return from my business trip to Columbia."

"Thank you, Lucas, for the kind offer of a meal, but I am tired and would prefer to go back to my hotel. Please thank the owner for my tour of Cotton Wood Plantation it was very interesting. They have indeed made an excellent job of the renovation," she said.

"You can thank him personally by accepting his offer of the position of Chief Executive for Overseas Business, reporting to me."

"You own! Cotton Plantation?" said Ebony with utter surprise.

"Yes I do, I intend to hire the house out for events, broadening the company's portfolio.

A striking building don't you think?" he replied. The car stopped and Ebony stunned by his reply got out of the car and went into the hotel. She made it to her room before what he had said had sunk in.

It was stuffy and hot in her room. She put on the air conditioning, stripped of to her underwear, and lay on the bed watching the fan turn above her head, enjoying the sweep of cooling air as it caught her body. Her mind was racing; she lay there pondering what Lucas had told her that he was now the owner of Cotton Wood Plantation, the mystery man she competed against for the purchase. In addition, what about the items found hidden behind the wooden cladding in the bedroom. The painting of Beth and her children, she knew of Will, but twins and one white, she needed to see the journal. Somehow, Ebony could not imagine Lucas putting his soul into the restoration of Cotton Wood Plantation. He did not strike her as having the depth of feeling necessary to put that much care and attention into the building.

"Mr McNally, this is Matthew Houghton, you have been highly recommended to me. I need a solicitor who can contest my father's Will. I would like to move on this matter as soon as possible," he said. He spent time explaining the situation to the solicitor, he was satisfied that following their conversation there were grounds to challenge the will. How could his father do this to him and his grandson? Matthew needed Ebony, where was she? He never felt so low.

Ebony had taken the position offered to her by Lucas. She was arranging her new office, when Laura her secretary whom she had insisted came with her, knocked on her office door,

"Lucas Houghton, to see you," said Laura.

"How are you settling in?" Lucas asked as he perched himself on her desk.

"Well, thank you," she replied. Ebony thought how dishy he looked in his Valentino suit.

"Good to hear. I have booked a table for dinner tonight I would very much like you to join me this evening," he said as he hovered at Ebony's door waiting for her reply.

"I would love to, but I cannot be late as I have a flight early tomorrow," said Ebony.

"I am impressed, Ebony, that you are getting down to business so quickly."

On her return from her business trip, she was feeling jetlagged and in need of caffeine; she paid for her latte from the street vender and with briefcase in hand walked towards her office building. She was pleased with the orders she had gained, she hoped Lucas would feel he had chosen the right person for the job. She smiled as she turned the corner. She could not believe her eyes, there sitting by the window in Luigi's Restaurant was Matthew and a younger women. She was very elegant, they were talking and laughing seemingly lost in their own world. Ebony walked past quickly hoping he would not see her. That was—their table where they always sat before going to work, how could he do that to her. Her tears fell uncontrollably down her cheek. "Get a grip of yourself; you should be pleased he is moving on, she told herself."

The orders where rolling in and Lucas had given Ebony a pay rise for achieving her targets. He made her the centre of attention at work involving her in many projects. She heard the rumours about them circulating the office but to her the truth was, he was just the boss, this was a business relationship only and she felt nothing else for him. However, they spent many hours in each other's company at dinner with clients or travelling together on business. He was handsome, charismatic and intellectual with the most amazing body. She found herself looking forward to seeing him, and disappointed if he did not accompany her at business meetings.

Ping, an e-mail from Lucas, Ebony opened it. Miss Marshall please bring me your Quarterly report, I need to go through it with you before our meeting tomorrow. I will be back in my office at seven pm. Lucas.

Ebony usually worked late. Everyone had left the office she appreciated the quiet time, which helped her to concentrate on the important paper work.

She glanced at her watch it was six forty five. Ebony took her handbag, went to the cloakroom, and tied back her hair with a pretty clip. She retouched her makeup, and sprayed some of her favourite perfume over her white blouse. She was so pleased she kept a supply of essential items in her office drawer, for those trips when she came straight from the airport to the office.

Having brushed her teeth, she scrutinised her appearance. She felt she was attractive and had curves in the right places. He would never be interested in her. Ebony felt she needed a relationship to take away the pain of losing Matthew. She sighed as she walked along the deserted dimly lit corridor to the lift. Lucas's office was on the top floor.

Ebony was feeling anxious but also excited at seeing him, especially alone. She was so attracted to him. He was not her type but she was spell bound. She could see the light was on in his office as she alighted from the lift. Her heart was pounding. She knocked on his office door and then straightened her blouse.

There was a pause; she was just about to knock again when he called.

"Come in?"

She found him at his desk he had removed his jacket, tie, and was looking very relaxed.

"The report you requested Lucas." Ebony handed it to him. Without a word, he took it and started to read it and then picking up a red pen started to correct parts of it. She felt awkward standing there as if she was back at school for he had never corrected her work before.

Lucas picked up her report and while still reading went to his office door and locked it and as he returned he said to Ebony. "Miss Marshal—bend over my desk." She wondered whether she had heard him correctly. Ebony hesitated.

"Do as I ask," he said in a commanding tone.

She instinctively did as he said placing her hands on his desk. She thought her heart would burst it was pounding so hard. Ebony knew that by the look in Lucas's eyes he wanted her yes—HER!

Ebony could not believe what was happening to her. She knew one thing she did not want him to stop.

Lucas then ran his fingers tantalizingly up her legs and reaching her thong slipped it down.

Ebony felt exposed with desire; she so wanted him.

He caressed her neck with his full generous lips, she moaned with delight. She was getting to the point of no return.

He removed her hair clip and her hair tumbled down around her shoulders.

Lucas grabbed her hair she was his. He entered her to screams of sheer delight and acceptance that she had at last what she wanted—Lucas."

Lucas turned her round and laid her on his desk knocking his paperwork onto the floor.

He kissed her passionately, slipped her skirt off, and undid her blouse revealing her breasts; he fondled them and slid his silky smooth tongue slowly down her curvaceous body.

"Your bodies beautiful" he said. Did she hear him correctly; was he talking about her—body? What he was doing with his tongue sent her into orbit, she did not want it to stop.

"Please, please!" Ebony let out a cry of anticipation, which reverberated around his office. Her legs could hardly hold her as he helped her off his desk, he whispered in her ear.

"Remember more errors—more punishment Miss Marshall.

"I will try not to make any more mistakes, Sir, but I cannot promise." she smiled and adjusted her clothes. "That's what I like, a woman with a sense of humour," he said as he smacked her on the bottom.

Ebony rolled over in Lucas's bed, stretching out to his side of the bed and found it empty.

A note for her was on his pillow. Have a lie in you deserve it; pick you up at eight for dinner. Lucas. Ebony put her head under the sheets, did she really sleep with him. Her body tingled at the thought of last night. This was just what she needed emotionless sex to numb her feelings of missing her dear Matthew. She laid there recalling the great sex she had from last night.

Matthew's son Joe called from the hallway, "Dad."

"I'm in the kitchen, son." Matthew replied. "Fancy some spare ribs and fries for dinner?"

"No thanks I am meeting Sara and her parents, I just popped home to change."

"Getting serious then, son?" Matthew replied.

"Yes, dad, she is the one. I am going to ask her father's permission to marry her, please be happy for me?" Joe said as he touched his father's shoulder in affection.

"Son, I only ever wanted the best for you. Since my father's death, I realise that having a truly strong bond between us is what is important. So yes I am very happy you have found the right woman for you." Joe hugged his dad and went to change. As he was about to leave he said "You know the right woman for you was Ebony, dad. I don't know what happened between you two, but if I were you I would get her back before someone else snaps her up," he gave his father a pat on the back as he went out the door.

"I have a reservation for two, Mr Lucas Houghton," Lucas said to the Maitre de that then showed them to their table. Lucas stopped to talk to a man sitting on his own at a table.

"Well, dear brother, this is a pleasant surprise how's life treating you?" in a sarcastic tone. Matthew ignored him and asked the Maitre de for his bill. Ebony blushed when Lucas put his arm around her and kissed her passionately, this was obviously for Matthew's benefit. She just wanted to curl up and die, poor Matthew.

She knew she had made a big mistake by letting Lucas into her life, how was she going to cool things between them, especially as she had just moved in with him.

The doorbell disturbed Ebony as she was eating her meal. Lucas was away on business and she was chilling out on a take away. Annoyed at being disturbed she answered the door, still keeping the chain on, as she was alone. Ebony peered through the slit in the door.

"Can I speak to Lucas Houghton" said a swarthy man, with weasel like features and with a cold demeanour.

"I'm afraid he is away at present," replied Ebony feeling uncomfortable.

"Can you tell me when he will be back?"

"Tomorrow, who shall I say called?"

"He won't know my name, I will call back." To Ebony's relief he left and she quickly locked her door.

She lay in bed thinking what a fool she had been she would be able to pack and leave while Lucas was away on business. Ebony set about moving her things out of his apartment. She was clearing her clothes from the walk-in wardrobe when she dropped a blue velvet box that held a pair of her diamond stud earrings. The box bounced on the carpet and opened throwing them out. Ebony found one but not the other, she must find it. She loved those earrings they were a gift from her mother. She rummaged around in the back of the wardrobe with no success. Perhaps it had bounced into the opposite wardrobe that held Lucas suits. They were so neat and in colour order with the jackets on top and trousers below. She knelt down and searched the floor inside moving boxes of shoes out of the way, when she felt something fall against her arms. It was a panel that had fallen from the back of the wardrobe. She found where the panel should fit and as she tried to replace it, she saw a laptop in the cavity. Ebony replaced the cover as best she could thinking how strange it was to keep a laptop hidden away, and set about closing her cases and shut the apartment door behind her.

Chapter Twenty-Two

Following Laura's experience, Ebony thought she would ring Joe, to see if he could help her in exposing the evils associated with human trafficking.

"Joe, its Ebony my friend's granddaughter, Jennifer was kidnapped, but thankfully she was found. I felt I needed to do something, so I am thinking of getting like-minded people together to start up a Web site, where we can provide awareness and information concerning Human Trafficking, will you help me?"

"Count me in; I will get my friend Craig, who is a web page designer to set up our site. It is great to hear from you, how have you been? I often think of you."

"Oh fine I miss you to." Ebony was dying to ask Joe how his father was. However, she did not want to hear about his new girlfriend it would be too painful. "Thank you, Joe, we can keep in touch through our e-mails, take care," she said.

Why did I leave it too late Matthew told himself he loved Ebony, why did he fight it. Since his father's death, it had taught him life was too short and that you must grab happiness when it comes along.

Business, money count for nothing if you do not have the one you love by your side. Joe was right someone had snapped her up but why Lucas, he had never felt so low. His family business, Cotton Wood Plantation, his son's future and now the woman he loved. He had taken it all. He poured his fourth whisky and with it in his hand, he sat down, finished the bottle, and then threw his empty glass against the wall in sheer anger.

Joe cleaned the glass up and woke his dad. He had fallen asleep drunk in his chair. "Dad, dad come on let's get you into the shower you'll feel better." Joe was concerned about him; he had never seen him like this before.

Lucas flung his briefcase down loosened his tie and poured a drink, and playfully shouted.

"Come here woman I need to bed you?" as he searched the rooms for Ebony. He went into the bedroom to see if she was in the shower, thinking, what a turn on it would be to join her. No sign of her, and then he noticed all her beauty products were gone, she had not mentioned she had a business trip. He walked into the dressing room and opened her wardrobe to find it empty. Then he saw his wardrobe closed. He never shut it because his suits' were silk and needed air flowing through to keep them in the best condition. Immediately he checked the bottom of his wardrobe, the panel was only slightly ajar but looked ok. He showered and took out his silk dressing gown and leather mules and slipped them on. "Ouch," he said as he took his left mule off his foot, out dropped a diamond earring. He picked it up and looked at it; hesitated for a moment then re-examined the panel and concluded that it had been disturbed Ebony must have found his hiding place. Panic consumed him. Then he noticed a folded piece of paper on his desk and opened it. I am leaving you, sorry, Ebony. Lucas was worried and had to think very carefully as to what to do next. He was playing with fire and he needed to watch his back. He had just crossed a drug baron and they do not play nicely.

Ebony was so angry with herself for having let Lucas into her life. He had swept her off her feet by his charm, the attention and promotion, and it all went to her head. She must put things right with Matthew. Silly, silly women she told herself as she cried herself to sleep.

Laura, Ebony's secretary handed her a letter as she walked into her office the following morning

"Human Resources delivered it by hand," said Laura.

"Thank you," replied Ebony.

Ebony could not believe what she read.—As from today your position of Chief Executive for Overseas Business has been terminated, due to you failure to reach your sales targets. Please vacate your office and return to sales as an assistant manager reporting to Tina Stoppard. You have an appointment at 10 o'clock with Mr Lucas Houghton.

Ebony fell into her chair; her body had gone into shock, she did not think he would be so ruthless and take her job from her. Yes, she had finished their relationship but she thought he was a better man than that. To get back at her through her job, how deluded she had been in believing in him. She looked at her watch 9.15 am. Ebony could feel the shock turning into anger.

How dare he destroy her career in seconds and humiliate her in front of her colleagues. When she thought of all the hard work, she had put into getting the business. Not reaching my targets, how dare he! Well he would see her now—she was ready for him. She barged past Jane.

"Mr Houghton can't see you now." Ebony took no notice and entered his office. "Sorry, Sir, I tried to stop her." "That's ok, Jane; hold all my calls for now, thank you." Jane closed the door. Ebony was furious. "How dare you treat me in this way our relationship I believed had nothing to do with my position in this company. I cannot believe that you would be so petty to do this to me. Ebony's heart was racing she just wanted to lash out at him for being so heartless.

"This meeting is concluded, if you are unhappy with your new position then you can always hand in your notice," he said in a cold and distant manner. Dismissing her, he looked down and continued with his paperwork on his desk. Ebony had never seen him like this before her anger turned to feeling hurt. How could she have allowed herself to be so deceived? She left work for home, parked her car outside the beach house, and descended the steps to the beach through her garden. Walking along the beach always calmed her down. Ebony then sat on her veranda staring out to sea. Ebony thought you will not drive me out Lucas, I will fight back, and if it means stepping backwards in my career then so be it, she said to herself defiantly.

As her mother used to say, today's news would be old news tomorrow She could weather the gossip at work, hold her head high and work hard to repair her damaged reputation, She would now know who her true friends were.

Ebony had an e-mail. Ebony, its Joe Houghton I was wondering if we could meet, we have so much catching up to do. What about Friday at Centuries bar Manhattan say eight o'clock? It will be great to see you again. Hope you can make it."

Dear Joe she thought, how she missed him, it would be good to catch up with his news.

She sat down in a booth at the side of the restaurant, it was ultra modern in design and she had never been there before. She was perusing the menu when she heard the waiter say.

"This is your table Sir." Ebony looked up to see Matthew. She blushed and felt awkward. "Sorry I was supposed to be meeting my son Joe," he said.

"So was I" Ebony replied. They both looked at each other and smiled. "We have been set up, I am so sorry I'll go," Matthew said. How Ebony had missed his amazing smile, it always sent a warm sensation through her body. "No please stay," she said warmly. The waiter took their order, she knew him so well that she knew what his choice would be from the menu. He would order pepper steak with fries and a glass of Chardonnay. The silence at the table was getting uncomfortable, at the same time they said, "How's work" and laughed.

"Don't mention work," said Ebony "My contract with the company was terminated today, because I have not fulfilled my new sales targets. This is so false, as I have secured several large orders. I must not bother you with my problems, I am just so angry," she said.

"I was surprised to see you and Lucas together. I would never have said he was your type." Matthew said as he poured her a glass of wine.

"Well I found out the hard way and have finished our relationship," she said.

"You do realise that's two Houghton's you have discarded." Matthew said with a smile on his face, he held his glass up and said cheers. Ebony clicked his wine glass, she so wanted to tell him how she had missed him. "Here I am telling you my woes, how are things with you?" she said as she leaned towards him. She had forgotten how easy it was to talk to him. With a teasing, smile on his face, Matthew said, "Well now I know you aren't a spy for Lucas, I can tell you I am fighting hard to get the family business back. I have a private detective watching him. I know nothing about him and mean to find out more."

They felt at ease with one another and chatted throughout the meal. "Well thank you for an enjoyable evening but I must go," said Ebony.

"Can I give you a lift home?" said Matthew. He was so hoping she would say yes. Ebony tried to hide her delight at his offer, "yes please."

They laughed and talked about work on the journey back and were soon at Ebony's house.

Matthew opened the car door for Ebony. As she stepped out onto her shingle driveway she lost her balance, Matthew quickly caught her. Ebony could not help herself she kissed him on the lips, with surprise he pulled away. Ebony felt embarrassed saying repeatedly "I am so sorry, of course you already have a partner, please forget what just happened." She searched for her keys in her handbag too embarrassed to look at him. She just wanted to get indoors and hide. Matthew turned her round, lifted her face and said, "I don't have any girlfriend at the moment, I do not know what you have heard?" he said looking puzzled at her.

"I saw you with a woman sitting in Luigi's two weeks ago; you looked very cosy, even sitting in our seats near the window."

"That was Melissa, my Cousin Jay's wife, he asked me to help her with regards to setting up her new P.R business. I invited her to breakfast, as I had no other time free to see her. Yes, it was our table and I must confess I always sit there, hoping you might walk in and order your usual mixed berry smoothie and toasted bagel. He cupped her face—and kissed her. They clung to each other not wanting to let go.

Chapter Twenty-Three

They awoke to a beautiful sunny morning wrapped together in the sheet from the bed. They laughed as they hobbled onto the veranda and looked out to sea. The warm sun touched their bodies. "I am so happy, Matthew, what a fool I have been, you do forgive me-don't you?"

"There is nothing to forgive; I was the fool in not snapping you up before someone else did." Ebony kissed his forehead, eye's and then his mouth and then they lay down on the sofa on the veranda and made love to the sound of the waves.

"Its Saturday tomorrow, why don't we have breakfast at our favourite restaurant Luigi's and then spend the day together at the Hampton's," said Matthew enthusiastically.

Ebony sat at Luigi's at their favourite table by the window. She loved to watch the world go by as she waited for Matthew to arrive. He had just popped into his apartment nearby to get a change of clothes for the day out. When he arrived he stopped to speak to Luigi, the owner, she watched him. To Ebony, he was her perfect man, he had a great sense of humour, and was attentive, valuing what she had to say, and she felt so blessed. Matthew returned and sat down.

"The days I've sat here wishing you were sitting in that chair. I am truly a lucky man, and I love you so much," he said as he clasped her hand over the table. "I have missed you so much, there is nowhere else I would rather be than right here with you," Ebony replied squeezing his fingers.

The waiter brought Ebony her favourite fruit smoothie, bagel, and soft cheese and placed it on the table in front of her. She opened her bagel to spread it with the soft cheese, and there lying on the inside was a diamond and ruby ring. She gasped and looked at Matthew, who got down on his knees and said "Ebony, would you do me the great honour and marry me?" She flung her arms around him "Yes, Yes" she replied.

There was a rapturous applause from all the other diners in the restaurant.

The sun was shining and the top was down on Matthew's sports car. It was an automatic so they were able to hold hands. She had not known such contentment for a very long time.

Ebony was busy cooking Spaghetti Bolognaise in her kitchen at her beach house, whilst Matthew was catching up with answering some e-mails on his laptop on the veranda. Ebony kept checking her engagement ring making sure it was not a dream. She must contact Ben to see if he would design her wedding gown. It was the happiest time of her life, she so wished she could have her mother there with her.

She heard his mobile ring while she plated the meal. She called to him "It's ready." Matthew put his mobile in his pocket.

"I have just had some very interesting news from the private detective I hired to watch Lucas. Apparently, he has some dealings with a well-known drug cartel and the C.I.A are watching him."

Ebony played with her food. "Matthew, I think there is something you should know." She explained to him about the laptop she found hidden in Lucas wardrobe. "If only we could get hold of it, he replied."

"Well actually I do still have my key to Lucas apartment; I often brought work back to the apartment and often forgot to take it with me, so I had a spare key cut."

Ebony sat nervously in her car, she had checked at work and knew Lucas had a dinner date with clients that evening. She kept watching the clock on the dashboard; Matthew had been gone thirty minutes it seemed like hours to her. They had arranged for her to ring him, to warn him if she noticed Lucas returning. A cab drew up outside the entrance to Lucas's apartment and he stepped out with a woman. She turned round and kissed him, it was Jane his P.A. Well there's a surprise thought Ebony. They stood on the sidewalk kissing and embracing each other before going through the entrance. Ebony quickly rang Matthew. Pick up please pick up she said anxiously to herself.

"What's the problem?" Matthew asked.

"Get out quickly Lucas is on his way up."

"I have what I need," he replied.

As Matthew made his way to the front door, he heard talking, then laughter and a key turning in the lock. His heart started to race and his hands were clammy as he held the laptop.

He hid behind the half open door of the bathroom and could just make them out.

"I hope you are ready for this," Lucas said in a teasing manner to Jane.

"I think you will find me more than ready." Jane replied seductively. Franticly they grabbed at each other's clothes and flinging them to the floor as they headed for the bedroom.

As soon as they were out of sight, Matthew made his move for the door, jumping over clothes and shoes strewn across the hallway floor.

It seemed like hours before Ebony saw Matthew leave the building and join her in the car.

"Phew that was close," Matthew said visibly shaken.

Ebony sighed with relief and quickly drove them back to Matthew's apartment.

"My good friend Stratford works for the CIA we were friends at Harvard, he might be able to help me." Matthew rang him and arranged to meet.

"It is so good to see you again, Stratford, how are you doing?" said Matthew, as he shook his hand. "Very well, sorry to hear about your father's death, I read it in the Times, "he replied.

"Thank you, what can I get you to drink?" said Matthew.

"A G & T please," Stratford replied. Matthew chose a quiet table where they could talk. Stratford said he would see what information he could find out for me.

Chapter Twenty-Four

Why did she have to report to Tina Stoppard? She would revel in her downfall.

Ebony had always had her own office, now being in an open office would come hard.

She was organising her desk when Meg, Tina's secretary popped her head round the partition

"Tina would like to see you, Ebony."

Tina looked up from working at her desk and with a motion of her hand directed her to sit down. Of course, there was no chair for her to sit on so Ebony had to get one. The bitch she thought. She made her wait and looking up said "I expect one hundred percent from my staff, no distractions. I want you to be responsible for the Spanish market, as you have had experience in that Country. You will be on a trial period of three months. Tina dismissed Ebony with a wave of her hand.

After all, those years working my way up through the company this is so humiliating. What a fool I have been she told herself. She was old news now as everyone was talking about Lucas and his new conquest Amanda head of HR. I bet she does not know about Jane, his PA that he is seeing at the same time. Then Ebony realized that he was more than likely seeing her to when he was with her. She must forget the past and concentrate on the future; things still could not dampen her feelings of joy at being engaged to Matthew.

After work, Ebony rushed through town to see Ben for her appointment to discuss her wedding gown. "Ben, these drawing are amazing," said Ebony as she looked at some designs he had laid out for her wedding gown. He had done well for himself.

"You can choose from these or I can design one just for you, which honestly I would prefer."

There was a knock on the door, in rushed a beautiful African American girl.

"Darling I managed . . . I am sorry I did not realize you had someone with you Ben."

He put his arm around her and kissed her forehead.

"Sweetheart, this is Ebony a friend. I am designing her wedding gown for her forthcoming wedding. Then looking at Ebony said, "This is my fiancée, Tiffany."

Tiffany smiled, "I am so pleased to meet you Ebony, you will look amazing in one of his gowns he has such a rare talent. She whispered in Ben's ear. Ebony noticed an engagement ring on her finger as she brushed her long curled hair out of her face. Tiffany kissed his cheek and left.

"We haven't been engaged very long and Tiffany has been arranging the wedding, she is so excited, "said Ben with a smile that radiated across his face.

"I am so happy for you both," said Ebony. She felt an uncomfortable feeling of jealousy, why should she feel that way. She loved Matthew and pushed the silly feeling away. She left Ben feeling excited about the wedding gown he had designed for her but felt confused at her feelings for him.

Ebony answered her mobile phone as she rummaged in her handbag for her car keys. She pressed the fob and threw her bag on to the passenger seat as she said, "Ebony Marshall speaking," trying to sound up beat as she settled into the driving seat of her car.

"I am calling from Manhattan Hospital; your sister Elizabeth Marshall has been involved in a car accident. We found your name and number in her diary in her handbag. As you are her next of kin, I am afraid I have to tell you she is very ill, we do not expect her to live. I suggest you get here as soon as possible."

Ebony's hands started to shake as she started her car. Thoughts flooded her mind, she must make it in time they only had each other now. Though they had never been close, she must be there for her and not let her die on her own.

"I have been informed my sister Elizabeth Marshall has been brought here, could you direct me to her room please. I am her next of kin Ebony Marshall." The nurse looked at her screen and then said "Room 12, second door on the right," she pointed down the corridor in a dismissive manner. Ebony found room 12 it was partially open and leaning over Elizabeth was a doctor; he turned on hearing her enter.

"I am Elizabeth's sister. How is she doing doctor?" she said focused and ready for his reply. The doctor drew her to a corner of the room. "Elizabeth has severe internal injuries and I do not expect her to make it through the night, I am sorry he said in a compassionate voice.

"Will you be staying with her, if so I will get the nurse to get you a drink and comfortable chair." as he put a sympathetic hand on her shoulder.

Ebony replied, "Yes I want to be with her," her voice gave way with emotion she managed to add, "She is not dying alone."

Ebony heard the door close behind her and moved to Elizabeth's bedside.

She thought how peaceful she looked. There was no sign of injury to her face she appeared to be asleep, if only that were true. She had so envied her the affection that her father had given her. She was beautiful and as far as Ebony was concerned, she had it all. As she sat at her bedside she realised she would have no family left when Elizabeth passed away. Ebony reached out for her hand and stroked it. Elizabeth stirred and started to mumble and opened her eyes and appeared to focus on Ebony's face.

"Is that you, Ebony?"

"Yes it's me,"

"I am sorry, so sorry Ebony. I was so unkind to you please forgive me," Elizabeth said breathlessly.

"You know I do—now rest. I'm here for you and will stay right by your side."

Elizabeth managed a weak smile and squeezed Ebony's hand, and then motioned her to come closer.

"I need to tell you something I have known for many years . . . her words faded as she struggled to breath. Elizabeth was getting anxious.

"Elizabeth please rest don't get upset," Ebony said with concern.

Elizabeth raised her head off the pillow desperate to impart something to Ebony she grabbed her arm and gasped for air. She then fell back onto the pillow. Then it went quiet. Ebony waited anxiously willing her to take her next breathe but it never came. She lay there still; all the pain that contorted her face had gone. "Nurse: nurse!" Ebony cried.

It had been two weeks since Elizabeth had died. She thought about the last words she had said to her and concluded she was not in her right mind with the pain relieving drugs and was trying to make amends.

Ebony's phone rang, "Can I speak to Ebony Marshall please?"

"Speaking," replied Ebony.

"This is Elizabeth Marshall's Solicitor, could you please call in to see me."

"I can call in tomorrow morning," replied Ebony.

Ebony moved nervously in her chair in the waiting room at the Solicitors.

"Your sister asked me to give you this envelope in the event of her death."

When Ebony returned home, she went out onto her veranda sat down in the rocking chair and proceeded to open the envelope.

Ebony, if you receive this letter then I have died without any heirs to leave the family business to. I know you will look after the company dad built up. You need to know that I have been researching a rumour I had heard at work concerning father's affair with his P.A twenty-eight years ago, apparently, she left work to have a baby. My research uncovered several facts, so you may find that someday there will be a knock at the door from another sibling. I am sorry for the way I treated you. Elizabeth.

So many questions and no one left to answer them, Ebony felt cheated. A roller coaster of emotions hit her. She felt elated at now owning the family business but also sadness that her adopted mother might have known that her husband had been unfaithful. How painful that must have been to bear and not being able to talk to anyone about it.

Matthew rushed through the door of the beach house saying "Hey Honey I have just had a meeting with Stratford," Matthew planted a kiss on her lips." I have some good news."

"Apparently Lucas has been under surveillance for six months, the information on the laptop was just the proof they needed." Matthew said reaching out for her hand.

"I notice that something is troubling you Ebony? Yes this is the letter that Elizabeth left for me," she said, as she handed it to Matthew.

"Wow, that s a turn up for the books, how do you feel honey?"

"Well there are a lot of questions unanswered and no one to answer them." Matthew gave her a cuddle.

"Darling, let's walk along the beach I need to blow away the cobwebs, said Ebony," after the day I've had at work." She told Matthew about being called in to see her new boss Tina Stoppard."

"Darling, you will be Mrs Houghton soon just think how that will annoy her. You can drop that bombshell on her when you hand in your notice letting her know you are leaving to run your multimillion-dollar family businesses. Then watch her face," he said.

Ebony kissed him and went to the bedroom to fetch her cardigan when her mobile rang. Matthew picked it up and passed it to her.

"This is Ebony Marshall speaking."

"Hi, Ebony, its Ben have you got a minute?"

"Of course I have Ben."

"I am afraid Tiffany won't be able to make it to your wedding, unfortunately we have finished our relationship. It will just be me, if you still want me to attend. "Ebony could hear by Ben's voice how upset he was.

"Oh Ben I am so sorry, would you like some company I can come over."

Matthew thought—what about our time together is she really going over to Ben's now.

He kept getting a feeling that he was excluded whenever Ben was around.

"No I'll be ok, I just wanted you to know there will be one less at the reception. Don't forget about your fitting on Friday, see you then bye."

"Poor Ben," she said to Matthew. Ben and Tiffany have finished and he sounds so upset. I think I will ring him back and insist I meet him."

"Hey honey—remember me, I am still here."

Matthew took her mobile from her hand and said. "Leave the poor guy alone because that is what he wants, now what about us and that walk along the beach?"

Matthew thought Ebony seemed distracted and he had a good idea why—Ben.

Ebony thought Matthew seemed quiet at dinner.

"What's wrong?" she asked.

"Well as you ask, are we alright?"

She was puzzled at his question. He explained.

"Well I have seen the way Ben looks at you and you do seem very happy in his company, do I have anything to worry about?"

Ebony was surprised at his comment.

"Don't be silly, he is a friend we have a lot in common. Oh, please do not look so concerned. I love you and only you," she said as she hugged him trying to reassure him.

Mathew held her and kissed her passionately desperate to show her how much he loved and needed her.

"Honey, I know we have thought of many venues for our wedding in Manhattan," Mathew said as he stirred his coffee at breakfast. "However there is another option we could consider as a wedding venue. I know how disappointed you were that you were unable to buy Cotton Wood Plantation. I have found out that Lucas has an agency in Charleston who lets it out for events and weddings. How do you feel about getting married there? Said Mathew, not sure how she would react.

"You are kidding me Matthew?" Ebony said in total surprise at his suggestion. Mathew at this point was not sure whether this was a good or bad idea, looking at her face he could not tell.

Beth felt emotion swell through her body at the thought of marrying at Cotton Wood Plantation. She looked down and tried to compose herself.

"Oh honey why tears? I am sorry it's a bad idea; forget it," he said cross with himself as he knelt down by her chair at the breakfast table."

"I think it is the most wonderful idea Matthew. Thank you darling it is so perfect. My mother cannot be there so to be married in the chapel that her ancestors were married in would be the next best thing. That is so very thoughtful of you darling, "Ebony said as she clung to him.

Mathew was relieved as his surprise was taking shape and Ebony would have the wedding she wanted.

Chapter Twenty-Five

⌘

Ebony tossed and turned in bed, she felt troubled. Was she in love with Ben? Did it show? Maybe as a friend, they just empathized on every level, and she so enjoyed his company. Should she be having feelings like this so close to her wedding day? She asked herself.

It was the day before her wedding. Ebony and her bridesmaids settled down in the aircraft seats for the flight to Charleston.

Matthew had booked them into the Royal Hotel Charleston for the night. He had paid Ebony's friends to fly and stay at different hotels to surprise her. She knew it would only be a small affair because of the distance. It was not going to stop him from making it a special day for her.

Matthew, Joe, Doug and Ben were flying out a day earlier to check everything was ready, as Matthew had organised an events company to set up a marquee in the grounds of Cotton Wood Plantation.

It was the morning of her wedding. Ebony's make up was finished and she sat in her dressing gown waiting for help from Ben to put on her wedding gown.

It hung on the bedroom wall. It was stunning, what a clever and talented man he was. How kind of him to design it for her as a wedding gift. She had so wanted her mother there fussing around her on her big day. The tears swelled up in her eyes, I must not ruin my eye makeup she told herself, as she dabbed her eyes. Ebony jumped as her mother's photo she had brought with her, fell from the table next to the bed onto the floor. She picked it up and looked at it.

"Hello, Mum, I know it's you," she sat there with her eyes closed and felt her loving arms surround her

"I'm so glad you came to me I love you." Ebony opened her eyes and smiled she was disturbed by a knock on the, door it was Ben.

Ben adjusted her wedding gown and standing back looked at it and then adjusted it again until he was happy with how it hung. He smiled at Ebony, kissed her cheek, and said, "Ebony, you look stunning." She thought Ben looked as if he had tears in his eyes. "I wish you happiness throughout your married life, you really deserve it." What a lovely man, so kind and thoughtful

"Thank you so much, Ben, I love my wedding gown—I have a favour to ask you, I was going to walk down the aisle on my own, as my father could not be here. So in his place would you do me the honour of walking me down the aisle?"

"You have no idea how proud that would make me feel," replied Ben.

There was a knock at the door and Joe entered. "Wow! My dad is a lucky fellow. You look beautiful; he kissed her on the cheek. I guess I will be calling you Mom in an hour's time," he laughed. "I think Ebony will do" she smiled.

"Ben has agreed to walk me down the aisle" beamed Ebony.

"Dad will be pleased," said Joe. "I know he was concerned about you walking down the aisle on your own."

Looking at Ben Joe said, "Ebony's dress looks amazing. Well I will see you two at the chapel," as he blew Ebony a kiss. "I must get back to perform my best man duties; dad will wonder where I am."

Laura, Sara and Jennifer came in excitedly into Ebony's bedroom. Laura took one look at Ebony and started to cry. "You look beautiful, Ebony," she hugged her. "What do you think of our dresses?" She said as each bridesmaid gave a twirl. "I love the colour jade and the white roses just finish the look. You all look gorgeous," said Ebony.

"You know, Ebony that Doug would give you away. I just have to ring him, it's not too late," said Laura anxiously.

"Thank you, Laura, but Ben has agreed to give me away." Laura tried not to look surprised but she knew Ebony well and that was what she wanted. She tried not to show that her feelings were hurt. There was a knock on the hotel door. "The limousines are here, Madam."

As Ebony's limousine drove down the avenue of Cotton Wood Plantation, she started to cry. It is like a fairy tale. My shining knight will be waiting for me in my dream castle. Could any woman be so lucky, she thought.

Ben passed her a tissue and a mirror; he was well prepared with a bag of essentials that he always carried on photo shoots. He looked at her concerned. "I am truly happy, Ben, these are tears of joy," said an emotional Ebony. He squeezed her hand and smiled." There are a lot of people who truly love you, Ebony, how could they not," and carefully dabbed away tears from the corners of her eyes. "We are here?" Said Ben

Ebony checked once again in the mirror.

Ben got out first and went around the limousine to help Ebony out. Once he adjusted her gown she took his arm then, they heard the unmistakable sound of the wedding march. There was a red carpet leading to the chapel entrance.

Ben said to her, "Now hold your head up, you look like a princess, Matthew's a lucky guy." Ebony smiled at him she thought he was the perfect person to give her away.

The chapel looked splendid with white roses, lilies and greenery with white ribbon tied in large bows at the end of each bench. The fragrance of the flowers filled the chapel. Candles sparkled in the dark corners and shards of sunlight streamed through the windows. Matthew stood nervously with Joe by his side.

Ebony had to hold her feelings in check. To be walking down the aisle of the chapel at Cotton Wood Plantation, the same aisle that her mother's ancestors had walked down, it was so magical. To have her beloved Matthew waiting for her flooded her mind with a mixture of emotions that made her feel lightheaded. She held on tightly to Ben and began to walk, she felt as if she was floating on air.

Ebony's voice broke with emotion as she said

"Matthew, as many before me have pledged their vows of love in this chapel.

I vow always to be there when you need me, to be on your side always. To cheer you up when you are sad and to look after you when you are ill.

I will be your companion, friend, confidant, and lover.

You will own my heart and enduring love for the rest of our lives."

Matthew squeezed her hand as he looked deeply into her eyes.

"Ebony, you have filled a large hole in my heart with your love.

I feel complete and utterly at peace when I am with you. I vow to look after you, protect you, and love you with a passion. I cannot wait to start our married life together. I look forward to walking hand in hand with you, for the rest of our lives until we are old and grey."

After the ceremony, Matthew said, "Darling, I have a wedding gift for you, but you must close your eyes—it's a surprise!"

"Keep your eyes closed, Darling," said Matthew. "We are nearly there." Ebony held on to her wedding gown while Matthew supported her arm. He positioned her at the front door of the Plantation house and said. "Ok you can open your eyes now." He had dreamt of this moment for so long and wanted it to go well. Ebony looked confused. "Don't say anything yet, just open the envelope on the front door." He motioned her to the big golden ribbon across it with a large envelope attached. "Open it." Matthew said excitedly. Written on it was Mrs Ebony Houghton. She opened it and pulled out paperwork, which looked like official documents. It was the title deeds to Cotton Wood Plantation. Ebony could not speak she had gone into shock and had to steady herself. Matthew lifted her into his arms and carried her into the study, and sat her on the desk chair

"Oh darling, let me explain. Stratford called, he needed to speak to me concerning Lucas, and we met at his office due to the sensitivity of the matter. It turns out Lucas was not Lucas Houghton. He had assumed the identity of my half brother that had passed away while at Harvard. He used his identity to get into a position that would be useful for bringing drugs into the U.S.A. When he inherited Houghton and Son, he found it was the perfect cover. Lucas had double-crossed a drug Baron and there was a contract out to have him killed. Unfortunately, for the person we knew as Lucas, the publicity he had generated when he took over the company had exposed him. They found his body in the boot of his car. My solicitor said, as my real half brother Lucas died before having any family, the property would revert to me.

Do you remember when you were on a business trip to Japan and I let myself into the beach house to retrieve the Castle contract." Ebony nodded "I hope that you will forgive me but I couldn't help looking at your mother's family tree that was on the dining room table. I recognised the surname Jackson on the family tree. I carried out further research since I was unaware of my family history and found out that her family had ostracized my mother, Rose Jackson, who was English by birth, after eloping to America with my father. Rose's father was Maliki Jackson the black twin son of Beth and Theodore. Jackson. So you see I am a direct descendent of Theodore that explains my lineage and why I am coloured. I now understand my position, which has been an enigma all my life. I wanted to return Cotton Wood Plantation to the rightful owners as it was Theodore's Legacy.

I bought Cotton Wood Plantation from Mr Pike who is a descendent of Sebastian Pike who was the stepson of Theodore who inherited the property on Theodore's death. Now from the evidence given in the journal, it is apparent that the rightful heirs should have been Theodore Jackson's twin son's Maliki and Isaac Jackson. That is why it was so important for me to buy Cotton Wood Plantation.

You must believe me when I tell you I did not know I was bidding against you Ebony.

I had kept this secret as I thought it would make the perfect wedding gift for you I came and saw the state of Cotton Wood Plantation. While renovation was being carried out in one of the bedrooms we discovered behind the wooden cladding a journal also a painted rolled canvas." Matthew handed the journal to Ebony.

It was a faded leather bound book. She gently held the fragile journal.

"My darling Matthew," she said. "I am overwhelmed, thank you from the bottom of my heart." She began to read it.

I Beth Jackson leave a record of my situation. Sebastian my husband's stepson informed me that he killed my husband Theodore, when he asked for his help as he lay wounded defending his estate.

I write this in great haste as he has locked my children and I in my bedchamber and threatened to kill us. Sebastian has convinced everyone that deserters have taken us hostage. He intends to have us sold into slavery and will then have control of Cotton Wood Plantation. Abel my first husband was not guilty of the murder of Miss Emma Jackson but Theodore had him hung. I witnessed Sebastian murder her. I bare witness Abel was falsely accused. I saw what happened that day but no one would believe a slave over a master. Please whoever finds my journal put the record straight for me. I take my children to my destiny, knowing that I have left a record of the true events. God bless my children and I. It was signed Beth Jackson. 1863

Matthew pointed to a painting of Beth and her children on the study wall. Ebony remembered Lucas showing her the canvas. Matthew had it framed for Ebony as a wedding gift and hung it back in the study where it probably was when Theodore was alive. Ebony got up clutching the journal to her chest, and faced Beth's portrait and said emotionally.

"Beth, I promise I will put the record straight for you and your children, you have my word." She clung to Matthew emotionally drained. On one side of Beth's portrait hung a picture of Theodore and on the other side Emma, his daughter with his first wife Martha. "So this is Emma, she was so pretty and the man himself, Theodore." Ebony remarked as she thought how real it all seemed now there were faces to the names. Ebony could now reconcile her adopted mother's ancestors with the family tree.

"I discovered these portraits in the back of the attic and had them cleaned and re-hung." Matthew said as he took Ebony's hand and guided her into the hallway.

"One more surprise, darling," he stopped by something covered on the hall wall. He removed the covering.

"Oh Matthew, she gasped, how wonderful our Family tree." Then she noticed their names at the bottom.

"My darling Ebony, we will bring our family up here and bring happiness into this wonderful house where there was once such sadness. Together we will continue our search to find out what happened to Beth and her children and put the record straight."

He gave her a glass of Champagne and proposed the toast. "To Beth and her children." They raised their glasses, and then hugged each other feeling as if all the previous generations had joined them for just this moment in time.

Chapter Twenty-Six

"We must get back to our guests," said Matthew.

"Darling, I must go and change for the evening reception. Would you ask Ben if he would help me out of my gown and into my evening one please?"

"Thank you, Darling, you know how much I love Cotton Wood Plantation and how I feel about getting the mistakes of the past corrected for the future," she leaned forward and kissed him. "This kiss is from my adopted mother, she would have been so excited if she was here, I love you so much, Matthew."

"Are you sure you would not like me to get you out of your dress," he said as he pulled her close to him. "Don't you think you should be seeing to our guests in the marquee?" Matthew gave her a passionate kiss. "There will be more of that later," he said playfully patting her bottom and leaving by the front door.

Ebony carefully lifted her gown up to negotiate the grand staircase. Was she dreaming, could this be real, to have married the man she loved and be able to live in the house she felt such an affinity with, so yes, for her—fairytales do come true.

Her beautiful scarlet strapless evening gown that was from Ben's summer collection lay on the bed. This was the first time she had been in the bedroom since she came with Cindy. She marvelled at its opulence. She looked out of the window. Her eyes drifted down the avenue of oak trees looking magnificent in their summer coat of green leaves that swayed in the summer breeze.

Ebony took her makeup bag from her case and placed it down on the top of a carved oak chest of drawers, a large gold ornate mirror hung above it. She heard a noise through the half open door.

"Come on in, Ben," she said looking in her makeup bag for her lipstick."

"My gowns beautiful, thank you so much, Ben, for designing it." As she lifted her head up to put her lipstick on in the mirror, she was shocked to see it was not Ben, but a stranger walking into her bedroom. She jumped and nervously stepped back. He appeared unsteady as he walked towards her. She knew he was not a guest as he was unkempt and scruffily dressed, she vaguely remembered him. It's him, the person who was hanging around outside last time she was here with Cindy, Ebony recalled.

"What do you want?" Ebony said as her voice quivered with fear as she moved further away from him.

"I want money the money you owe me." Seb said threateningly as he produced a knife from his pocket.

Ebony knew she had to think quickly on her feet.

"There might be some in the safe in the study?" thinking she had more chance if she was downstairs where there would be more people around.

Seb put his arm around her neck and pointed the knife into her back as he directed her out of her bedroom and down the staircase. He knew his way to the study, as it had been his grandfather's house.

He pushed her into the study.

"Get the money—Now!" Ebony noticed the hand with the knife was shaking.

Ben saw Ebony in the study through the open door as he entered the house via the hallway.

"What are you doing downstairs we need to get you changed, Mrs Houghton." he teased, as he walked towards the study door unaware of what was happening.

"Ben, help me?" Ebony cried.

Then as Ben got closer, he saw the man with the knife.

"Now put that knife down," he said calmly "We don't want anyone hurt, do we?"

Ben could tell from the young man's eyes that he was on drugs. "I'm owed money and I want it"

Seb said anxiously as perspiration rolled down his face.

"I can get some money but you must let Ebony go first. "Ben could see Seb thinking about it and then he pushed Ebony away from him.

"Ok, now I want my money?"

"Ebony, get over here?" Ben shouted to her.

"No she stays here until you bring me the money." Seb replied.

Ebony made a move towards Ben and Seb tried to grab her, slashing her arm. Ebony cried out as the knife struck her.

Ben dived towards Seb pushing her to the side of the room. A fight ensued and Ben made a gasping sound as he realised he had been stabbed in the stomach. He fell to the study floor as Seb ran off.

"Ben, oh Ben," cried Ebony. She knelt down and put her arm under his head to support it. Ben was struggling to breathe as he said to Beth.

"Stay . . . with me, please . . . don't leave . . . me."

"I am right here, Ben," Ebony said as her voice broke with emotion.

"Help: Help!" Ebony screamed. Matthew came rushing into the study.

"My God what has happened, Ebony?"

"Call 911—NOW! Matthew."

"Stay with me, Ben," she begged.

Ben looked at her as if he wanted to say something. Ebony placed her ear close to his mouth. He whispered in her ear and then went limp in her arms.

"The ambulance is on its way," said Matthew as he knelt down by Ben's body.

Matthew was concerned at the way Ebony was behaving, she would not speak she just clung to Ben fiercely.

She was in shock. When the paramedics arrived to put him into the ambulance Beth would not let go of him.

"Come on now, Ebony," said Matthew as he tried to pull her away from Ben.

"No-no you can't take him," sobbed Ebony. "You don't understand," she cried as she held tightly to him.

"Please help him," she begged the paramedics as they put him into the ambulance.

"Who's the next of kin?" asked the paramedic.

"I am—he is my, twin brother," said Ebony." As she climbed into the ambulance in her blood soaked wedding gown, holding her wounded arm. The doors of the ambulance closed and it sped down the avenue of Cotton Wood Plantation.

Matthew stood confused as he watched the ambulance leave; he knew Ebony had a strong bond with Ben. Saying that she was his twin sister so she could go with him in the ambulance and on our wedding day makes it hard to understand he thought—should he be worried. Mathew returned to his wedding guests and announced that Ebony and Ben had been injured and taken to the hospital and that he would be joining them.

"Please help, my brother," Ebony cried repeatedly as she followed the medical staff down the hospital corridor. A team of doctors were waiting and Ben was wheeled into a room."

"No you can't go in you must wait outside," said the nurse as she pulled Ebony away from Ben's side.

"I want to be with, my brother." Ebony begged.

The nurse took her by the arm and sat her outside the room where Ben was receiving life saving treatment.

"You can watch through the window," said the nurse as she tried to calm Ebony.

She waited outside whilst the doctors rushed around trying to save Ben. She did not want to leave him. She looked through the window and watched as he lay there fighting for his life. She said Ben fight, with every part of you, please I need you, don't leave me." Ebony fought to control her emotions.

"Are you the next of kin?" asked a nurse holding paperwork in her hand.

"Ah . . . Yes I am."

"Could you fill this form in for me please," she said.

Ebony tried to focus on the form, her tears mixed with the blood from the cut to her arm staining the form.

Ok, she thought name of patient—Ben. She did not know his surname, but of course, she did, it was hers 'rather theirs—Marshall.

His address was next on the form.

She realised she knew very little about her twin brother.

Age—28 that she did know, a spark of comfort flooded her body at the thought that they had been born on the same day, then sadness at the twenty-eight years apart from one another.

"Are you the next of Kin?" asked a dishevelled looking doctor.

"Yes, I am Ben's twin sister, Ebony replied emotionally.

"We have managed to stabilize Ben but he is not out of the woods yet," the doctor looked at Ebony's wedding dress covered in blood and her wounded arm.

"Let's look at your arm first; this must have been a traumatic day for you. Why don't you go home and have a rest, we will call you if there is a change in Ben's condition."

"No please, I just want to sit by my brother's bed. I don't want to leave him," Ebony said pleading with him. "May I go in and sit with him?"

"The nurse will sort out your injured arm and then you can sit with Ben—ok?" said the doctor. looking at her over his black rimmed glasses.

Ebony nodded.

The nurse examined Ebony's arm and cleaned around the wound.

She then asked Ebony her name.

"Ebony Marshall . . . no sorry it's Houghton. I was married today," she replied.

The nurse informed the doctor that the wound to Ebony's arm would require stitches. While the nurse stitched and dressed the wound, Ebony felt calmer knowing Ben was in safe hands.

She settled down in the chair next to his bed and reached out for his hand. She leant forward and spoke to him.

"Well we have finally found each other, my dear brother. I knew you existed in my heart for I always felt a part of me was missing. We have so much catching up to do. Questions I want to ask you, silly things like do you like bagels. I love Soul music do you? We have each other now and I will always be here for you. I will not leave your side.

Please fight to recover Ben we have many years ahead of us to enjoy. Can you hear me Ben?

She touched his face—I love you." Ebony was so distressed she could hardly breathe.

"Could you finish this form for me please said an impatient nurse?" as she thrust the form at Ebony.

"I am sorry but I have only just found out today that Ben is my brother."

"Well let me see," the nurse pulled Bens wallet from his bloodstained jacket, which lay on a chair, with his, shoes and tie.

"I will give this to you as you are his next of kin, perhaps the information you need you will find in the wallet," she said as she handed it to Ebony and left the room.

Ebony felt uncomfortable opening it. She pulled out his driving licence and took a sharp intake of breath. Benjamin Marshall-Ferris. Marshall—the proof was right in front of her, Yes, Ben was her twin brother. Then her mother's maiden name must be Ferris.

Ebony then found a donor card, several hundred-dollar bills and some of Ben's business cards. Tucked in a side slit she found a card for the City Hospital in Manhattan and a folded piece of paper, which she opened. It had list of items written on it. Tiffany's photo stared back at her; Ben obviously still had feelings for her. She must ring her. She went out to the corridor and found a coffee machine, got herself a drink and settled down in a chair and phoned Tiffany.

"Hello this is Tiffany Gardner, speaking."

"Tiffany, it's Ebony," the line went quiet.

"Ebony, this is a pleasant surprise what can I do for you?"

"Are you on your own?"

"No actually I'm staying at my sister's house."

"Good," said Ebony, as she did not want to give her bad news when she was on her own.

"Tiffany I have some bad news. Ben has been stabbed at my wedding he is in Charleston Hospital. His operation went well but he is still unconscious, but stable.

"Oh my God, he will be alright—won't he?" said a distressed Tiffany.

"The doctor told me he is not out of the woods yet."

"I will get the next flight out, if in the meantime he regains consciousness, please tell him I send him my love."

"Of course, there is something I need to ask you, Tiffany? Ben told me when we were waiting for the ambulance to arrive that he was my twin brother. Did you know?"

There was silence once again.

"No I did not, but it explains everything. You see I thought he loved you and we had so many rows because I was so jealous of you that it tore us apart."

"Did Ben have any family Tiffany?"

"Yes a mother." Ebony's heart started to pound.

"Do you have her address as I would like to be the one to tell her about Ben?"

"We'll . . ." there was a pause from Tiffany's end.

Ebony sensed Tiffanies' reluctance in telling her.

"Please, Tiffany—just tell me." Ebony was feeling very anxious now.

"Ben has been visiting his . . . *your* mother in Manhattan Hospital. She has been poorly of late and has had to have an operation."

"What do you mean an operation? You must tell me what you know, Tiffany, "Ebony said."

"For a brain tumour, I am so sorry. Look, Ebony, I have to rush, as I need to book that flight to see Ben. Thank you so much for telling me, take care."

Ebony's brain was finding it hard to take in all that had happened over the last twenty-four hours. So much had happened to her on her wedding day the gift of Cotton Wood Plantation, discovering her twin brother and finding her real mother. She may well lose both of them when she had only just found them.

She rushed back to Ben's bedside to find him still unconscious. She held his hand and stroked it. She thought about how she had envisaged what her mother would look like and how as a child she dreamt so many times that, she would come and get her. Now she was on the threshold of meeting her biological mother, it somehow did not feel real. Ebony had never imagined having a sibling, let alone a twin, it all made sense now. She always knew that there was part of her missing but now she knew it was because she had a twin out there. Then she felt her hand squeezed.

"Hi, Sis," said Ben woozy from the painkillers.

"Oh, Ben, I was so worried I thought I had lost you." Ebony lent forward and stroked Ben's wayward hair off his face.

"You can't get rid of me that easy. I found our birth certificates when I was a teenager and I swore as soon as I was old enough I would come and find you. However, mother became very ill and you were getting married and were so happy, I decided to wait until Mum was better.

Ben looked concerned, Ebony, I need to get a message to Mum, she will be wondering where I am. I told her I would be away two day's at my friend's wedding, you see there has only ever been us two." Ebony could see Ben was getting agitated."

"Ben, you must stay calm, I will fly back and see our mother." She thought how wonderful that sounded to her, but frightening to. "I rang Tiffney she is flying here as we speak and can stay with you. I hope you did not mind me ringing her. However, I needed to find information for the admittance form and had to look in your wallet. I saw Tiffany's photo and knew you would have wanted her here."

"That's what twins have, that something special at knowing what the other feels, it's a gift. Give Mum . . . my . . . love . . ." Ebony could see Ben was tired and his eyelids were getting heavy.

"Rest now, I won't be far," said a very happy and relieved Ebony. "Ebony went out into the corridor and got a coffee while Ben slept and checked for messages left on her phone.

There were five missed calls from Matthew. Ebony rang him.

Hello Darling?"

"Hi honey, how is Ben?"

"I've spoken to him, he is through the worst. Darling I am so sorry to leave you on our wedding day but my twin brother needed me."

"So it's true, Ben is your twin?"

"Yes darling isn't it wonderful," she said as her face glowed with the thought.

"Thank goodness for that, I really was beginning to think you had married the wrong man."

"You can see why I was so drawn to him, he told me my mother is alive but she has just undergone an operation, she has a brain tumour." Ebony's voice faltered.

"Honey, I am so sorry, would you like me to come over and bring you home."

"Darling I have booked a flight this afternoon back to Manhattan to see my mother and look after her while Ben recovers. I promised Ben I would do it. Tiffany's flying out to be with Ben. I hope you do not mind, I need to do this she has no one else. I could lose her and I need to see her."

"Honey, do you want me to come with you?"

"No I need to do this myself; you finish up and return to Manhattan. Then we can enjoy our honeymoon. Love you."

"Love you to," said Matthew.

Ebony sat in her seat on the flight to New York, she felt easier knowing that Ben had Tiffany with him. As she reflected she thought of poor Matthew having to stay behind and sort out the aftermath of the wedding, it was a shame they had to delay their honeymoon. He knew how important her newfound family were to her and that her brother and mother needed her.

Chapter Twenty-Seven

Ebony walked into the Manhattan hospital, that distinctive smell of antiseptic assaulted her nose. She clutched a colourful bunch of flowers as she approached reception. A thin, grey-faced woman wearing a colourful pair of spectacles smiled. "Can I help you?"

"Could you please tell me which room Miss Ferris is in?" The receptionist looked at her screen intently.

Room 33 straight ahead through the double doors and turn right, she said indicating with her hand.

"Thank you," replied Ebony.

Her stomach was churning with anxiety at meeting her mother for the first time.

Would she look how she expected as she imagined in her many dreams? She went through the double doors and turned right. The sign-indicated rooms 30-36 pointed to a corridor, where a young nurse sat at a desk working at her computer. She looked up at Ebony and said "May I help you?"

"Yes please, I was told by reception that Miss Ferris was in room 33." Ebony felt her heart pounding in her chest, the nurse looked down her list.

"Are you related to the patient?" asked the nurse. Ebony was reluctant to say daughter until she had spoken to her Mother so she replied family.

The nurse seemed to accept her reply.

She was feeling sick with anxiety now; her mouth was dry all she could hear was her heart thudding in her chest. She found door 33, and peered through the little window in the door.

Ebony saw a frail black woman sitting in the armchair by the side of her bed. Her head bandaged she wore a red dressing gown and slippers she appeared to be asleep.

Well this was her mother Ebony felt panic. She suddenly felt like a little child again, very vulnerable.

She opened the door with a shaky hand the silence broken by the sound of the wrapping around the bunch of the flowers in her hand as she closed the door behind her.

Ebony walked over to her mother. She jumped when she opened her eyes, although sunken, you could see that they were large, dark brown and beautiful, they stared at her.

"Do I know you?" she quizzed Ebony.

"I am a friend of your son Ben," replied Ebony trying to control her nervousness.

"I was worried when he did not arrive this morning, he is such a good son he promised to bring some things in for me from home that I need. I am sorry I did not get your name?"

Ebony moved uncomfortably. "Mrs Houghton, Ben came to my wedding, he made my beautiful wedding gown." Ebony so wanted to say—Mum its Ebony your daughter but she could not overload her. Just telling her mother about Ben was enough worry for her when recovering from a major operation.

"Ah, so you are the lady, Ben made the wedding gown for; he never stopped talking about you and your big event. Where is he?" the tone of her voice showing her concern.

Ebony said "May I sit down?" as she pulled up a chair.

"Of course," her mother replied.

"Ben was taken ill at my wedding, he will be fine." Ebony added quickly. "He just needs to rest for a while. He asked me if I would visit and see to your needs until he is well enough to fly back. Which I said I would be pleased to help, as your son is such a good friend of mine. He asked me to tell you not to worry; he is fine and sends you his love."

There was a pause, Ebony wondered whether her mother had heard her or not, and then she saw tears run down her face. Ebony's heart went out to her she could see the strong bond between mother and son. How she wished she had that closeness with her.

She took a tissue from her tray and dried her eyes "Please forgive me but I feel so helpless. I should be visiting my son he should not be worrying about me when he is ill. He is such a kind and loving boy. Ebony just wanted to pick her up and take her home. She so desperately wanted to tell her who she was but in her condition, the shock could endanger her life.

"Ben has given me the list of items you need and with your permission I will bring them in for you tomorrow," Beth said sounding upbeat.

"That is very kind of you dear," she replied.

"These flowers are from Ben," she said and handed them to her, although she had bought the flowers herself, she knew Ben would have brought some for his mother if he could.

The door flew open and a stout nurse entered.

"Miss Ferris time for your scan," the nurse's eyes fell on the flowers in her mother's hands. They are beautiful flowers, I will get you a vase," said the nurse and walked off with them.

It was a cue for Ebony to leave. "Shall I take your apartment key and then I can collect your things today and bring them in tomorrow for you Miss Ferris."

"Dear that would be so kind of you, please pass me my handbag and I will get them for you. Ebony passed the red, leather handbag to her; she found the keys and gave them to her.

Ebony said "I will ring Ben and tell him I have seen you, do you have any messages you wish me to give him?"

"Oh yes please, tell him not to worry about me and to concentrate on getting better and that I am thinking of him and send my love."

"Well until tomorrow," said Ebony as she smiled and left the room. She made it to her car and as she closed the door, the tears flowed uncontrollably. I do not know how I feel. I have waited all my life to meet my mother and I just feel numb. Ebony felt a mixture of so many emotions.

She found her mother's apartment block. It was in a rundown area and Ebony felt uncomfortable as she locked her car door. She looked at the address number 139 and entered the building. The lifts were out of order, so she climbed the stairs; 130-140 the sign indicated that this was the floor. Ebony opened the door and walked along a balcony. She ducked several washing lines in her search for no 139. Ebony finally found the apartment and opened the door with her mother's key.

She smelt Lavender when she walked in. She found the sparsely furnished lounge that was spotlessly cleans. The Lavender plant stood in pride of place in the centre of the dining table. On the windowsill were some photographs. Ebony recognised one of Ben when he was younger and another more recent one of him receiving a qualification. In addition, there was a wedding photograph, which must have been her parents as she thought her mother had not married.

Ebony was sad to think she was not there in her mother's past. She delved into her handbag for the list Ben had given her. I must stay focused she told herself as she collected the items required, her mobile rang, it was Matthew

"Honey, how are you bearing up?" he said concerned.

"Oh darling, thank you for ringing."

"How did your visit go with your mother?"

"I felt guilty thinking that my adopted mother would have been upset by my visit. However, I needed to meet her. I wanted to tell her that I was her daughter, but she was too frail. I cannot burden her now, this isn't the right time Matthew," she suddenly thought of her brother. "How's Ben?"

"I called in to see him as you asked, he is on the mend, he was delighted to see Tiffany," replied Matthew.

"I am so pleased," Ebony went quiet.

"Honey, tell me what's wrong?"

"I am in my mother's apartment; it's so sparse and cold. I keep thinking of her living on her own. It is not a very nice neighbourhood and she must feel isolated. How lonely she must have felt having only those moments to look forward to when Ben could visit her, she doesn't even have a car." Ebony broke down in tears.

"Honey, don't upset yourself. You have found your brother and mother now and with the fortune you and your brother have inherited you can help her. It is not possible to do everything in one day. In time it will all work out, you'll see," said Matthew trying to calm her. "I'll be back tomorrow evening. I am here on the other end of the phone if you need me."

"Thank you, Darling, I look forward to my cuddles then, love you, bye."

Ebony returned to Matthew's apartment with her mother's things. She thought how wonderful it would be to see him. They would be staying at Matthew's apartment while they saw to their businesses in Manhattan. She would be glad when her brother Ben would be able to join her at the helm of their fathers business, how so very proud she would feel.

She was exhausted from all the events that had taken place during the day, she crashed out feeling mentally, and physically exhausted.

"Ebony struggled up the hospital corridor with her mother's belongings that she had collected from her apartment, plus magazines and fruit.

"She got to her room to find it empty. Panic overtook Ebony. Where was her mother? No, no she cannot have! She dropped all her mothers' belongings in the room and rushed to the nurse's station, but there were no nurses there. She had started to hyperventilate when she discovered a nurse she was unable to speak.

"Sit down." said the nurse and blow into this bag. Ebony regained her breath.

"Miss . . . Ferris . . . room . . . 33," she said breathlessly. "She is not there anymore?"

"Sit here I will go and find out what has happened," she said.

Ebony tried to keep herself-calm she could not lose her mother now she felt as if her heart would burst it was pounding so hard.

The nurse tapped her on the shoulder and said," Come with me?"

She took her down another corridor and opened a door. Her mother was sitting in bed, with her bandage removed and there was a large closed wound to her head held together with metal clips.

The nurse said nothing but just smiled at her.

"I was so worried you would not find me," said her mother seeming perkier." The doctor told me that the operation went well and everything is healing as expected, would you please tell my son when you speak to him?"

"I will ring him as soon as I leave the hospital," reassured Ebony trying to control her emotions, as she wanted to cry with relief.

She smiled not letting on how concerned she had been.

"I have brought everything on the list Ben gave me. If there is anything else you need just ask."

"Thank you so much, I do not know what I would have done without you."

The only words that registered in Ebony's stressed state were 'without you.' She felt tears well up in her eyes and she could not stop them flowing. She turned her face away to hide her tears as she rearranged her mother's belongings in bags on the chair.

"Ben is well and sends you his love, he is improving day by day the doctors say."

"I have been so worried about him. I wondered if you would be kind enough to buy some writing paper and stamps so I can correspond with him."

"Of course, I will get you some from the hospital shop on level 1."

"Thank you, that is very kind of you."

Ebony was grateful to leave her mother's room as she was finding it hard to control her emotions. As she walked to the hospital shop, she thought how blessed she was that her mother was recovering well and that she'd had this precious time alone with her, even if she was not aware she was her daughter. Soon she would be well enough to tell her.

After leaving the hospital, she arrived back at their apartment. She popped into the shower, dried herself, and creamed her legs. She looked in her wardrobe for the strappy number Matthew liked. She thought how wonderful it would be to see him.

She smiled with contentment as she piled her hair up in the mirror. There had been no time to enjoy the afterglow of her wedding day. Knowing her mother and brother were being looked after she could think about Matthew.

They awoke together locked in each other's arms, for this was the first time they had been intimate since their wedding day.

"Darling, I'm sorry I have to leave you but I promised my mother I would visit her."

"We'll, honey, I need to call into the office and then perhaps we could meet for lunch at Luigi's would you like that Mrs Houghton?"

"That would be perfect, my darling." Ebony smiled as she dressed.

They kissed and she rushed out the door.

"Hello, Miss Ferris," Ebony said as she smiled walking through the door of her mother's hospital room, feeling much more positive at her mother's progress.

"Please, call me Clio."

"Ok, thank you." She thought her mother looked cheerful as she sat in the chair by her bed.

"I had a phone call from Ben, he has been cleared by the doctor and he can fly home. Tiffany is making the arrangements. I am so glad they are back together, she is such a nice girl." Her mother paused. "I never asked you about your wedding?"

"It was the happiest day of my life, in so many unexpected ways. "If only you knew she thought.

"I can see by your face you have the radiant look of a new bride."

"I am very lucky Matthew is a wonderful man."

"I never experienced a wedding day, it was not to be," a sad expression crossed her mother's face.

"Is there anything I can do for you before I leave? I am sure Ben and Tiffany will be in tomorrow to see you."

"Yes please, would you kindly pass me the menu; I have to select my meals for the day."

Ebony passed the form to her. "Eggs Benedict and Bagels, I have so missed my bagels." That's sad isn't it to be so excited about food." she smiled at her.

I have the same taste as her, Ebony thought. Just a simple thing that they both enjoyed meant so much to her. "I will leave you now;

my husband's expecting me for lunch so I must run. "It was lovely to have met you . . . Cleo." Ebony said feeling uncomfortable at calling her mother by her Christian name.

"Perhaps we can meet up and have coffee when you are fully recovered?" Ebony said not wanting to let her mother go without arranging to see her again.

"I would like that, thank you so much for your help dear. "Ebony smiled at her mother.

"Good bye Clio." Ebony said as she picked up her handbag and headed for the door.

"Take care . . . EBONY," said her mother.

Ebony froze unable to move. Did she hear her correctly? How did she know my name?

It seemed as if she stood rooted to the spot for ages. She bravely turned and faced her mother. Her gaze fell on her large, beautiful eyes that where knowing and full of warmth.

"Mother," Ebony swallowed hard and started to shake with emotion.

"Come here my child? I am *so, so* pleased to meet you." Ebony knelt down, placed her head on her mother's lap, and sobbed uncontrollably. Her mother caressed her head and her tears flowed.

Ebony controlled her tears, she asked her mother. "How did you know?"

"A mother knows her child; it is a bond that can never be broken. You have your brother's mannerisms you even rub the top of your lip when concerned, just like Ben. You are kind natured and I see a lot of myself in you," she paused—"I know there is a burning question you want to ask me." Her mother struggled to find the right words to explain to Ebony the painful truth—"Why were you given away?"

Her voice broke with emotion, not able to look her daughter in the eyes. Ebony took her hand—her mother continued. "When I found out I was pregnant I thought your father would leave his wife and marry me. I was heartbroken when he broke off our relationship he told me his family was the most important thing to him and that they must never know. He agreed to make provision for the baby and make regular maintenance payments into an account on the condition that I kept quiet. She wiped her eyes as she continued. "I had to leave my job because I was starting to show. When you twins were born I suffered from severe postnatal depression my elderly parents helped me as much as they could. Then when my mother died, I found I could no longer cope without her help and my nerves got the better of me. My father realised that I needed professional help and reluctantly had me committed to a psychiatric hospital. My father looked after you and Ben until he was unable to cope and thought by giving you to your father to bring up this would solve the situation. Therefore, he took you to your father's beach house and left you on the house steps, he waited there out of sight to ensure your safety.

He knew he had failing health and that perhaps I would be able to cope with just one baby when I was well enough to return home. Although every day I continued to struggle with depression, I was just able to look after Ben. I did not blame my father after all he was only looking after me. Since I lost you, there has always been a piece of me missing but I realised that your father could provide you with a much better start in life than I could. Knowing you were out there and having another women's love was a pain I carried every day.

Ben was looking for you, and when you walked through the door that first day I knew you were *my Ebony*," she cupped Ebony's face. "I have always loved you and there was never a day that passed that I didn't think of you—please say you will forgive me?"

Ebony looked at her mother and said with optimism and feeling. "There is nothing to forgive, everything was done out of love. That is all behind us, we are a family now with a future to look forward too.

The nurse came in and said "Miss Ferris, good news the doctor has cleared you to go home tomorrow.

"Who is your next of kin?"

Ebony turned to the nurse with pride and said, "I'm her daughter, she will be coming home with me."

Ben and Tiffany were delighted to hear that his mother was well enough to come out of hospital and had booked their flights to South Carolina.

Ebony stood on the steps of Cotton Wood Plantation waiting excitedly for her family to arrive, reflecting on the cycle of events that had led her to find her mother and twin brother. She realised her destiny had been predetermined by this wonderful house.

Matthew being the direct descendent of Theodore Jackson had brought the rightful owners back to Cotton Wood Plantation. It would be their duty to ensure that 'The Legacy' would pass onto the next generation.

Ebony knew that somewhere—Theodore and Beth would be smiling.

Lightning Source UK Ltd.
Milton Keynes UK
UKOW05f0859101013

218784UK00002B/183/P